AF491344

FEELS LIKE THE FIRST TIME

A NOVEL

KIMBERLY PACKARD

abalos
publishing

Book cover designed by okay creations.
Edited by C.A. Szarek
The text in this book is set in Baskerville.
Library of Congress Cataloging-in-Publication Data
Available Upon Request

ISBN eBook: 979-8-9904395-2-8

ISBN Print: 979-8-9904395-3-5

AWARD WINNING AUTHOR

KIMBERLY PACKARD

For Audra, Susie, Sarah and Chrissy.
You did it. You finally made me a romance writer.

CHAPTER 1
1996

I can't seem to get the butt right. The model is all roundness and steely muscle in the right places, but when I sketch the flex in his right cheek it looks like the time I accidentally backed my mom's Volvo into the mailbox.

"That's an interesting perspective there, Murray," Ross, the Art Composition TA, says, sneaking up behind me.

He calls all of us by our last names, which is really pretty badass. Like I've finally shed the too-tight skin of teenage years and, finally moving into my twenties, I'm free to be more than Emily Murray, or even Em.

I'm Murray, a modern woman eager to blaze into the new millennium with a change-the-world-career—and a rock star boyfriend.

"So, Murray," Ross says. "I suggest waiting to explore Impressionism once you've mastered the techniques of realism. I mean, if you continue with art and you're not just satisfying a credit."

"Oh yeah, I was trying..." The heat of embarrassment incinerates my witty comeback.

Not even waiting for me to finish my sentence, he moves on to Fleur, a French exchange student with dreads, a nose ring, and, I'd bet my trusty Hardrock bike, a birth certificate that shows she was born in Paris, Texas, not Paris, France.

"Nice, Fleur, you've captured not just the contours, but the struggles of the modern man as well."

"*Merci*, Ross," she says, rolling her R with as much fervor as I roll my eyes.

"Em, psst, psst."

I crane my neck to the cracked classroom door.

Wick waves me over.

A quick glance tells me Ross has moved on to the next hot, arty girl with indecipherable art to fawn over.

I announce the need for a bathroom break—not that anyone cares—drop my charcoal and head over to the door.

"Hey babe, gonna need your help with load in," Wick says. His eighth-natural-wonder blue eyes briefly connect with mine before he looks over my head into the art lab. "Sam at the club said there's a scout from L.A. coming. We talked him into letting us in this afternoon so we can make sure the sound is bitchin'."

"Okay, sure, I'll come over right after class."

He shakes his head, messy blond curls slapping his cheeks. "No *bueno*, babe. We need your help loading the gear into the van and then back out at the club."

I glance over my shoulder. My unoccupied easel is as empty as my talent. I've never let a thing like talent stop me. Talent is a shortcut. I prefer the long-cut.

"We just have another hour left." I hear the faltering in my voice and instantly hate those vocal cords for their weakness. "I can meet you at the club, help unload and get the gear set up."

Wick's shoulders fall forward, like the kid I used to babysit in high school when I wouldn't let him stay up past his bedtime right before the temper tantrum commenced. "I thought you wanted this for me," he says with a whine that rivals a five-year-old. "For us. This could change everything, but if I get all sweaty with load in, then imagine how bad I'll look when the scout comes by." He crosses his arms over his broad chest. "Anyway, didn't you change your major to art just to piss off your dad? Don't get me wrong, but your art is pretty juvenile compared to someone like Fleur."

On cue, a *bonjour* floats out of the classroom—and nicks my heart.

Sure, I've had a half dozen different majors in the two years I've attended college. I'm waiting for my heart to sing like a chorus of angels when I find my home in this institution of higher education, but so far the only music is the droning of professors who care more about their own voices and research than inspiring the next generation.

I'm pretty sure Daddy was bluffing when he said he's cutting off the college fund after this semester.

At least, I hope.

"You know what, you're right," I say. "Let me gather my stuff and we can head to the house."

"Sweet, thanks babe, I'll meet you there." He leans forward and plants a kiss on my forehead.

"Give me a few and I can grab my bike and ride with you."

"Sorry, babe. I need to pick up grub for the boys. Let yourself in when you get there and start pulling out the gear," he says, backpedaling down the hall.

Likely his hasty retreat is because I'm projecting a look like I'm contemplating how I'll get rid of his body. That semester as a criminal justice major might pay off after all.

"I'll be back at the casa soon," he says, waving.

No one seems to notice as I load up my gear. Maybe art is graded on a bell curve and just my mere presence brings everyone else's grade down.

With my well-worn backpack strapped on and my sketchpad tucked under my arm, I hurry to the stable of students' bikes, and unlock my bright red bike. I wasn't looking forward to the climb up the hill—because of course, Wick lives uphill from campus—in the late August Texas heat.

Halfway up, and I'm regretting my decision to try to hold on to the sweet parking spot for my Jeep as long as possible this semester. Sure, the old girl's AC isn't what it used to be, but we can't all stay cool forever.

Most people don't realize the work that goes into dating the lead singer of a band. Date nights end up being on nights when clubs are dark, or when there's no practice, or when there's no rumors of a label exec from L.A. in town checking out a rival local band.

Dating a future rock god is not for the faint of heart.

Luckily, my heart is made of fucking steel.

I finally get to his street, and I hear Pearl Jam's guitar licks coming up behind me.

Wick drives alongside me in his gray van, half of a French fry dangling out of his mouth like a cigarette. "Babe! Race you!"

He probably didn't see me when I flipped him off, but it sure as hell made me feel better.

At the band's communal house, Wick hands out bags of burgers and fries while the guys pull their equipment out of the crooked garage.

"Where's mine?" I ask, knowing damn well he didn't get me anything. I'm not hungry, but he doesn't need to know that.

Sometimes relationships are about reminding the other person you're still there.

He drops his shoulders again.

The more he does this five-year-old pre-tantrum routine the more I get the feeling I'm dating a toddler.

"You didn't tell me you wanted anything, babe. I'd give you mine, but you know I need to fuel up."

I wave him off. Point proven. "It's fine, I'll get something later."

It's never *fine*, but I don't need to say that.

I never had intentions to be the girl dating a lead singer. Well, I mean, I had plans to marry Kurt Cobain when I was in high school, but Courtney Love got to him first.

I had just changed my major from Pre-Law to Art at the start of the Spring semester. It was my first day of Art Theory and I was trying to find the best seat. A place between where the been-drawing-since-diapers artists sat and the taking-it-to-satisfy-an-arts-credit students sat.

There was no section for me. The trying-to-piss-off-daddy-by-not-getting-a-law-degree section.

There was Wick. Sitting in the back of the room. His dirty blond hair hanging down to his shoulders in messy ringlets. Knees poking through the holes in his jeans, a faded New York Dolls T-shirt covering his broad, lanky frame. Even though this was a lecture class, he sat there without a pen, notebook or even a backpack.

I dropped into the seat next to him, leaned over and leveled my gaze into those ice blue eyes. "This seems like a suitable start to our sordid love affair," I'd said.

It was probably the most badass thing I've ever done, but I had also just gone to the Lilith Fair the weekend before so I was hyped up on female empowerment.

It worked; we're six months into the most serious, longest relationship of my life.

With the van loaded, and the other guys following in the lead guitarist's beat-up sedan, I assume my spot in the passenger seat throne next to Wick.

He starts the cranky old van and turns in his seat. "Emily, you know I couldn't do any of this without you, right? You ground me. You lift me up."

"If you say I'm the wind beneath your wings, I will beat you up."

He quirks one side of his gorgeous mouth. "I wouldn't dream of it. But, I just know that I don't always say thank you."

The boys load in and run through sound check, playing halfway through their songs, enough for Wick to declare that they're ready.

I leave them to their pre-show prep. Meditation. Shots. Yoga. A hit off a dubious joint. Wick losing his shit because he's questioning the talent of the rest of the band.

I've been in the green room once or twice with them, and it's always the same. It's better not to be around Wick's neuroses.

I find my best friend, Josie, in the growing crowd. We push our way forward just right of center stage.

"Is it true?" she shouts over the piped in music. "Could this be their big break?"

I nod. "Yeah, scout from L.A. The guys had a good meet and greet. This could be it!"

As if on cue, the music stops and the club owner's voice fills the hot and humid venue. "Put your hands together for San Marcos's own Neon Reverie."

The crowd surges. A collective soul eager to pray to their rock gods.

A guitar riff slices through the screams.

Wick counts down before launching into their biggest hit on the college station, *'Firefly Sky.'*

They sound tight.

Wick's voice is deep, with just enough sandpaper to make girls swoon and guys try to mimic when they're alone in the car. The crowd sings along, a harmony to my boyfriend's lead vocals.

My eyes sting. I'd like to think it's the cigarette smoke from the guy next to me blowing into my face, but deep down, I can't deny it's more than that.

It's pride at seeing someone I love in his element. Winning. Being adored by so many of our friends.

Standing on the fulcrum of his future.

It hits me in a flash. Record deal. Major label debut. Music videos in heavy rotation on MTV. World tour. Late night television appearances.

Mansions. Swimming pools. Groupies he brushes off because he sees me waiting for him after every show.

The dying chords of *'Firefly Sky'* fade away and Wick pulls his guitar over his head. He starts thrumming a gritty acoustic riff. One that matches my own heartbeat. Literally. Wick wrote it one night after laying his head on my chest. *Bom. Bombom. Bom.*

"I want to crawl inside you," he sings, his voice grittier than usual. "I want to be you. I want to see me like you see me."

I close my eyes and remember the night he wrote the song. It was more intimate than sex. Sitting there in our underwear, Wick with an old acoustic guitar, writing *'Be You.'* A song about wanting to see himself the way that I see him. A perfect way to cap a conversation we'd just had about how I see what he is capable of with much more clarity. That he wished he could see himself through my eyes.

The song hit the bridge and I pop my eyes open.

Wick is on his knees. Hand reaching into the audience center stage. A hand reaches up, fingers entwined with his.

It's a move I've seen dozens of times. A way to connect with the audience.

I follow the fingers of the fan to a tanned arm. The arm down to hemp sundress with dreadlocks draped over one shoulder. The shoulder up the thin neck to the arty, yet beautiful face of Fleur.

"I want to see me like you see me," Wick sings the refrain—*our* refrain—to the girl whose face I want to punch.

CHAPTER 2

The scout from L.A. is impressed.

Very impressed.

I linger just outside the green room.

"Such a unique sound," the scout says. "A good bridge between grunge and the resurgence of pop with just an edge of metal."

I wrinkle my nose. None of that would appeal to Wick.

"Yeah man," Wick says. "It's exactly what we're going for. You get us."

Is that what it takes to achieve your dream? Absorbing someone else's interpretation and wearing it like it's your own?

Signatures scratch across stacks of paper. Rights signed away. Futures secured.

A horde of our friends comes down the hall, high on a great night of music and the promise of an epic after party.

I get swallowed up by the patchouli-drenched crowd, sweeping out into the night, pulsing with co-eds eager to blow off steam and live a life of ultimate freedom, no parental curfews and no responsibilities.

Just living in this moment.

I put Wick and his band's impending success out of my mind and let myself give in to the energy buzzing all around me.

The promise of a new millennium just four years away. An era of equality and technology. Women will be able to do even more than our mothers could. Our grandmothers.

We're finally becoming equals.

I won't let Wick's fame change my path.

Nope, I'll be a very different partner of a rock star. My own life, goals, dreams, will stay mine. Once we get settled in L.A., I'll enroll in college there, maybe find a major that will allow me to work in the industry. Hell, maybe I'll even make my dad happy and become an entertainment lawyer.

"Em!" Josie's voice cuts across the din of drunk college students. "How'd it go?"

I rush to her, sweeping my long, sweaty hair into a ponytail. "He loves them! Neon Reverie is going to be famous."

We scream and jump around like a couple of drunk twenty year olds.

"Jo, you know what this means, right? I'm going to go with Wick to L.A."

My best friend's smile flips to a frown, as fast as turning off a light.

We've been best friends since second grade, never being apart for more than a few weeks at a time. Josie is more than my best friend, more than a sister.

She's my person.

"You guys already talked about that?"

"Lots of times," I say.

It's not a lie. We've had lots of conversations about what our life would be like when the band made it big. The mansion we'd buy. The cars. A ridiculous pool with a slide that the guys will play on when they're between tours.

She nods, but I see the concern wrinkles on her forehead in the dim streetlight.

If she's not careful, those will become permanent in about ten years.

"Okay, well, if you're going to be leaving me, we should hit the afterparty and celebrate their big break."

That's what we do. We hit Greek row and flow between the fraternity houses, mixing Jello shots with cheap beer with potent liquor that no one over the age of twenty-three would be caught dead drinking.

I switch to water once faces start blending into one another. At some point, Wick and the guys will arrive and I want to remember the moment of the 1990s version of a hero coming home from battle.

The cheers. Handshakes. Slaps on the back.

I want to be sober-ish when Wick spots me in the crowd, people parting like the Red Sea as he makes his way to sweep me up in a grand romantic kiss.

The alcohol, combined with water, hits me at the worst moment. After spending twenty minutes waiting in a bathroom line that never moves, I gotta do what every Texas girl has been raised to do.

Pee in the bushes.

I'm squatting between two boxwoods when I spot Wick's tall figure walking down the street. He's not alone.

Fleur walks beside him, their shoulders touching as they walk. His hands are in his pockets, and hers are wrapped in a jacket she's carrying.

They're two friends walking together. That's all.

I mean, sure he sang our song to her, but it's his thing.

He sings to a girl at every show. If I'd positioned myself center stage he would've sang to me. I'm not a possessive girlfriend, so I was happy to watch from the sidelines.

I finish the marathon pee and rush out of the bushes, only to find myself falling forward. The toe of my sandal jammed on an exposed root. I catch myself, but instead of finding soft grass, the palm of my hand lands on a broken beer bottle.

Damn frat boys.

A string of curse words that would embarrass a sailor erupts from the angry volcano of my mouth.

"Em?"

Leave it to Josie to hear my distress in the profanity.

She finds me on my knees, cradling my bleeding hand.

Pain and embarrassment flares through my body like fireworks.

"Oh, honey," she says, prying my fingers open to examine the angry gash, despite the dark. "Let's go home and get this cleaned up." My best friend pulls me to standing.

"But Wick." Is all I manage to get out before a sob closes up my throat. I hate that I still have the childish reaction to cry when I get hurt. It has to be neurological. Or maybe it's deeper. A childhood wound of divorced parents who were more concerned with out-achieving the other to pay attention to when their daughter tumbled off playground equipment.

"I'll call his house when we get home and leave a message letting him know where you are," she says, obviously thinking I'm concerned he'll worry about me.

I don't put up a fight as Josie ushers me into her on-its-last-legs Subaru.

We make the quick drive back to our apartment, and she went into mom-mode, holding my right hand under the sink, gently washing away the dirt and checking for glass in my wound before pouring peroxide over it.

It strikes me that she's in her element. Wiping away tears, fixing boo-boos. She'll be an amazing mom. It's a sore subject, but I secretly hope she'll reconnect with her high school crush, Daniel. They would be the most amazing parents.

Nothing like mine.

Once Josie bandages up my hand, exhaustion drains me.

I sleep the dreamless sleep of the dead. Or buzzed, sleep-deprived college students. Same difference.

The incessant ringing of my phone startles me awake.

Spears of sunlight pierce my eyes as I flutter them open. My alarm clock flashes the God-awful early time of 9:10 a.m.

"*Hi, this is Jo, and Em,*" our joint answering machine message clicks on in the kitchen. "*If this is our parents, we're studying hard in the library. If this is our friends, we're down at the river.*" We burst into giggles before the beep.

I'm pretty sure we were drinking when we recorded that.

"Emily, it's your father. I'm sure you remember we're having brunch this morning at the club in Austin. I'll see you there at 10."

I shoot out of bed.

Crap on a cracker.

Dad's in town for a trial next week and I'd agreed to brunch when I ran out of suitable excuses.

I'm still holding out hope that aliens will abduct me before I get there, but seeing it's now the light of day, and there's no little gray alien in sight, I have to put my big girl panties on.

"Daddy," I say, grabbing the phone before it cuts off. "Hi! Yes, I'm just getting dressed. See you there."

I hang up and rush into the bathroom.

Of course, Dad chose to stay at a country club on the northwest side of Austin, so it'll take me at least forty-five minutes to get there.

The good news is I can be back before Wick even gets up, so I can swing by his house and see when we're leaving for L.A.

With no time for a shower, I wipe my armpits and layer on the perfume. My dark hair is greasy from the heat of the bar and reeks of stale cigarette smoke. I pull it back into a low bun and douse it with sticky-sweet hairspray.

Half the counter is taken over with Wick's stuff. His house doesn't have AC, so he spent the better part of the summer shacked up with Josie and me.

I push his toothbrush and electric razor aside to pull out my makeup bag. It's been a long time since I've been Dad's perfect country club princess, but I can't poke the bear today. Especially since there's a good chance this will be the last semester he'll fund.

With my fresh-faced Texas pageant queen makeup on, I whip a black and white polka dot sundress over my head. Before I head out the door, I throw my grandmother's pearls on for good luck.

I leap into Scarlett, the red Jeep Dad got me for my sweet sixteen. I'm halfway there before cool air finally blows out of the vents. I could probably ask him for a new car, but that feels like a betrayal of Scarlett. This car has been there for me during first loves and heartbreaks. Through carefree days with Josie and Sofia, our other best friend, and in the dark, lonely moments when Dad was off living his new life in Houston, and Mom was building her real estate business. Neither of them seeming to remember their daughter had a volleyball game.

Scarlett's always been there for me. So, it's only fair that I stick with her until her wheels fall off.

I pull into the valet, barely putting the Jeep into park before launching out. I'm ten minutes late, even though Dad is likely entertaining elected officials and CEOs dropping by his favorite table with practiced ease.

The storm clouds of his annoyance wash over me from outside the lavish building.

"Be kind to her," I tell the college kid reaching for my door. "Give her some water and shade, she had a hard ride over."

I speedwalk until I get to the dining room and slow to a normal pace, reminding myself to take a breath.

As suspected, Dad is there in his Saturday best, which is just a gray suit without a tie. He doesn't do casual.

A partner at a large Houston law firm, Dad works twenty-four seven. He's speaking with a man in a golf shirt and khakis.

A state senator, I think.

Once Dad sees me, he reaches out to side hug me. "There she is." The more jubilant his voice sounds, the more annoyed he is.

Judging by how happy he sounds to see me; I'm in for an uncomfortable brunch.

I wonder if I can sweet-talk the bartender into sending over bottomless mimosas.

"Clyde, have you met my daughter Emily? She's starting her junior year at San Marcos."

"It's nice to meet you," I say, playing the role of the dutiful daughter with such believability that I should get a damn Oscar.

As soon as the senator is out of earshot, Dad switches to his normal judgmental self. "You're late."

"There was traffic," I shoot back.

"It's Saturday."

"Have you never been on I-35?" Honestly, there wasn't much traffic, but I also know he wouldn't fight me on that.

His true fight was something else.

My future.

We make polite small talk. I ask about the firm. Dad shows me something called a Palm Pilot, claims it'll revolutionize how he works, but it just looks like the boring, ugly cousin of the Game Boy.

He asks about everything but the thing he wants to talk about. School.

"So, Emily," he says, leaning his elbows on the table once the waiter removes his eggs Benedict. "I think we both know why I'm here."

"To see your only child?" I slap on a sweet smile and bat my eyelashes.

"Well, of course, that," he stumbles slightly. "But as my only child, I'm deeply invested in your future."

"Do you mean that emotionally or financially?" Maybe my boldness was born out of the fact that soon Wick and I will be off to L.A. and that I won't need Daddy and his money. Or, maybe it's the fact that my hand hurts like a mother-effer and I just don't have the patience to do the dutiful daughter dance.

"Both." He flings the word at me. "Obviously, your emotional fulfillment is important but considering that you're starting your junior year, and you seem to be an art major, I'm now questioning my financial investment."

I shrug. "You know what they say, if you love what you do, you'll never work a day in your life."

"That's what I'm worried about, Emily. That you'll never work a day in your life and will remain on my payroll for longer than necessary."

I drop the muffin I'd been nibbling on. "But you have more money than God, what does it matter?"

"It matters because I raised you better than this."

His words are a cold drink to my face.

"*You* raised me?" My voice is louder than I'd expected. "You saw me only a handful of times a year, and even then, I spent more time with your housekeeper."

The clattering silverware silenced, and I can feel the gaze of Austin's elite on my back.

"Sure, you gave me a credit card and a car, and you're paying for college, but *I* raised me. And I think I did a pretty damn good job of it." I stand so quickly the heavy dining chair turned over behind me.

"Emily, you're causing a scene," my father drawls, his blue eyes—the same as mine—flare with barely controlled anger.

"Of course, that's what you take away from all that." I grab my purse and fish around for cash for the valet but only find bar receipts. I hate stiffing the poor kid, but there's no way I'm asking Dad to spot me. Hopefully all these old rich dudes over-tip. "You know what, *Father*, don't worry about me. I've got my future planned out and I don't need you for it." I escape the silence of the country club, and with a million apologies to the valet, I hop back into Scarlett.

Hot furious tears sting my eyes, but I hold them back. I didn't cry when my parents had plate-breaking arguments in the middle of the night. I didn't cry when I moved with my mom back to her hometown at the start of second grade. I didn't even cry when instead of showing up the morning of my sixteenth birthday, my dad sent a flatbed truck with a shiny red Jeep on the back.

Scarlett's AC did nothing to soothe the fury burning inside me.

I pull into a parking lot to remove my Jeep's top. It's when I'm fighting with the snaps, my right hand throbbing, that I see it.

A neon sign in the shape of a palm with an eye in the middle of it. The word 'psychic' blinks on and off one letter at a time.

A winking invitation.

CHAPTER 3

The sign sits in front of a lavender clapboard house sandwiched between two strip malls. The wind blows, stirring about twenty chimes hanging off the porch in all shapes and sizes.

My feet lead me there on their own, as if pulled by some magnetic vortex.

I push open the front door, and stumble onto an uneven floor.

The front room is filled with crystals and amethyst gourds of all shapes and sizes. A sage green hutch sits open to one side, filled with brown bags of various herbs.

I peruse them, half looking to see if one might contain eye of newt, when I hear a chair creak in the next room.

"You're early," a voice full of gravel says from behind the beaded curtain separating the rooms.

I laugh. "I bet you say that to all the girls."

A woman parts the curtain.

She's old, but that indecipherable kind of old. Like she'd been old for most of her life. Her gray hair hangs long down her back. A purple chiffon shirt tucked into an equally gauzy purple skirt with silver star appliqués.

She dismisses me with a wave. "Thought you were my sister. You here for crystals, herbs, maybe something to smudge a room?"

I chew on the inside of my cheek. Josie had once suggested we visit a psychic but I'd laughed. She'd just wanted to ask about Daniel, but she'd have better luck driving all over the state than asking a con artist to tell her what she wanted to hear.

Maybe this is what I need. What was that term I learned in my marketing class?

Confirmation bias.

Maybe *this* con artist can confirm what I already know.

That I don't need my dad. He's my past. Wick is my future.

"So, are you really a psychic?" I ask.

"If the neon sign says so." She goes behind the counter and starts tidying a stack of receipts.

"Yeah, so what am I thinking?"

"That I'm full of shit," the lady says with a scoff. "But your body language is saying all that. I'm Astrid, and yes that's my real name."

"Emily. Also my real name."

"So, Emily, you look like you need a reading. Follow me." Astrid leads me down the hall to a smaller room.

A round table sits inside the dark room. Purple scarves are draped over the one window, giving the room a twilight glow.

She points to a chair for me and lights a series of candles on a side table while murmuring under her breath. "Angels and guides, protect me, protect Emily. Grant me clarity to give her a vision into her future."

She sits in the chair opposite me and reaches toward me, her palms upturned. "Take my hands, dear."

I place mine in hers, and she jumps.

"Oh," she says on a gasp.

"Please tell me I have a future." I laugh nervously, but I felt it too.

I tell myself the zip of electricity was likely nothing more than the woman shuffling down the worn rug in the hallway. A simple parlor trick.

Astrid turns over my right palm, the same one that'd been on the losing end of a broken beer bottle the night before. "May I?" She doesn't wait for a response before peeling back the bandage. "Hmm… this cut straight through your lifeline."

"Don't tell me my clumsiness cut my life in half," I scoff.

"Not in half, it's just not going to be a straight path."

"Oh, I'm up for an adventure. I might have one soon—"

She holds up a hand to shush me and closes her eyes. A groan starts low in her chest while she sways in loose circles. "You've got a long journey coming up. You'll be far away, but close by." Her face is blank, then she scrunches her nose like she smells something rancid. "I see you standing there, wrapped in armor."

"Am I going to war? Do I look like someone who takes orders?"

Astrid flutters her eyes open. "Sometimes the way to win the battle is to surrender. Put down your shield."

Surrender.

Maybe that's what I need to do. Surrender the fight with my dad, because I'll never live up to his expectations. Surrender to Wick— maybe the road to my future truly lies in L.A. and not in Texas.

Surrender.

It's the most terrifying word in the English language, but if Astrid says I'm going on a long journey and I have to surrender, that means I need to get home and pack for Los Angeles.

CHAPTER 4

A long journey.

The words sang through my head the entire way home. Los Angeles is a long way from Austin. Is Wick the home she spoke of when she said I'll be close to home? It's a given that he'll ask me to go with them. I'll be leaving Josie in a bind without a roommate, but maybe I can get the university to refund my tuition directly to me, and I can give her what I owe for the rest of the year.

It's freeing, really, seeing my whole life laid out in front of me.

Moving to L.A. Being there for Wick while Neon Reverie records their first album. I'll enroll in UCLA to have my own life and purpose while they're on tour. After their second album, the band will take a break and we'll get married and I'll get pregnant on our wedding night, because that's just so poetic.

By the time I roll back into San Marcos, I've not only named our children, but all of our pets—three dogs, two cats and a turtle.

Instead of going home, I turn, driving down to Wick's house.

The typical college street—there's always a solid line of cars parked along the curb. The moving truck halfway down stands out like a zit on a supermodel's forehead.

I stop across the street from the bustle of the guys loading gear and random furniture into the back.

"Hey, Matt," I shout at the drummer, standing up in the seat of my Jeep. "What's going on?"

"Em, perfect timing, Wick's been looking for you."

Excitement nips at my heels like a hyper puppy. He's been looking for me.

It's time for me to surrender.

I bound out of the Jeep like a woman running toward the love of her life in a cheesy movie.

The house has never been stuffed with furniture, but now it looks even more barren. The couch had a questionable origin story; thankfully it looks like it's going to be left behind.

Wick's bed has a wonky spring that pokes at tender areas in the middle of the night. Maybe I can talk him into swinging by my apartment for my bed instead.

I'm making my packing list—definitely need my Doc Martens, I could probably leave my overalls behind, are Birkenstocks still cool in California?—when I run into Wick coming out of his bedroom.

"Hey babe! You're here," he says over a trash bag stuffed with T-shirts and boxers. "Did you get my message?" He glances down at my dress. "Oh shit, did someone die?"

When did black and white polka dots become funeral attire?

"No, I had brunch with my dad, and this was clean. Ish. Anyway, he was being so annoying and authoritarian and all 'get a job' and he had the balls to admit he's more financially invested in me than emotionally. I mean, thanks, Dad, that'll save me a lot of therapy with you just admitting exactly what you think of me." I take a big breath. I know I'm word vomiting all over him, but I'm high on our future. "Anyway, long story short, I pulled into a parking lot for a psychic and yeah, I know, load of shit because we're in charge of our own destinies and all, but she told me the craziest thing, that we're going on a long journey, and..." I whip out my arms to the quickly emptying house. "She's right!"

Wick drops the bag of his clothes and grips my upper arms,

meeting my eyes, staring hard with arched eyebrows. "Babe, are you high?"

"What? No, you know me. I'm too much of a control freak for that stuff. It's just so empowering to be free of my dad and finally in control of my own future." I flash a smile.

He exhales and straightens. "Good, I'm glad to hear you finally stood up to him. That's really badass of you, Em."

"I know, I mean, it's a little scary because we'll be going to L.A. without the safety net of his money, and I plan to use his credit card until it gets cut off, so I'll get us as far as I can, but after that we can see if the label will give you guys an advance, and if not, that's fine. I can wait tables or bartend. People like me—"

He tilts his head and his too-long bangs fall in his face. "Wait, back up, what do you mean 'we'?"

"'We,' the pronoun that means you and I, and the rest of the band, of course."

Wick sighs and runs his hands through his tangled curls. "Emily, sit with me." He grabs my hand and pulls me back into his bedroom.

The bed screams a protest as we sit.

"Look, I first want to say thank you for everything you've done for me. And the guys. I can honestly say that Neon Reverie wouldn't be where we are today without you. You'll definitely get a mention in the liner notes. But this is our shot at our dreams, and to have a chance, a *real* chance, at reaching them, we need to be one hundred percent focused."

I'm nodding along as he speaks. "You got it. I'm here to support you every step of the way so you guys can stay focused. But don't worry about me, my parents trained me for taking care of my own needs. Think of me as a latch-key girlfriend."

Wick grips my hands, squeezing my sliced palm to the point that pain burns down my arm, but I don't flinch.

We're having a moment and I don't want to do anything to ruin it.

"Em, babe, listen. *Neon Reverie* is going to L.A. *You* are staying here. And I think you should, well, explore other options."

The words float past me, but none of them sink in. "Explore other options?"

"Yeah, I mean, you have your whole life ahead of you, and Em, you are seriously the most badass babe I've ever met. You are so independent and strong and—"

"Explore other options?" I repeat. "Like what does that even mean?"

"You know, date other guys."

A buzzing sound vibrates under his words, like the overhead lights snapping on in a classroom.

"But why would I do that? We've been together for, like, six months."

Wick sighs again and looks up to the ceiling. "We had a good run, a really good run, but it's time to move on. You even said it yourself the day we met, that we'd have a sordid love affair."

The pain that'd been burning up my arm took a left turn and flared into my heart.

His words don't feel real. None of it feels real.

Astrid said I'd be going on a journey. That I had to surrender myself.

Fine, if that's what it takes, I'll surrender.

I drop from the bed to my knees. "What? Wait. Wick, you just said, we've had a good run."

"Yeah, *had*, past tense." He glances at the door.

The buzzing grows louder, as if a colony of bees made a home in the walls.

"Why are you doing this? I was going to go with you. You guys need me."

The little bird of panic wakes in my chest and ruffles her feathers, eager to let loose and send me into a tailspin.

Wick stands stiffly, as if avoiding touching me. "Babe, please don't make this any harder than it has to be. It's time for us both to move on. Next chapter and all."

The panic bird gets shoved aside by the jealousy hog, grunting about what's hers is hers.

"Wait, is Fleur going with you?"

"Who? Fleur? The French girl?" His brows draw tight, his blue eyes narrowing as if trying to remember an answer to a test.

"She's from Paris, Texas. But yes, the Parisian Texan chick. I saw you last night, you sang our song to her and then you guys went to the frat house together."

Wick shuffles away from the side of the bed, angling, as if he needs to make a run for the door.

Which probably isn't a bad move to make.

"Okay, yeah, you know the routine, so sure, Fleur happened to be the girl in the front row last night, and I saw her again as I was walking up to the party, but that's it." He glances out the door as his bandmates shuffle by carrying out random stuff. "Look, Em, I never meant to hurt you. I'll be honest, I always thought you'd be the one to break my heart. But long distance won't work. I know it hurts now, but trust me, you'll thank me later. I hope we can still be friends."

I laugh.

Friends? No, we're not going to be friends.

Because my friends would never choose their career over me. But I don't say that, because I know what will happen next.

He'll be stuck in a van with his bandmates for hours and there will be stretches between radio stations where the only way to break the monotony is to tell the story of his crazy ex-girlfriend, Emily, who begged on her knees for him to take her to Los Angeles and who had named their children, and their three dogs, two cats and a turtle before he'd even told her he loved her.

I refuse to be a road trip story, or—I swallow down rising bile—the subject of a terrible break up song.

"Of course, I wish you nothing but the best," I say, letting Wick give me a hand to my feet.

He leans in for a hug and I inhale his scent. Patchouli and sweat with a hint of old yeast.

The buzzing quiets just a bit, but it's still there. Maybe it's best that the guys leave if this house is infested with bees.

"You really are the best, Em."

I hug each of the guys and wish them luck before climbing back into Scarlett.

Head held high, I drive slowly back to my apartment, processing how my future had gone from clear and defined to *what-the-fuck* in the span of an hour.

Maybe I should switch back to pre-law. It'll at least make my dad happy, and a happy dad is a charitable dad.

That's the long journey Astrid had spoken of. Law school. Studying for the bar. Years working evenings and weekends to prove myself with no social life. That's also the surrender she'd mentioned.

I have to surrender to my dad. To the financial sway he held over me.

The armor? That's me tucking my disappointment and heartbreak so deep down inside that no one can touch it.

Not even me.

I pull into the apartment parking lot and scan for Josie's car. There's nothing more I want in the world than to crawl in bed with Jo and have her hold me while I cry, but her faded blue Subaru is nowhere to be found.

The apartment is as quiet as the library during finals. A note with her hurried handwriting is stabbed with a pushpin to our cork board in the kitchen.

Lunch with the parents. See you tonight!

Was I really this close to skipping town with my boyfriend without saying goodbye to my best friend?

I trudge into my bedroom, eager to sleep for the rest of the day, semester. Hell, I wouldn't even mind going to sleep for a few years letting my shattered heart repair itself, letting Wick and Neon Reverie have all the fame and fortune while I snooze away. Rip Van Winkle would have nothing on me.

Sleep until it doesn't hurt anymore.

I strip off the stupid polka dot sundress. I'm done with being the country club princess. In the bathroom, I tug my hair free of the bun and study my reflection. Long brunette hair hangs straight to my elbows. Wick always joked that half of my five-foot-two frame was made up of hair.

Bloodshot blue eyes stare back at me. When I'm feeling goth, I'll layer dark eye shadow on to make the blue stand out, but no more.

I don't want anyone to look at me anymore. I want to fade into the background, like a favorite song you've heard so many times that when you hear it now, it doesn't even register.

I rifle through my messy bathroom counter for makeup remover. Half of the crap belongs to Wick. Will he stop by to get it? Or, does he think it'll be easier to just replace it all, so he doesn't have to encounter his clingy ex-girlfriend again?

I snatch his electric razor, trying to remember the last time he even used it. The heft of it set something alive in me.

My mind blanks, and I switch it on, letting it hum in my injured palm, feeling the vibration all the way down to my bare feet.

In one quick move, I run the razor from the middle of my forehead as far back as I can reach. Long strands fall to the side. Virginal white scalp starkly stands out against a sea of black.

A laugh wrapped in a sob escapes my chest and I run the razor in haphazard streaks across my scalp.

With each razor swipe, I feel the future I'd so very clearly figured out float further and further away.

Gone are the adorable children Wick and I would have. I release the rescue dogs we'd save, wishing them luck with whoever they end up with.

I even cry for the turtle, for no other reason than I'd always begged my mom for one and she'd quip that she could barely keep me alive, much less a turtle.

As more of my hair falls away, my head feels lighter, like I'm unloading more than hair, but the essence of who I am.

The buzzing of the razor grows louder, like it's not just coming from my hand but from all around me. From inside me.

Did the bees follow me home?

The small bathroom shrinks even more. Gone is the shower, the toilet. It's just the vanity. My reflection.

Even that is collapsing on itself.

With a final swipe across the back of my head, the last of my long locks falls away.

I stare at the new me. The smaller me. Mascara dripping down my face. Wearing nothing but panties. Chest heaving.

The razor in my hand pulses again, this time sending a numbing shock through my body. I drop it in the sink, and my legs buckle like a rag doll.

Discarded hair cushions me as I land hard on the linoleum floor. Even though the razor is off, the buzzing grows louder.

My vision grows darker, as if my hair is crawling over me, demanding to know why I didn't want it anymore.

I don't have an answer.

Why doesn't anyone want me anymore, I silently ask my tresses before letting the darkness overtake me.

CHAPTER 5

Pattering rain wakes me. Did I put the top up on Scarlett? I was pretty catatonic when I got to our apartment, so probably not. Great, another thing I lost.

My Jeep.

I stretch and snuggle deeper into the softest bed I've ever felt.

Am I in Josie's bed? I'm sure she found me lying on the bathroom floor in a puddle of shaved hair with dried mascara caked down my face.

It would be so very Josie to put me in her bed to keep a watchful eye on me and make sure I don't do something else stupid, like shave off my eyebrows next.

God, what was I thinking?

Easy answer. I wasn't.

I just wanted to disappear, and somehow shaving my head seemed like the best way to do that.

I roll over and wipe the hair off my face.

Wait…

Hair?

I blink and it hits me. The sound of rain is coming from *inside*, not *outside*. Then there's the sound of a man singing. Deeper than Wick's voice, singing a song I've never heard before.

"What the what?" I whisper.

Pain pinches my temple, like a cheap wine hangover.

Did Josie and I go out when she got home?

I reach into my memory but all I'm coming up with is shaving my head and passing out.

When I manage to sit up, a thick white comforter falls away. The room around me is completely foreign. The walls are painted a soft sage green, with black and white pictures filling the space to my left. To my right, double French doors look out to a patio, and the sun glints off a pool.

A picture frame on the nightstand snags my attention. I reach for the frame with my left hand, still babying the slice through my other palm from the night before.

The twinkling spark from my ring finger catches my eye. A ginormous rock sits below my knuckle. Square diamond cushioned by smaller diamonds that taper into a band filled with pavés.

Whose ring is this?

Does she know I'm wearing it?

I grab the frame and study the picture. It's me, but my hair is shoulder-length in big loose waves. Tight jeans cover my legs with a loose sweater on top.

A tall, handsome man stands behind me, his arms wrap around me and I'm gripping those strong arms, huge diamond winking at the camera.

I bring the frame closer, my eyes uncharacteristically bleary. Whoever this man is, he's hot, even if he's not my type. Clean cut brown hair, square jaw, broad shoulders.

We're both smiling, so if this is a hostage situation I'm not putting up much of a fight.

The opposite. I look…happy.

The shower shuts off.

I drop the frame and grab a peony-filled vase, making my way to the open bathroom door.

Drawing on all the spy movies I've seen, I peek around the corner.

The bathroom is as huge as my apartment bedroom. Steam fills the air, masking a very naked man drying off in the shower. It's the same man in the frame, and as suspected, he definitely works out.

He looks up. A slow, sexy smile crosses his face.

"You're staring," he drawls.

Is this a sex dream? I can honestly say I've never had one, but always assumed they featured someone I'd know, or at least would've fantasized about having sex with, like Ethan Hawke or Brad Pitt.

"And if I weren't running late to catch my flight, I'd drag you right into this shower with me."

The timbre of his voice hits me right in that tingly place. Yep, this is definitely a sex dream. Maybe this is my bruised ego trying to get over Wick.

I put the vase on the counter and step toward the half-naked man, tugging on the towel around his waist. "So how does this work," I ask the dream man. "Do you want me to be a slutty flight attendant? Strangers on a flight joining the mile high club?"

He smells incredible. Freshly showered with a hint of peppermint. Water droplets dangle off light brown hair that's dusted with a touch of gray. His eyes are the lightest shade of brown, so light they are almost gold. Even though he's like thirty years older than me, he's hot as sin.

My broken psyche done me right.

He laughs. "Seriously, Em, I've gotta leave for the airport in twenty minutes. You know how unpredictable traffic is heading to Bergstrom." The man leans down and plants the softest, gentlest kiss on my lips.

While the kiss might've been barely there, my reaction certainly isn't.

The feel of his lips against mine was like the first drop of a roller coaster, pulling my stomach down to my feet. I press forward, trying to deepen the kiss, but he pulls back, resting his forehead against mine.

"You're determined to make me miss this conference. I'll be back in three days, and I promise we can fulfill whatever fantasy you want then, but Gary's counting on me to be at that podium with him." He steps into the closet.

I shiver at the loss of his warmth, but it's more than body heat. The way I gravitated toward him, like he's north and I'm a magnet, everything in my being pointed toward him.

My legs give out, and I fall onto an ottoman in the middle of the bathroom, mindlessly rubbing my sore palm but it's no longer sore. I flip it over. The skin is as smooth as ice, only a faint scar bisects the line in my palm.

What did Astrid call that?

The mystery man dresses in the closet, chatting about this conference—a medical thing from what I can gather—and how he wished I could be there, but he understood that it would be difficult to reschedule all my clients.

I want to stop him to ask what kind of clients I have, but he rushes past me, clothed in khakis that make his butt look amazing and a sports coat.

He pulls me to standing and this time lays an honest-to-God kiss on me, but the feeling that this might not be a sex dream is too overwhelming for me to respond.

"I'll text you when I land in Boston. And when I get back, let's nail down some of the wedding plans," he says. "I love you, Em."

I sit back down. His words wash over me.

In the first wave is the realization he was going to an airport that isn't yet complete. They'd only just started work on that big new airport.

When I catch my breath from that wave, the next one hits me.

He was going to text me.

What the hell does that mean?

Then, the mother of all tidal waves.

Wedding plans.

What kind of sex dream ends in marriage?

Not *mine*. For sure. Unless it's with Wick. At this point, I'd get off more on strangling him.

I head out of the luxurious bathroom back to the enormously fluffy bed.

A slip of paper on the night table catches my eye. Card stock, like an invitation.

I bring it closer. Did I hit my head passing out?

Is that why my vision is fuzzy?

It's the same picture I saw in the frame. Me with the handsome man who made me feel like my stomach is full of fireflies.

I flip it over.

Save the date for Emily and Craig's wedding.

May 16, 2026.

The invitation falls from my hand and I run back to the bathroom. I'd been so focused on the hot half-naked guy, I never looked in the mirror.

It was a dream, why would I? I know what I look like. And, it's nothing like the reflection staring back at me.

I have hair, that's the most noticeable difference. Like the picture, my hair is shoulder length, sleep-messy, more subdued than the raven hue that I'd spent my life finding around the house. I lean into the mirror, my face coming into focus. Fine lines fan out from the outside of my eyes, and two distinct lines form an eleven between them.

I'm me, just...*old.*

"This dream really sucks," I tell my reflection.

Maybe if I go back to bed, I'll wake up in an actual sex dream.

Maybe...

Although somewhere in my heart I know, *something is fucked up.*

CHAPTER 6

A buzzing sound pulls me toward the light. The same bedroom is now brightly lit with the full force of the sun.

The buzz is coming from my nightstand. That dark rectangular thing has come alive, showing a picture of a gorgeous Black woman.

Monique Lillet flashes under her smiling face.

I should reach for it, but I hesitate.

A line across the bottom says *"Swipe to Answer."* I don't know anyone named Monique.

What does that mean? What is this thing?

I leave the buzzing thing on the night table, as if it's full of an electric charge and might be deadly to the touch.

Besides that, *why* am I still in this dream?

I listen for running water, thinking that perhaps the dream started over and this time I'll finally get to see what the half-naked hot-guy is made of. It's as silent as my childhood home in the aftermath of one of my parents' shouting matches.

I push out of the bed. The room is exactly as it was before. The same pictures on the wall, same framed photograph of me and—*what was his name, oh yes*—Craig.

My feet carry me into the bathroom. The same middle-aged version of my reflection stares back from the mirror.

A grumble from my stomach echoes around the bathroom. Have I ever felt hunger in dreams?

This feels so different from any I've had before. It feels as real as when I stopped by Wick's house, and the band was moving out with the fury of a criminal on the run. Which itself felt otherworldly.

Would he have left town without telling me?

Without saying goodbye?

Would that mother-trucker have left without breaking up with me?

Angry tears burn at my eyes. I'm not going to let him have anything else of mine, especially my tears.

My stomach groans; a sound like my PopPop getting out of the recliner. I guess if I'm dream-hungry, I should find some dream-food.

I head out of the bedroom and wander through a bright living room. A row of sliding doors open to the pool I'd seen from the bedroom, giving a better view of the outside living area. There are Christmas lights strung around the patio and expensive-looking outdoor furniture.

I pass the front door. The foyer's floor is covered in dark gray tile with a modern door with opaque glass cutouts. A sleek dining room table sits alone in a room under a chandelier that looks like one of those atomic mobiles we had to make in high school chemistry.

Finally, I turn the corner and find the kitchen. On cue, my stomach gives an appreciative moan.

The kitchen is bright, filled with natural light and a large island in the middle. A flat planter sits in the middle of the island, filled with tiny succulents.

So far, this house looks like something my mom would've staged for one of her upscale clients. Aside from the frame of me and Craig, there are no personal items. No shoes kicked off in random places, or a bra left on the floor by the front door.

No pictures of Josie, Sofia, and me on the fridge. No stubs from our latest concerts impaled on a cork board. No backpack dropped in the middle of the floor. No whiteboard by the phone—wait, where *is* the phone?

Unable to fight the hunger monster, I pull open the fridge.

Foreign objects stare back at me.

Cottage cheese. Ugh, that smells like sweaty feet.

Greek yogurt. What is *that*?

Oat milk. I'd love to see someone milk an oat.

I tug at the freezer next. Frozen berries. Frozen pizzas with cauliflower crusts. Thank goodness for some frozen tamales.

Then I see it. The lid of something forbidden.

Ice cream.

Not just any ice cream. Mint chocolate chip.

My salvation.

I grab it and furiously pull open drawers until I find a spoon before settling in with the tub of ice cream while I replay the last twenty-four hours.

Meeting Dad for brunch and being reminded that I'll never live up to his expectations. Essentially excommunicating myself from the Bank of Dad. The psychic telling me I was going on a long journey.

Gah, how wrong was she?

Then Wick.

I was right when we'd met. It was a sordid love affair. Except I might have put my emphasis on 'love' while he was focused on 'affair.'

What I can't figure out is how I'd gone from shaving my head to waking up with hair but not like before I shaved it, a haircut I've never had before.

Then there was Craig. If he was a dream, why did kissing him feel like…home?

I suck on a spoonful of ice cream, half imagining it's his lips when a chime echoes through the house.

Like a thief, I freeze. With the picture of Craig and me, and our wedding invitation, I'd assumed this was our house. What if we're squatters?

The bell chimes again, followed by knocking on the front door.

I put down the ice cream, but hold tight to the spoon, just in case I have to defend myself.

Right when I reach for the door, keys jangle in the lock. I jump back.

The door narrowly misses me.

I scream, holding the spoon in front of my face.

The woman screams, and one of her hands flies up to her chest.

It's in the space after our screams that I recognize her. It's Monique, the lady from that rectangular thing on the nightstand.

"What in God's name are you trying to do? If you give me a heart attack, I'm going to need that gorgeous fiancé of yours to give me mouth to mouth," she says, her voice like warm honey with a lovely lyrical accent. "You've been warned. Why aren't you at the office? Since you didn't answer my texts or call, I had to come all the way over here to make sure you're still alive. You owe me coffee." She pushes past me and heads into the kitchen like she's done that a hundred times. Monique picks up the ice cream carton. "Really, doc? No coffee but you're having ice cream for breakfast?" She *tsks* as she puts the ice cream back in the freezer.

Like with Craig, I process her words slowly. Not only do I have a job I'm supposed to be at, but she also called me *doc*. Is that some sort of nickname? I can't be an actual doctor, right?

Monique gets to work grinding coffee beans and putting them into what can best be described as a chemistry set. The spicy, earthy notes waft through the air, almost giving me a contact high with the promise of warmth and clear thinking. Once the coffee is brewing, she turns to me and hitches her hands on her hips.

"You okay?" she says, her dark eyes narrow, studying me. She feels my forehead with the back of her hand. "Huh, yeah, you're a bit warm. I'll cancel your appointments for today. Why don't you get back in bed and spend the day catching up on Netflix? Text me if you need anything."

Text. That word again. What is this place?

Monique grabs a coffee tumbler from the pantry and pours some of the oat milk in before adding coffee.

It's obvious we're good friends from how she knows the way around this kitchen.

"For the trip over here," she says, toasting with the tumbler. "You'll text me, right?"

I nod, words failing to form in my mind. "Monique? What's today?"

She quirks an immaculate eyebrow. "Monday. March second. You sure you're going to be okay? When does Craig get home?"

Heat rushes up my body, threatening to consume me right there in the middle of the foyer.

"Three days," I mumble, willing myself to breathe and stay upright.

A sympathetic smile crosses her face. "Go to bed, Em. Get some rest. You've been burning yourself out."

After she leaves, after her footsteps fade away and a car starts up outside, I release the hold on my legs and fall to the floor. The cool air a balm to the heat flooding my body.

It was August twenty-third when I met Dad for brunch. When I saw my boyfriend moving to L.A. to live his rock and roll dream without me. When, in a moment of panic, I shaved my head.

How did six months pass? A little voice whispers deep down inside, from that place that tells the truths I never want to hear.

More than six months has passed.

A lot more.

CHAPTER 7

I pick myself off the foyer floor and head back for the ice cream. I don't care what Monique says, this is my mental breakdown, and I can eat ice cream for breakfast if I want to.

There has to be some explanation.

Maybe I dropped Wick's electric razor in the tub, and I electrocuted myself and this is my life passing in front of my eyes. The part I didn't live. Or maybe I'm still asleep.

This could be one of those weird dreams within a dream within a dream.

I just need to wake myself up.

An idea strikes me like a match catching fire. During high school slumber parties, we always tried to get some unsuspecting girl to pee herself by putting her hand in warm water.

I flip open the cabinets until I find one with a set of mixing bowls and fill it with warm water. If I put my dream-hand in it, maybe it'll make me have to real-life pee and I'll wake up to whatever messed-up world's waiting for me.

While my hand soaks in water, thoughts tumble around my brain like over-caffeinated bunnies.

How do I have a fiancé, and an upcoming wedding date, when I broke up with my boyfriend just mere hours ago? Then this *house*?

Maybe it's one my mom is selling and it's stuck in my head like some annoying pop song.

Monique calling me 'doc.'

I threw up when we had to dissect earthworms in biology, I could never make it through an actual surgery of an actual person. And, there's no way I'm looking at people's toenail funk or getting sneezed on.

No, that has to be a nickname.

The water cools and I turn my hand over. In the bright, overhead kitchen lights a silver line across my palm catches my attention.

It runs lengthwise down my palm from my ring finger stopping midway down.

How could that be?

Just a couple of days ago I sliced it open on a broken beer bottle and now it's not just healed, but—I bring my palm closer to my face— now it looks like a faded memory.

A cut I got two days ago is now a scar.

An *old* scar.

Instead of waking myself up from a deep sleep and sprinting to the bathroom, my fingers are as wrinkly as my nana's thighs.

Holy shit.

"Is this real?" I say aloud to the empty house, not expecting an answer, but it would be great if some voice-over could fill me in.

I leave the now-cool water on the counter and study the rest of the kitchen. Really, it's everything I could ever want in a kitchen. White and light gray with splashes of red accent. Everything is tidy.

Just because my head—and my life—is a mess doesn't mean I want my living space to be that way. I always need everything neat. Orderly.

Deep down where I hide the crush on a high school geek, is another secret I can't tell Josie and Sof. I *love* organization.

My feet act on their own and carry me into the adjacent living room. A huge TV hangs on the wall. How deep is the cut-out in the wall for that TV?

Like the kitchen, the living room is exactly something from my dream home. A plush, dark blue sectional takes up the majority of the room. Two horizontal paintings hang on the wall, opposite the windows facing the pool.

The paintings remind me of day and night; one is awash in oranges and red, the other reminds me of twilight.

I continue around the corner and find another room. Like the bedroom, it has a wall of French doors opening to the back patio, but this one is smaller, with a white desk sitting in the center. Matching bookshelves line the wall across from me, filled with books, random bits of decor and picture frames.

I scoop up the first frame I find. It's Josie, Sofia and me. Not one of our high school pictures, or even a picture we'd taken when the three of us managed to catch up during a college break.

We're older.

Sofia's normally dark hair is a bit faded with a few wisps of gray. Her face is leaner, her cheeks sag just a touch.

Josie is in the middle. She still has her strawberry blonde hair hanging in loose waves, but lines radiate from the sides of her eyes.

Then there's me. My hair is shorter than now. In the photograph, it's tucked behind my ears with layers only reaching my jawline.

It's more than how we look. Josie in the middle with a white dress and white bouquet is very much a bride, Sof and I are in identical dusty pink dresses with wildflower bouquets of our own. How in the world did we let her talk us into wearing pink?

Okay, so Josie is married in this strange world. It looks recent. I'd always assumed she would have married after college, maybe find her way back to Daniel and have kids.

My gaze snags on a beam of light thrown my way from the rock on my hand. I'm poised to take my own trip down the aisle.

I put that frame down and pick up another. The photo a bit grainier. In this picture, my hair is much shorter, a cute, spiky pixie cut. An auburn-haired girl of about eight stands behind me, her little arms draped over my shoulders. A little boy with floppy blond hair and tiny dark-framed glasses sit on his adorable nose sits in my lap. We're all grinning at the camera.

Wait.

Do I have *kids*?

I lift up my shirt, searching my stomach for the same stretch marks my mom constantly complained that I gave her, but only flatness and unmarked skin stares back at me. Then the words around the frame snag my attention.

World's Best Aunt.

Ah, yes, the little girl is very definitely Josie's.

Three large frames sit on the wall behind my desk, each holding a diploma. One is for a Bachelor of Science in May 1999.

Science?

I was an art major yesterday.

The other is a Master of Science in Psychology, awarded in December 2001.

The final one proclaimed me a Doctor of Psychology in May 2006.

"Okay, so no cutting people open," I say aloud. "I just get inside their heads in other ways."

A wave of wooziness washes over me, like too many shots on an empty stomach. This is all too much. My best friend's wedding that I don't remember. Her adorable children. Me spending more than a decade in college. Gah, I hope I patched things up with my dad and he paid for all of that.

Suddenly, the need to talk to my best friend hits me. My gaze tears through the office—*my* office—looking for a phone, but this must be some sort of sacred space.

I head back to the kitchen, my fingers run along the walls thinking that maybe there's some super-secret phone cabinet.

Nothing.

Like a baby chimp, I clammer through the house, my eyes on the wall looking for a phone jack. The only thing I find are electrical outlets with weird slits in them.

After scouring every single inch of the huge house, including finding a nicely made bedroom and one that's obviously a junk room, I head back into my room, flopping onto the bed like a teenager on the verge of a meltdown.

A buzzing catches my attention.

That same rectangular thing on my nightstand is lit up.

It reminds me of the thing Dad showed me at brunch, what was it, a Palm Piper? No, Palm *Pilot*.

This time it's a picture of Craig and me taking up the face of it. Midway down is a smaller green rectangle. The words Craig "McFine Ass" Harrison are in bold. Under that are more words.

> Landed. Flight was fine, but coffeemaker was
> broken. Think they were trying to kill us. I'll call
> you tonight…

And, the words vanish.

More words pop up next.

> Of course, if there's any other fantasies you
> want to explore I'd be game.

Followed by a winking smiley face.

I gently pick the thing up. When I look at it, it snaps alive. I touch the green bubble and the glass cover changes, bringing up a keyboard on the bottom and the words from Craig just above it. I touch it and the words pull down, showing more than what had just popped up.

CRAIG "MCFINE ASS" HARRISON

Want sushi?

> I'm always down for sushi.

CRAIG "MCFINE ASS" HARRISON

Working late. Busy night in neuro. May just
stay at the downtown place.

> Okay, take care of your patients AND yourself.

CRAIG "MCFINE ASS" HARRISON

Have I told you lately how much I love you?

> I love you, McFine Ass. Can't wait to spend
> forever with you.

I continue reading more messages that appear to be between Craig and me. Mostly mundane stuff, letting one know when the other was leaving work, asking for fro-yo and, a testament to my occasional laziness, asking him to bring me a glass of water.

Then there are notes of love and adoration. Funny comics or short videos. Even a few pictures. One of him in scrubs and a face mask with what looks like a cap made for a child's head. Even with the mask covering his mouth, I can see the laugh from the way his hazel eyes crinkle at the sides.

A photo of Monique and me in a dark bar, toasting with martinis.

My finger traces the glass, the words flying all the way to his last message. I tap the bottom to pull up the keyboard. After reading our past messages, the need to respond to him rushes over me like diving off a cliff. I don't know why I'm doing it, but it feels like the thing to do.

> Hi! Yes! Call me. It'll help me find the phone.

A bubble pops up, then disappears. Pops up and disappears. Finally, words come through.

> CRAIG "MCFINE ASS" HARRISON
> Where are you texting me from?

Like that trip to Mexico after my third semester of Spanish, everything suddenly makes sense. The language of this strange place—time? —whatever this is, comes into focus.

Another message, a *text*, pops up.

> CRAIG "MCFINE ASS" HARRISON
> It was on your nightstand this morning.

This is my phone? I flip it over, study the smooth metal back. This is something out of a sci-fi movie. Wait, will this beam me somewhere?

Like back to my bathroom covered in my shaved-off hair. Back to my cut hand and broken heart. Back to a future—past?— that's about as certain as whatever my next major will be.

I touch the screen again and study the boxes. There's one for the weather. My calendar. Then, blessedly, one shaped like a phone.

When I tap it, a list of names pulls up. Some of the names I recognize. Craig. Josie. Sofia. Daniel. Mom. Dad. Now, Monique. Some unfamiliar.

My finger hovers over Josie's name. My person. The one who's always been there for me. When my parents were too caught up in their own divorce drama to take me back to school shopping, Josie and her mom had always been quick to rush me off to the mall.

When my dad was too busy with a trial to make it to the father-daughter dance, Josie's dad proudly strode in with both of us on his arm.

Then, when I thought that Wick might actually, finally, be 'the one,' Josie was there to give me a hug and whisper words I know she regretted ignoring. *Don't let him go.*

I rub away the burn of furious tears.

I should have whispered those words to him.

Don't let me go.

Josie shouldn't have to come to my rescue. Not yet. This is what adulthood is about. It's about finding a career that makes the heart sing and keeps my dad from grumbling that he's wasting his money. It's about making mistakes and messing things up but also having the independence to be accountable only to myself.

Adulthood is about navigating the headwinds of the future.

Adulthood is about falling in love and having that person love me back.

I find my way back and click and tap my way around my phone.

One square takes me to my bank account. Maybe this *is* the afterlife because there's no way I have this much money while alive.

Another square called Facebook opens and I scroll through photos and long messages from both people I know and don't know. After a click on my own picture, I'm taken to a bigger version of that picture. Like the photo down in the study, my hair hangs just past my chin. The face is still very much my own, but it reminds me of my mom. The cheeks a little softer, the skin a little duller, fine lines fan out from my eyes.

According to the description below, I have my own counseling practice, creatively known as, "Dr. Emily Murray, Counseling."

I scroll down a bit and come to the picture from my study of Josie,

Sof and me, but there's more with it. It's part of an album titled, "Josie and Daniel's Wedding."

"Oh good, they finally hooked up," I say to the device.

Whatever place this is, at least they finally pulled their heads out to admit they belong together.

I click through the rest of the pictures. A photo of Craig and me—he's handsome in a dark suit—laughing down as I stare head on at the camera. Me with the teenage redhead, looking more like Josie in the photo. Finally, a picture of me laughing, holding a just-tossed bouquet high over my head.

The bedroom goes from bright to dusky gray, and then darkness rolls in like a fog. I scroll through my history. Birthday wishes. Vacation photos. Faces I know. Most I don't. Through commenting on national events and mindless musings.

It's only when the light coming into the windows shifts from black to purple that I notice the time at the top of the phone. *6:10 a.m.*

I stare out the window at the lightening sky. My eyes are tired and bleary from staring at this tiny thing all night. Exhaustion swallows my mind, too. Like cramming-for-a-final-in-a-class-I'm-not-passing exhausted.

What is happening to me?

How can I go from a heartbroken twenty-year-old to an engaged middle-aged woman?

I can barely keep my own shit together, but somehow, I counsel other people.

I rub at the scar on my hand. Astrid said my life wouldn't be a straight path. She also said I'd be going on a long journey.

Her words play through my head as if I heard them yesterday.

Which I *did*.

My stomach curls in on itself, as if it knows what my brain can't quite comprehend. This is no amnesia. Or a dream. I'm not dead—abducted by aliens and being ruthlessly experimented on.

Like my nana used to say, *'Blink, and your life will be half over.'*

I just never thought she meant that literally.

CHAPTER 8

According to the calendar, I have a full day of clients ahead of me. Considering I'm barely qualified to give advice to a stuffed monkey, much less an actual human who has actual problems, it's probably best I avoid all contact with people.

I pull up my texts with Monique and type.

> Still not feeling great, so need to take another day off.

This is a pretty awesome way to communicate. No need to fake a cough or hold my nose to make it sound like I'm stuffy. If this is truly the future, it does not suck.

After another hour going through photos on my phone, I finally feel brave enough to call the one person who would call BS on me faster than a turd could hit the ground. The person who grounds me when thoughts swirl throughout my mind like a tornado.

With a deep breath burning my lungs, I press my best friend's name on my phone and wait for her to answer.

"Hey," Josie's voice is that first sip of a margarita, warms my soul while cooling the anxiety that's tightening like a boa constrictor. "I'm driving so you're on speaker, and I have minors in the car."

"So, keep it PG?"

When she laughs, it hits me that the Josie I'm talking to doesn't sound like the Josie who'd cleaned the cut across my palm. Like the scar, her voice is a little rougher, like the brightness of youth and the promise of a full life has worn it down like a boulder in a river.

"Why start now?" she says. "R-rated is perfectly acceptable. What's up?"

Shyness washes over me, like I'm talking to a celebrity. What am I going to say to her?

She's the person who knows me best. What if this is really just some sort of hiccup my brain is having and I'm truly a functional adult with a hot-doctor fiancé?

Maybe my memory is clogged at the day I shaved my head, and I need Josie to plunge it free.

"Feeling under the weather so called in sick." I nibble on my lower lip. "And I've been thinking about Wick, and that time I, uh, shaved my head."

"Huh, didn't have hearing his name on my Bingo card for today," she says with a half-hearted laugh. "He's lucky I never saw him again because I would be in jail right now." My best friend's voice is as sharp as a knife.

I believe she would've shanked him.

"What's this all about? You haven't mentioned that bastard since college," she adds.

My mind thumbs through what to say next and lands on what I think is least likely to have Jo questioning my sanity. "I have a client who might be going through something similar with a friend, and I was wondering what it was like when you found me. What I was like?"

It's her turn to pause.

Through the phone I hear the hum of the car and Josie giving instructions to her kids for the school day ahead.

"Aubrey has finally worn Peter and me down, so we'll be car shopping soon," she says at the end of a chorus of *have a good day* and *make good choices*.

Peter. Josie's ex-husband. I read through enough texts and Facebook to know that while they have an amicable relationship, their divorce brings up a bitter aftertaste like a swig of soured milk.

"Anyway," Josie says, the hum of the car back under her voice. "Back to Wick. It was terrifying. When I found you there, I freaked and checked your wrists." She takes a deep breath. "The hardest part though was having to finish what you'd started. You had missed some spots in the back, and it was all I could do to hold myself together while I shaved those parts. In some weird way, I felt like as much of an asshole as Wick."

The pain in my best friend's voice is a paper cut to my heart. Small, but stings like hell. I stand and pace the length of the bedroom.

None of this feels real.

Her words don't unleash a downpour of memories. I'm still stuck with a clogged memory bank.

"Hey, the office is beeping in," Josie says, cutting into my self-loathing. "You okay?"

I nod—not like she could see it. Could she? Hell, I could be hologrammed into her car for all I know. "Yeah." I clear my throat of something that feels an awful lot like sadness, but had to be allergies. "This is helpful. For my client, you know."

I end the call and continue my pacing. The past twenty-four hours makes about as much sense as the first day of class my freshman year of college when I'd misread a room number and stumbled into Calc 3 instead of 18th Century English Lit. Class had nearly been over when I realized my mistake.

If a conversation with Josie didn't unlock a lifetime of memories, maybe getting out of the house will?

After the best shower of my life, I rummage through a ridiculously large closet. I gravitate to Craig's side first; my fingers skip lightly over a few suits, flip through jeans and casual button-down shirts. Whether by his choice or encroachment, my side of the closet takes up three quarters to his one.

I stop in front of one section and tilt my head. Does my mom live with us?

Suits, both skirt and pants, stare back at me. A few solids; blue, tan and black, and a few patterned. Do I really need three different houndstooth jackets?

The side with my dresses is marginally better. Some long, a few that look like they'd hit my knees and, thankfully, still some stuck in the back short enough to have me consider my underwear choice.

After settling on the softest pair of jeans, with frayed hems and a T-shirt that says, '*Keep Talking. I'm diagnosing you,*' I emerge, ready to explore this new-to-me world.

For some reason, I expected to find Scarlett in the garage. Instead, I find the most beautiful creature in the world.

Also red, the car sitting in the garage—which has to be mine—is a sleek two-door BMW. Even though she's sitting still, it looks as if she's racing through a winding mountain road.

I fall into the driver's side, the black leather welcoming me like a warm hug from my Nana. This car is damn sexy. Apparently so futuristic it doesn't have a place to put the key.

"I don't know if you have a name yet," I murmur. "But we're going to call you Ruby." I hit Ruby's start button in the center console, and nothing happens. "Oh, don't do me like that," I say to my new love.

After several useless minutes of trying to figure out how to make the car start, I'm relieved to find that at least we still have manuals in the glove box, and this beautiful girl hums to life.

Turns out, I live in a pretty nice neighborhood in west Austin. A neighborhood that wasn't too far from the country club where I'd just met my dad for a chastisement with a side of eggs.

Some of the houses look familiar, but with a freshness to them. Like seeing that dirty-hot guy in art class show up in a tux with a fresh haircut.

I circumvent the streets, aimlessly going into the communities without a gate, following the curves of the roads, climbing the hills. Ruby, the gorgeous beast that she is, glides effortlessly, almost bored.

Driving has always been my therapy. A place where I'm alone, but at my own choosing. Not where my mom spent every minute showing clients homes. Or when I'd go to Houston to see my dad but end up spending more time with his housekeeper and her family when he pulled all-nighters at his firm.

Here in my car, it's just me. As me. I'm not a daughter or best friend. Or loser college student with zero talent and even less pull toward a career path. I'm not a girlfriend so desperate to be with a guy destined for fame that I lost myself.

I'm not even whoever the hell I am now.

Someone who might be dead or dying, or an amnesiac, or maybe never even existed.

Without thinking, I turn left onto a busier road filled with shopping centers and bumper-to-bumper cars.

In between the gleaming new buildings sits a lavender clapboard house. The neon 'Psychic' sign blinks a little slower as it lights up one letter at a time. The sign with the palm and eye is still there, but it's either dead or not turned on.

As if my car has a mind of its own—which frankly, wouldn't surprise me—I pull into the parking lot.

The inside is how I remember it, but a little dimmer. The hutch that was sage green a few days ago is now a muted gray. A dusty zebra print upholstered chair sits in one corner, with a purple shawl thrown over one of the wingbacks.

"You're late," that same scotch-on-the-rocks voice speaks from the depths of the building. The beads leading to the back swing open and Astrid appears.

A little more hunched, her long gray hair is now pulled back in a braid. She wore a similar outfit of a gauzy shirt and skirt, this time instead of purple it's a vibrant teal with the skirt a few shades darker than the shirt.

"Last time, I was early," I try to make my voice light and airy, but it has the energy of a dying balloon.

"Thought you were my niece." Astrid narrows her eyes. "You've been here before."

It wasn't a question.

"Yeah, about thirty years ago, although, it literally feels like yesterday to me." I thrust out my palm, eager to cut right to it. "Long story short, I don't remember anything since I left here at the start of my junior year of college, so can you do your thing and tell me everything I missed?"

The woman glances at my outstretched hand and pulls up ballerina straight. She closes her eyes, and a shudder rocks her body.

Just as I'm starting to wonder if the old lady was going to die on me, her eyes pop open, sharp, like a bird of prey.

Astrid reaches for my hand, her calloused thumb rubbing the scar. "There's nothing to tell."

"What do you mean? Look, apparently, I'm rich, so I'll pay you whatever for however long it takes, just help me remember."

"There's nothing to remember." She drops my palm and turns toward the back of her shop.

I follow her down the short hallway to the same room where she'd read my future.

"The Spirits should've warned me you'd be back," she says, her back to me as she lights candles around the room. "They like to mess with me sometimes. Guess that's how they get their kicks."

Her words float by me like dandelion seeds, making me scrunch my nose and hold my breath for fear I'll have a deadly allergic reaction to whatever she says next. "I don't understand. You told me I'd be going on a journey. Well, maybe it was a journey of single-hood, because as soon as I left here my boyfriend dropped the bomb that he was moving to L.A. Without me."

Astrid reaches for my palm again. "It's this cut, what did I say? It sliced your lifeline?"

"That my life wouldn't be a straight path, and honestly, that sums up most twenty-year-olds who've already had eight different majors."

She closes her eyes and sways in a circle again, that same groan building from deep inside her. "Yes, you've gone on a long journey, but you're close to home. You skipped ahead, like a stone skipping on water; you went from one age and leapt ahead to now. That's how your lifeline was cut."

I pull my hand back, her touch suddenly searing my palm. Her words scorching my brain.

"Wait, you mean I skipped thirty years of my life?" My heart bangs in my ribcage like an inconsiderate roommate. "I'm fifty? More than half my life is gone?"

Astrid closes her eyes again, her chin dropping. If it wasn't from the sound deep inside her chest, I would've guessed she fell asleep.

Several seconds pass before her eyes reopen. She shrugs. "The Spirits said this is where, *when*, you're supposed to be."

"No! Send me back!"

This is real.

This is mother-clucking real.

My heart has gone from an inconsiderate neighbor to an entire frat house jumping to some college party anthem. "I don't care that Wick left, and I did the dumbest thing in the world. I'll deal with that and major in whatever makes my dad happy, just please, send me back."

Where am I in 1996? Did Josie come back to our apartment to find a puddle of shaved hair and me gone? Or am I lying there unconscious?

Fiery tears fall down my face, scalding my cheeks. I cry for the choices I didn't make in my life, but I'm now, for better or worse, living the result of.

I grieve for the loss of years like the loss of a beloved grandparent. I sob for myself. I already know I've missed so much. Like a young person who died too soon, I'm being cheated out of so much life. "Please, Astrid, send me back." My voice is quieter this time. Pleading.

A cool, surprisingly soft hand cups the side of my face. "If it were up to me, I would. But Emily, the Spirits are emphatic that *this* is your path. Know this, they wouldn't do this if they didn't think you could handle it."

I sit there for a few more minutes, waiting for the storm of tears to pass. This is too much for my mind to comprehend. I'm thirty years in the future, a therapist and engaged to a man I don't know.

When I feel strong enough to lift my gaze from the table, I meet Astrid's milky eyes. They remind me so much of my Nana's. Kind, wise, but also not one to coddle.

With a nod and a sniff, I stand to leave.

"Emily," Astrid says, pausing my hasty retreat. "Remember the last thing I said? You're going to have to fight for something. I wish I knew what it was, to at least make that easier for you."

"But the Spirits want me to figure it out for myself?" I finish her thought and practically flee the small building.

I wish I could say the Spirits are screwing with the wrong girl, but nope, they are absolutely screwing with the right girl.

The one who has no flipping clue how to function in this world or find her way back to the past.

CHAPTER 9

I stare into the bathroom mirror for at least fifty years. Or maybe it was only five minutes. Time feels less like a constant, and more like something that hot guy in philosophy class railed against as being a man-made construct to keep humans under the power of corporate overlords. Or whatever the hell he was saying.

The steam from the insanely awesome shower clouds the mirror, hiding the finer details of my reflection, but showing my outline.

It feels appropriate to view myself like this. A shape devoid of a lifetime of memories.

Hollow on the inside.

After leaving Astrid's, I spent another night going through my phone. This feels like an anxiety-fueled dream. The one where I'm halfway through the semester when I realize I've completely forgotten I signed up for something super hard, like Calc 12, but it's too late to drop the class and I have a major test coming up.

Unfortunately, if Astrid and her Spirits are right, this is going to be harder than Calc 12, and I'm cramming for the hardest test ever.

My life.

It'd be so much easier to just hop in my super-fancy car and drive away.

Where would I go?

To Josie's, where I'm closer in mental age to her daughter than my best friend and where I would just get in the way of her and Daniel's newlywed bliss?

Or, to my mom, who, through the breadcrumbs of Facebook and text messages, has retired to the Colorado mountains with a handsome widower.

Or, even my dad? It doesn't surprise me that he isn't on the Facebook thing, and that we text so infrequently, that the ones I read are only a smattering of 'Happy Birthdays' and 'Merry Christmases' with nothing in between.

There's nowhere for me to go. Except to the office, where apparently, I'm not just a fully functioning adult, but a damn good therapist if the reviews are to be believed and it wasn't just Josie making up fake names—which I can see her doing as a symbol of her unwavering friendship.

I wipe away the steam, and my reflection comes into focus. For a middle-aged woman, I look pretty darn good. My skin is still smooth with the faintest of lines between my eyes. A check for gray hairs as intense as checking for head lice comes up empty—of both gray hair and lice.

"Alright, Em, you got this. Just put on pants and give good advice," I tell my reflection.

Twenty minutes later, I'm not just wearing pants, but a cropped, blue plaid blazer that matches my eyes, and a pair of nude stilettos. My shoulder-length hair is loose with waves that I never knew existed.

Ever since I can remember, and until just a few days ago when I shaved it, my hair hung mostly straight to the middle of my back.

Thankfully, my car is way smarter than me and has my office address programmed in. All I have to do is follow the mechanical, and somewhat judgmental, voice telling me to turn. What I don't account for is all the traffic. Austin's always had terrible traffic, but this is like next level *Super Mario Kart*.

After nearly dying at least twenty times and probably making a mortal enemy for life in another driver, I arrive at my office.

It's in another residential neighborhood on a street made up of businesses housed in former residences.

The yellow, clapboard house for my practice is a duplex, and the other side is a yoga studio. A weathered wooden sign claims that Dr. Emily Murray, therapist, works here—and knows what she's doing.

Even though my first appointment isn't for another hour, the door is unlocked. I hear a honey-laced voice that has to be Monique singing somewhere from the back.

I take in the lobby. The yellow from outside is carried inside as well, but it's more of a muted butter color.

A wooden desk sits to the right of the front door, the top shiny and tidy with just a computer—so small that when folded it's the size of a spiral notebook.

Across the room is a modest seating area, with just a love seat flanked by two mid-century modern armchairs surrounding a glass coffee table.

Bright nondescript artwork adorns the walls. I lean in to see if perhaps I got any better at art and painted these, but it appears my artistic ability still hovers around that of a drunk chimp.

Footsteps echo off the hardwood floor, pulling me out of the crime-scene-thorough examination of my office lobby.

Monique rounds the corner and draws up short. "Lordy, my heart just fell out of my chest." As if to prove her point, she holds one hand against her sternum. "What are you doing here so early? You usually fly in like a jet-propelled munchkin five minutes before your first appointment."

Guess some things haven't changed in thirty years.

I smirk. "I just thought I'd try something new. Get here early, prepare, you know, maturity and shit."

She eyes me like a pickpocket in a jewelry store, a *hmm-mmm* rumbling in her throat.

"I'll get the coffee going," she says. "You're going to crash later."

My office sits at the end of a short hallway. Like the lobby, the same butter yellow paint covers the walls, with only one large painting behind my desk.

The other wall is a replica of my office at home, holding framed diplomas, and the far wall has a large window looking out over an ivy-covered wall.

Much to my dismay for future naps, there's no therapist's couch, just a small seating area with four modest, yet comfy-looking chairs surrounding a table.

The only thing that makes this look like a therapist's office, aside from the diploma porn, is the box of tissue sitting in the middle of the coffee table awaiting some massive breakthrough.

I pull my computer from my bag and open it on my desk. The *This is Your Life* forensics exercise from yesterday taught me how to use it, and, not surprisingly, my password was my first guess, Scarlett92.

What I couldn't figure out, for the life of me, was how to read up on my clients' background.

"Hey Mo?" I call out.

She pops her head around the corner, steam from her coffee cup wafting around her face gives her an ethereal glow.

Like she's the angel to save me from myself.

"Yeah doc?"

I laugh nervously. It's practiced. Practiced so much that I hope it sounds natural, because something tells me Monique has an impeccable bullshit reader.

"Can you remind me how to get to client files? Obviously still getting over whatever it was I had." A serious case of the time warps, it seems.

She makes that *hmm-mmm* sound again. "I think your brain reset while you were sick," she says, crossing the room to log into my computer.

Somehow, I'm not surprised she has my password. I feel like we have that kind of relationship. The kind where she knows me better than myself. The kind where she steps into the Cat 5 hurricane of my life and cleans up the debris and straightens the plastic chairs.

"Do you remember when I started? Your filing system looked like a three-year-old did it. Some clients' filed by first name, others by last name and then there were a few who were filed by what I could only describe as a HIPAA violation," Monique is more speaking to herself, but I cling to this bit of history, even if I should be mildly offended.

Then again, I'm not surprised.

"To keep you from ruining my system, I link the client file in the calendar item," she adds, twirling the computer around to show me.

My first appointment stares back at me in paper form. Olivia Bentham. Twenty-six year-old marketing manager dealing with, and, this might as well be a clinical term, an asshole boss.

Olivia is a semi-regular client. She's probably canceled or rescheduled as many appointments as she's kept. From my notes, we haven't delved too much into her family history. Middle kid, parents are still together. Has two roommates and is still with her college boyfriend. Seems that the majority of our conversations about her trying to change her boss.

Monique knocks on my door. "Doc, Olivia is here." She quirks an eyebrow, possibly over the fact that Olivia was indeed there, or the fact that I look like I'm cramming for a test in a completely foreign language.

"Sure, yeah, send her in, because I am absolutely ready for this."

I am so not ready for this.

Olivia appears in my doorway with Mo pulling the door shut behind her.

She looks young, even to my youngish eyes. Olivia's hair is so blonde it's nearly white, and it stands out against her warm complexion and Brooke Shields-like eyebrows.

It's not that alone which makes her stunning, but the fact that she's at least six feet tall. Is she a model?

Maybe that's why she's got a toxic work environment.

"Hey, Dr. Murray." Her voice is as calm as a spring day. "Feeling better? Monique said you were under the weather when she had to reschedule us."

"Yeah, much better. Thank you for asking. Wanna get started?"

I wait for Olivia to take a seat, which she does and immediately kicks off her ballet flats, and tucks her long legs under her.

With a notepad in hand, I take the seat next to her and wait. What for, I'm not sure. Divine intervention?

To suddenly have thirty years of knowledge pop into my brain like an answer to a question on a final exam from the first week of class?

After a few seconds of a silence so uncomfortable I started to wonder if my parents were in the room, I say, "So, want to tell me how you're doing?"

That's all it took.

Olivia took a deep breath. "Yeah, so Cliff is up to his old tricks again. We'll have a meeting about a promotional campaign, and he'll give me very specific ideas of what he'd like to see. Then when I implement it, it's not what he wanted, and he loses his shit and yells at me. I tried some of the things you taught me. I stood my ground and pushed back, but he just kept yelling and started waving his arms all around. Like he didn't even realize he knocked a full coffee cup all over my desk.

"And then I walked out of my *own* office, mostly to get paper towels to clean up *his* mess, but also to diffuse the situation, like you'd said. He just followed me to the kitchen, now yelling at me in front of the whole office. I mean, it's not like it hasn't happened to all of us, but it's just so embarrassing."

At her break to breathe, I jump in. "You should quit."

She looks at me with big, confused eyes. "Quit what?"

"Your job."

"But I love my job. The products we make are really great for the environment, and I love my coworkers. I just want Cliff to change so it can be an amazing place."

I tap my pen on my notepad, looking down at the flowers I doodled instead of notes I should have taken. "How old is Cliff, give or take?"

She shrugs. "I dunno, early fifties."

"And this is his company, yes?"

Olivia nods.

"Girlfriend," I say, leaning forward and resting my forearms on my thighs. "He's not going to change. So, you're going to have to."

Her eyes grow shiny and lower lip trembles just slightly. "But you said to try to shift the power dynamic. To stand up and diffuse."

I shake my head. "Sometimes the best way to stand up for yourself is to walk away." Gah, how I wish I would've had someone say those words to me when I was running all over campus for Wick.

Something in the girl shifts. Her eyes go sharp, and that tremor in her lower lip grows steely as it presses into her top lip. "So let me get this straight. I've been coming here for nearly a year and for nearly a year you've been telling me I can change him."

"I doubt—"

"You know my insurance doesn't pay for this, right?" she says. "Like it paid for the first five appointments but after that I've been paying two hundred each time I come. I only make forty-five thousand a year, so between rent and student loans, I sometimes have to choose between seeing you and getting groceries."

"Olivia, I didn't know—"

"So, all those times I chose *you* over groceries, I did that thinking I could make things better at a job that I truly love. And for *what*? To find out that I could've saved myself *thousands of dollars* and have eaten a few more good meals because the answer all along was to *quit*?" She unfurls her legs and shoves her feet back into her shoes. "Well, you know what, you're right. I should quit. I quit you, this." Olivia waves her arms in the air. "And," she says, pausing with her hand on the doorknob. "You better believe that I will post about this on social and leave you a one-star Google review." With the dramatic flair of a soap opera star, my patient—correction, former patient—clomps down the hall and out the front door.

I blink. Dumbfounded. Did I really string this poor girl along? Not to mention, charge her two hundred dollars an hour?

Narcissists are narcissists. There's no changing them.

Why didn't I tell her this from the beginning?

I deserve a one-star Google review, whatever that is.

"You okay, doc?" Monique's warm voice reaches in and gives me the hug I need at this moment.

"You heard all that?"

"I think the entire block heard all that." Mo sits in the chair Olivia had just vacated. "You weren't wrong. Telling her to try. Giving her the tools to stand up for herself. If you would've told her to quit right away, that's what she would've done for the rest of her life when things are tough. Quit. Sad she had to practice that with you, but maybe you're the first step for her. Come on, I'll make you a cup of jet fuel."

Jet fuel, it turns out, is my favorite way to have coffee, but due to the caffeine-sugar combo, Mo only lets me have it on special occasions.

Like getting chewed out by a patient.

I watch as she fills a large mug with two teaspoons of sugar, then half-full of coffee, followed by a heavy pour of creamer topped off with a double shot of espresso.

That first sip is like a shot of adrenaline to a stopped heart. Or bruised ego.

Both hurt just the same.

We're sitting in the kitchen in a companionable silence when the front door chimes.

"Must be a delivery," Mo says, setting her cup down. "Too early for your next appointment."

A second later, she calls me.

Jet fuel still in hand, I head into the lobby. There's another twenty-something. This time, a young man with dark brown hair that's grown out in the back and up top but shaved on the sides.

Are mullets still a thing in the future?

That's unfortunate.

He's medium height and lean, wearing dark jeans and loafers, complimented by a teal V-neck T-shirt under a navy blazer.

"Dr. Murray?" he says, thrusting a hand in my direction. "Crispin Dunne."

I take his hand. It's soft with incredibly well-groomed nails. "Hi, Crispin, you've come at the right time, my first appointment finished early, and I've got some time before my next."

"He's not here for an appointment," Mo says, the Caribbean-lilt is gone. Instead, her voice is as flat and dry as a desert.

"Yeah, what I was telling your assistant here..."

Mo does her signature *mmm-hmm* at that and turns away.

"Is that I just opened a practice down the street, Zenith Therapy, because we'll get you to the top of your potential." He pauses to flash an expensive smile. "Anyway, I wanted to come say hello, let you know that I'm here, and start the conversation about your future."

"My future?" I can't even have a conversation about my past, and this mullet-having, blazer and V-neck wearing guy wants to talk about my future?

"Yeah, I mean, you've been in practice for a while now, and I studied your website. No offering for virtual behavioral health, no mention of how to manifest your goals or to navigate the comparisonitis that runs rampant among today's teens and twenty-somethings thanks to social media. You're not even creating content."

I take a sip of jet fuel and wait to see if what he just said makes any more sense.

It doesn't.

"Truth be told, you're rather old school. Which is cool, in a very throwback nineties sort of way, but—" he takes a step in. "Emily, may I call you that? You know, peer to peer. That just doesn't work in today's world."

"Okay, sorry, what was your name again? Crispy?"

"Crispin."

"Anyway, Chippy, I don't know if your kindergarten teacher taught you this, but this is not how you make friends. By coming into their business and calling them old."

His blue eyes widen in practiced earnestness. "No, Emily, Dr. Murray, that's not what I'm saying. It's just, perhaps it's time to pass the torch. You know, to the next generation." Crispin shifts his feet, as if gearing up for another strategy. "You're like, what, fifty? That's how old my mom is, and she's preparing to retire. So, I was thinking you might like to retire and hand off your clients to me for a fresh approach." He finishes his sentence with another overly bright smile, like a kid who made poo-poo in the big boy potty.

"I have no intention to retire. My clients are perfectly happy with me."

He shifts again, this time leaning against one of the chairs in the lobby, crossing his ankles and his arms across his chest. "Oh, like Olivia? Yeah, ran into her outside. Not once did you talk to her about a vision board for her growth."

I match his stance. "What's a vision board going to do? Sometimes the best thing is to know when to quit."

Crispin nods. "I'm glad you agree. Well, anyway, I've always been a fan of meeting your opponent face-to-face." He pulls a business card from his pocket and hands it over. "Whenever you're ready to take your own advice, just text." He walks out the door, and follows the path to the sidewalk, where he hops on a scooter and zooms away.

Really, a scooter? Is he twelve?

Mo joins me. "You know you walked right into that one, doc."

I take a sip of lukewarm jet fuel. "Yep. You know I could break him in half, right?"

She takes a sip from her cup. "Yep. You know I hope you do, right?"

I've never hated mullets and scooters more in my life.

CHAPTER 10

I am utterly exhausted when I finally finish for the day. Luckily, I dial it back for the next appointments. Somehow, I manage to dish out some good advice without making it seem like I'd been sitting on the answer this whole time and milking my poor clients for everything they've got.

With the last client seen, and their next appointment booked, Monique and I lock up for the day.

"Hey doc," she says, turning toward me on the porch shared with the yoga studio next door.

Neither of us seem to be in a hurry to leave.

It's one of those perfect central Texas spring days, the humidity is low, a cool breeze dances in the newly sprouted leaves and the sun is at that perfect place in the sky where it reminds us pale-skinned, easy-to-burn chicks that it's not all bad, just a gentle giant orb in the sky.

"You're not actually considering that little man's offer, are you?" Mo hitches her large, colorful tote higher on her shoulder. "You'll tell me if I need to start looking for another job? You know, mouth to feed and all, and the more I feed him, the more he grows. It's a vicious cycle."

In my infinite perusal of the pictures on my phone, I found a whole series of Monique and me with the most adorable little boy on the planet. Large brown eyes framed by impossibly long lashes with a wide, snaggletoothed smile. That kid will break hearts. Mine included.

"I meant what I said. I may not break him physically, even if I want to, because that would be illegal, but I won't let that twerp close us down."

She looks into the studio next door. I follow her gaze, and several sticking-up butts greet us.

"But he's not wrong, about needing to make a few updates," she adds, staring at the yogis next door instead of talking to me.

Even if I don't speak the language of this century, I understand what she's saying.

I nod. "Yeah, you're right. Can you help me with that?"

My wonderful assistant turns, unleashing a smile brighter than the setting sun. "Absolutely, doc. I'll start making some notes tonight." She leans in. "Now, go give that hot brain surgeon a welcome home that will make him never want to leave again."

Craig. That's right.

Today's the day he gets back home from the conference in Boston. We've traded a few texts, but nothing deeper than him telling me about drunk doctors singing karaoke, and me telling him I was feeling a bit under the weather, but nothing to worry about.

A new car is in the garage when I pull in. His much more sensible mid-size SUV compared to my little red rocket.

Country music greets me when I come in through the utility room. A rich voice harmonizes with the artist, singing along distractedly, but pausing long enough to call my name.

I drop my bag in the hall and step toward the kitchen. A swarm of butterflies wrestle in my stomach as I take in the handsome man donning a frilly apron and up to his elbows in flour.

"Hey, gorgeous," he says, looking up from a countertop full of flour.

Wait, did he make me ravioli?

"I opened up a Montepulciano." Craig nods to a wine bottle on the opposite counter with an empty glass beside it. "I'd pour you some but…" He holds up two flour-covered hands and grins like a kid caught making mud pies.

How did I greet him before? Was it long, sultry kiss? Or, did we dish about our days?

People have their routines. Their rhythms. What's ours?

"Dinner will be served at seven," Craig says, saving me from trying to figure out our rhythm. "Figured a healthy dose of carbs will get you back to your charming self in no time."

Despite my best effort to play it cool, the teasing snark in his voice hits me in my warm, gooey center.

"I've never met a carb I didn't love." I top off his glass and fill mine before taking a seat on the opposite side of the island to watch him work…and study the man I'm apparently marrying in just a few months.

I calm my internal panic in a long sip of wine.

I can see why future me is attracted to him. A thick head of dark brown hair is laced with the lightest dusting of gray, just enough to give him dimension without adding years. A light tan covers his face, and the faintest of stubble dusts a sturdy jaw.

His T-shirt fit perfectly, loose where it needs to be loose and tight where it needs to be tight. I can only see the top of his jeans from where I sit, but the memory of the low-slung towel from a few days ago rises up like the undead.

However, who's the man underneath that very hot and fit exterior?

Does he call his mother every day to check in on her? Is he someone who helps people in need, or does he only serve those who can pay insanely high medical bills?

I'd like to think I wouldn't be with someone more like the latter, but I let myself get lost in Wick and his dreams.

Not to mention, I'd charged a poor girl a lot of money for nearly a year only to tell her the solution to all her problems was to simply quit. My character barometer is obviously very, very off.

Maybe I should be less worried about who this man is and more worried about who *I* am.

"Want to talk about it?" Craig's voice pulls me back into the kitchen. He's brushing olive oil on the ravioli, but his hazel eyes are focused on me. "You're obviously processing something. I'm used to a Cat 5 Hurricane Emily when I get home, but this," he points the food brush at me. "Feels like a volcano waiting to erupt. Want to get it out before you blow?"

I laugh. Mostly because of his description of me as two different types of natural disasters, but because not once in the months that Wick and I dated did he ever ask how I was.

Not even that time I threw caution to the wind and indulged in questionable, yet delicious, road-side chicken enchiladas and spent two days camped out in my bathroom.

"Just a really long day catching up on appointments." I swirl the wine in my glass, watching the liquid cling to the side. What did Mom call this? Oh yes, legs. Even though I wasn't twenty-one yet, my mom believed that if alcohol wasn't taboo, I'd be less likely to fall victim to college party life. What she failed to realize is that teaching me how to drink wine and make a good, dry martini didn't exactly sync up to the college curriculum of beer pong and trashcan punch.

"This guy came in," I say, as Craig gently drops the ravioli into a pot of boiling water. "He's opening a practice down the street and asked me to retire and transition my clients to him."

He pauses and glances over his shoulder. "Are the police going to knock on our door tonight? Do I need to give the lawyer a heads up?"

A laugh nearly causes the sip of wine to spew from my nose. Maybe I fell for his humor first. I laughed at Wick's jokes, but truthfully, they weren't really all that funny. I laughed because I felt like I needed to.

"No, he walked out on his own, with no broken bones." I pause, trying to find the words I want to say to a man I don't know. "It's just..."

He turns from the cooking pasta and leans on the countertop; his face just inches from mine. "I get it. Every new generation thinks they have all the answers the previous one doesn't. And sure, the residents I work with today are coming out of school with newer, different skills. Many of them grew up playing video games, so robotic surgery is just another video game to them. But we have experience and patience, and better taste in wine." Craig leans in and kisses my forehead. "And I doubt those are things you had when you first opened your practice. All right, dinner will be ready in fifteen. Want to throw together a salad to balance this carb invasion?"

We settle in at the small kitchen table.

Turns out, Craig spent more than a few hours preparing butternut squash ravioli, just because he had the time and knew it was my favorite dish.

I savored each bite with the appreciation of a dying woman having her last meal.

While I do my best to tamp down a foodgasm, Craig tells me about the conference.

The other doctors he admires, the ones he doesn't. He talks about the breakout sessions he sat in on, and even how his own presentation went. I really only understand every other word, but it's not his *words* I'm focused on. It's how I feel, sitting here with a total stranger who somehow knows me better than the man, okay, *boy*, I'd dated for the last six months. Knows me better than I know myself in this time. Maybe it's the combination of the wine, the food, the fact that he's more interested in me than telling me all about him, or even that in a very weird, crush-on-a-friend's-dad sort of way I'm incredibly, physically drawn to him.

I volunteer for clean up so Craig can unpack from his trip and catch up on work. Just as I'm inspecting my handiwork, movement in the doorway catches my eye.

He stands there, barefoot in pajama pants and T-shirt. The smile on his face is equal parts admiring and mischievous.

"Hi," I breathe it more than say it.

He takes three steps toward me. "Hi." Craig leans in and instinctively I lift my chin, preparing for the same kiss that just days ago zapped me like an unsuspecting bug. His mouth bypasses my lips and goes straight to a spot on my neck, just behind my ear.

No one has ever kissed me there. Probably a good thing, because there seems to be a direct line to my legs, cutting off all communication commanding them to stand.

A laugh rumbles in his chest as he catches me.

"Works every time," he whispers, which like the kiss, has magical powers over my nervous system.

Craig switches to the same spot behind the other ear, liquifying the few remaining bones in my body.

"What was that fantasy you were tempting me with the other day? Hot flight attendant? Mile high club?"

The other day.

He means the day I woke up having skipped more than half my life.

The day *after* I happened to drive by Wick's house at the right time to find that he was going to leave me without a goodbye. The day after my father tells me that unless I pick a real major, the college fund was officially closed.

The day after I let the unrequited love of an okay-boy crush me.

Standing here with a man who knows my body, who knows how to feed me and make me laugh. Who apparently loves me and asks about my day before even telling me about his.

I should grab him by the hand see what other secrets he knows about me, but how can I? How can I give myself to him when I don't even know who I am, or what I have to give?

I step back and clear my throat, trying to ignore the confusion written across his face. "You're probably exhausted," I say. "And I need to catch up on some work. Maybe later?" The smile I give him is as weak as my excuse. I duck my head as I push past him, escaping to my office.

I slide down the closed door and wrap my arms around my knees, holding myself like I wish I could let Craig hold me, as waves of homesickness—for a time, not a place— threatens to pull me under like a riptide.

CHAPTER 11

I t's nearly midnight when I crawl into bed next to Craig's sleeping form. He stirs only slightly, rolling over to tuck an arm around me, pulling me toward him.

I don't even remember falling asleep. Yet another way this mystery man is magical, his mere presence calms the hyperactive thought bunnies bouncing through my head.

When I wake, his side of the bed is empty and the bathroom is quiet. I grab my phone and see a text from him.

Early rounds this morning. Start my on-call shift this evening. I'll keep you posted on how today's looking. Love you.

Were we one of those couples who confess our undying love at every opportunity, or did we save them for private moments, trading the declarations like precious diamonds?

Can I say the words when the time comes?

Luckily the second day at the office starts off much smoother. Monique is leaving early today to pick her son up from school, so she has her head down doing whatever she does to keep my business from running off a cliff.

My clients today aren't too taxing. First up is Maya, a shy, quiet college student who struggles with both her confidence and her weight. Her parents sent her to me in hopes I could convince her to eat better and workout more. Unfortunately, I suspect her parents have a lot to do with the struggles that sent her to me.

"Maya, can I ask you a question and have you answer me honestly?" I lean forward and set my notepad aside. "I know what your parents think we should talk about here, but what do *you* want to talk about?"

"Um," she says, glancing toward the door like her parents might be listening on the other side.

"You're an adult. Our conversations are private. We can talk about the weather, how school's going, or we can talk about nothing at all and sit here in uncomfortable silence." I smile, hoping humor will slice through the nervousness.

She sits for several long minutes, staring at her entwined hands and takes a big breath. "Have you ever felt like you don't belong in your own family? Everyone else is tall, blond and thin, and I'm nothing but recessive genes." Maya straightens, as if letting those words out unleashed a long-held weight. "Mom and Dad both want me to follow their footsteps and go to law school. Mom is so worried that if I don't lose weight, I'll never meet a nice boy to marry. But what I can't bring myself to do is tell them I don't want to be a lawyer and I don't like boys." The girl's chest heaves and red splotches her neck and cheeks.

"Yes, to answer your question, my parents divorced when I was young, so I didn't really feel like I had a family. After that, my mom got her real estate license and went to work building a business. I'll just say, I felt more at home at my babysitter's house than mine." I pause, waiting to see how those words land with Maya.

There's probably some rule about therapists not sharing personal details, but considering I never actually studied for this I'm not responsible for rules I don't know. "I was an art major and my dad threatened to cut me off if I didn't switch to law and follow in his footsteps."

Her eyes widen. "What happened?"

I shrug. "I didn't major in law." Maybe the funding was cut off, maybe it wasn't. Either way, my answer was the truth. "Maya, when was the last time you did something just for yourself?"

"I had a pint of cookies and cream ice cream Mom would go nuclear if she knew I ate."

And there we go. "Do you think you had that because *you* wanted it or you were hungry, or was it because that's how you feel you can control your life?"

She didn't answer me.

Didn't need to.

The tears streaming down her face said everything.

I glance at my watch. We still have ten minutes left, but I think this is as far as I can go with her today. "Maya," I say as she's blowing her nose. "Before our next appointment, will you do me a favor? Will you do something just for yourself? And, if it's to eat ice cream, that's fine, but think about something else. Like maybe sign up for a class you've wanted to take, or ask a girl out that you have a crush on. It can be little or big, as long as it's what *you* want."

She nods and pulls out another wad of tissue before escaping my office.

I follow her out and find Monique smiling, watching the girl walk down the front porch.

"Does it mean I broke them if they're crying?" I ask.

"No, doc, it means you made her see her truth. Vision board be damned, sometimes all people need is someone on their side."

Isn't that all we can ask for?

To know we have someone, hopefully lots of someones, on our side.

My thoughts flutter to the people on my side. Mom and Dad, in their own ways. Monique, Craig, Josie.

Aside from a quick conversation and a handful of texts, I haven't seen my best friend in this present. I'll call her and see if she's free this evening. Maybe seeing her in person will unlock whatever memories from the last few decades are secreted away in my brain.

My after-lunch appointment abruptly canceled. I peek at her files, another twenty-something who wanted me to cure her of all her negative energy and help her manifest her way to becoming a social influencer. Whatever the hell any of that means.

The next two clients are easy enough to manage as my mind chews through my own issues.

One of them wants me to dissect everything she deems as unfair to help her find a way to validate that the other person wronged her. It takes everything I have to not tell her sometimes bad shit happens to decent people, like a twenty-year-old college student whose dad threatens to cut her off, then she happens to catch her boyfriend at the exact minute he was leaving town to become a rock star only to go home and in a fit of anger shave her head and wake up thirty years later.

See, sister, it could be so much worse.

The last client of the day is a woman about my age, and from the joined accounts, I discover her teenage son is also a client, but they don't come together. From my files, Julia is one of my longest standing clients, coming to me when she was a young mother who just needed to get stuff off her chest.

Her youngest son, Tyler, is about to finish his junior year of high school, so our conversations have gone from how she can carve out 'me-time' to how to prepare to be an empty nester.

Mo is already gone by the time Julia arrives, so instead of going back to my office, we sit in the lobby waiting area.

After an hour of what truly feels more like two girlfriends catching up on life, Julia stands and stretches.

"You know, Em, I like this approach you took today," she says.

Honestly, this was the only way I *knew* to approach my time with Julia. Even though physically we're close in age, mentally and emotionally I felt much more at ease with the younger patients so far. At least the ones I didn't manage to piss off.

"Oh yeah?"

Julia gathers her purse. "Yeah, it felt less, preachy? Not that you were ever preachy before, but I always felt like you were you and I'm me, and today we were just, *we*." She laughs. "You'll probably spend between now and our next appointment analyzing that." She snaps her fingers. "That reminds me. Tyler. I need to cancel his next appointment."

"Sure, no problem." I cross to Mo's desk and rummage for a pen and paper, knowing better than to tackle the scheduling system on my own. "When does he want to reschedule?"

She shakes her head. "Em, I said cancel, not reschedule." She takes a deep breath and drops her arms in exasperation. "It's really a stupid reason, I think, but he found this new therapist on social media, Crispin something or other. Anyway, he's been watching some of his videos and feels like he might be a better fit. But Em—Dr. Murray, please know he said it's not anything you did wrong; he just felt that someone, well, someone younger would be a better fit."

I have to focus on what expression I'm giving her. To keep my smile from dropping like a tray of glasses in a clumsy waitress's hands. To keep my eyes from narrowing like I could shoot lasers through the window all the way down the street to a competing office. To keep a slew of curse words that would make a sailor proud from slipping out of my mouth.

"But don't worry, I'm not going anywhere. You've been there for me through so much it feels only right that I stay with you through this."

I shift my concentration to my chest. To keep the spear of her pity from piercing my heart.

CHAPTER 12

After Julia leaves, I call the one person who will not only lift my spirits but help me plot that little twerp's murder and hide the body. No matter what sort of time warp flung me into the future, I know in my bones she'll be there.

"I was just thinking about you," Josie says as a way of greeting.

"Were you thinking that you need happy hour with your BFF, because I'm definitely thinking that."

She pauses, not awkwardly so, just long enough to let a seed of doubt plant in my heart. "I can! Sorry, just had to make sure I didn't have some sort of kid-related thing. Let me text Aubrey to remind her to bring Ben home from school, and I'll be on my way. Meet at the usual?"

"Err…" It's my turn for the awkward pause. Luckily, I quickly find in my maps that I routinely go to a bar called The Usual. "Yep, sounds great. See you soon."

Fifteen minutes later, I'm walking into a dimly lit bar with dark, worn wooden floors, cracked pleather banquets and a wall full of eighties era video games. No wonder Jo and I come here so often.

With a dirty martini in hand—because this is totally a dirty martini type of bar—I grab a table in the middle of the room and wait to see my best friend for the first time in—well, I guess thirty years.

I've seen pictures of her, so it's not that I wouldn't recognize her physically.

Would we recognize each other on the same level today that we did when I saw her last?

I rub the scar on my palm. Is she still the person who cleans glass and dirt out of a cut on my hand while murmuring ways to kneecap my shitty boyfriend?

Am I still the person she called when a broken heart threatened to strangle her after letting Daniel go back in high school?

A few sips into my drink, the door opens again and she's there.

Future Josie isn't really all that different than the one I've always known as well as I know myself. Her hair is still long, but a few inches shorter than the length that fell to the middle of her back. The strawberry blond is a bit muted.

Once the door closes behind her and my eyes adjust to study her face, I take in how much she reminds me of both her parents—the shape of her mom's face with her dad's warm, sly smile.

I nearly knock over my drink as I hop up from the table and wrap my best friend in a tight hug.

"Sweetie, you okay?" she whispers in my hair.

The need to tell her the truth burns my gut. I'm so far from okay I couldn't find it on a map. That I don't know what's worse, the fact I'm nursing a broken heart, but also engaged, and incredibly attracted to, a man I just met.

I want to cry to her about how my life is more than half over, and how I experienced none of it. That I feel like a character plucked out of *"The Oregon Trail,"* forced to figure out how to live in this new world, where phones aren't used for talking, my car can parallel park better than me, and any bit of random trivia is an internet search away.

All of those words and feelings, grow cold feet and climb back down my throat, back into my heart where I'll keep them safe from a cruel world.

We break the hug, and Josie tucks a strand of my hair behind my ear.

"Get a drink," I tell her. "And then I'll fill you in on my latest work drama."

With her own dirty martini, Jo sits across from me. "That looked like a good idea," she says, nodding to my now half-full drink. "Why didn't you tell me running your own business would be this hard?"

"Because I can't be the only one having all the fun." It's an answer I'd say at any point in my life. "Want to talk about it?"

She shrugs. "Same old, same old. I have the world's best team, but sometimes I feel like I have twenty children instead of two. And, my own teenagers are more mature than the grown-ass adults who work for me. But what about you? You never have work drama. Is everything okay with Mo?"

"Mo is great," I rush the words out, because they're true. From social media and my photos, I learned that Monique joins Josie, Sofia and me often on girls' nights. The much-needed fourth leg of our three-legged stool. "If anything, she'll keep me out of jail. It's this new therapist who opened an office down the street. He came by to introduce himself, and to tell me it's time to hang up the therapy couch. That I'm..." I take a deep breath. "Too old."

Josie glances to the left and right and leans in, dropping her voice. "Blink twice if you need help burying his body."

A much-needed laugh erupts from my chest. The kind only the person who knows you best can coax out of you when all you feel like doing is crawling into your childhood bed and cuddling with a musty old stuffed animal.

"Funny, Craig said something very similar. Do I really scream murderess that much?"

"Absolutely." Josie takes a drink of her martini. "Competition sucks. But, it also keeps you on your toes. When I started Mamacita, there were just a handful of other small companies doing the same thing. Now, big corporations are trying their own small business-like all-natural cleaning products. And sure, sales always take a dip when one of those companies launch their product line, but we always even back out after that. Plus, your clients love you, and more importantly, they *trust* you. They won't jump ship for him."

I throw back the rest of my martini, flirting with getting a second like it's the hot guy at the bar. Ultimately, deciding, like that hot guy at the bar, I'll regret it deeply when daylight comes. "They're already jumping," I mumble, not especially eager to admit defeat. "He swooped in and stole a client as she was leaving. And, the son of one of my longest clients told his mom that he wanted someone younger. That's just the first two days."

"Shit," Josie says on an exhale.

"Shit," I agree.

"It feels like yesterday we were the young punks ready to take over the world," Josie says, tracing her finger around the rim of her nearly-empty martini glass. "We should get another round. Craig and Daniel won't mind driving us home. Again."

"I wish I could, but Craig is working late." I can't tell her the real reason I'm afraid to have another. That the alcohol will dislodge the truth midway through the next drink, and I'll be blubbering about how it was literally last week that Wick was leaving me and I was shaving my head. Ever practical Josie will listen intently while texting Craig under the table that something is seriously wrong with me.

She wouldn't be wrong.

"Yeah, another downside to getting old. We can't drink on a school night and be a fully functioning adult the next day anymore." Josie's blue-green eyes study me, the way a doctor studies a longtime patient to check for any underlying conditions.

I steady myself, hoping that the terror at being misplaced in time isn't shining through my eyes. If there is anyone in the world who'd pick it up, it's Josie.

"You're going to be okay, Em," she says. "And, I know you don't like change—"

"What? No, I'm always up for trying something new." I cut her off, because how could someone who changed her major a million times her first two years of college not like change? I love change. New hobbies, jumping out of airplanes, hopping in the car for a road trip with no destination in mind. I thrive on that stuff.

Josie smiles, and it screams being patient with child. "Yes, you do love trying something new, but only if you can go back to your comfort zone. It's not a dig, Em, I swear. But you always ran when someone got too close, until Craig. And you never had to market your business because you're just so damn good at it, until this guy showed up. So yeah, a wedding and a business competitor. It's new, but it's also change."

Damn.

This is why I called Josie. To be the mirror I couldn't be. To tell me the truths I couldn't tell myself.

"So, what do I do?"

Josie grabs my hand and leans over the table. "You marry the love of your life, and you kick that little punk's ass. But purely in a business sense for the latter. I'm pretty sure we'll hurt ourselves trying to discard a body these days."

CHAPTER 13

I'm buzzing on my drive home. Not from that strong-enough-to-put-hair-on-my-chest martini, but from that hour of time spent with my best friend. Seeing Josie, seeing with my own eyes that she's still the same person to me and I'm still the same person to her gives me confidence to navigate this strange world.

Ruby rings as soon as I turn into my neighborhood, which is probably really my phone that seems to be magically connected to my car, like some sort of hive mind. Craig's name flashes on the small screen.

"Hi," I say after pushing the accept button. Too bad I never invested in technology stock—then again, not sure how rich a twenty-dollar investment would make me today. Or if I even know *how* to make an investment.

"Do you have dinner plans?" he asks.

It might have been the martini's influence, but it sounds like his voice wobbles on a fulcrum of nerves.

Were we not the happy couple our messages and social media led me to believe?

"A third-year resident offered to stay up at the hospital tonight and said she'll call if I'm needed," Craig says. "I can grill some steaks, open some wine for you."

The way to my heart is a path lined with delicious food, including a perfect steak.

"Sure! I met Jo for a drink but almost home now."

"Great." The smile in his voice plays over the car's speakers. "See you soon."

Thirty minutes later, Craig arrives with steaks, asparagus and a bottle of wine. He pours a glass of wine for me and iced tea for himself, since he's on call, and I settle in on an outside chaise lounge while my *fiancé*—a word still so foreign I sometimes feel like I also woke up in another country instead of a another century—prepares the steaks while the grill warms up.

"Oh and cook mine just on the—"

"The other side of mooing," Craig finishes my usual cooking instructions. "The day you ask for it well done will be the day when I wonder if you've been replaced by a clone." He chuckles. "How's Jo? Should Daniel and I prepare to be prison husbands or were you on good behavior?"

I cringe at my flub. Of course, he knows how I like my steak cooked. He probably also knows what sushi I like best, better than me, considering that I'd only been able to afford California rolls on my college-student budget. He probably even knows what wine I like best. By the way the rich fruit and leathery texture explodes in my mouth with a sip, is *this* wine.

Six months of dating Wick and he couldn't even remember to ask if I wanted anything when he was picking up burgers for the band.

As cliché as it sounds, is this the difference between dating a man and a boy?

"All good with Jo, just catching up and talking about work."

"How was your day?" He asks over the sizzle of flipping a steak. "Better than yesterday?"

I throw him a glance. Even though his focus is on the grill, I can also tell he's equally intent on our conversation, on my responses. "Marginally," I say, and go on to recount my conversation with Julia. "Deep down inside, I'm his age." I say about Julia's son. It's a lie. It's not that deep down, it's on the surface, and I'm probably younger than Crispin by a good seven years.

Craig pulls the steaks off the grill and replaces them with asparagus. "Yeah, I know what you mean. Some days I feel sixteen, then I go run a few miles on the hard pavement and my knees remind me that I'm in my fifties."

We take advantage of the perfect weather before summer and mosquitoes descend over Austin and eat outside.

The conversation flows easily, meandering from the latest with his work colleagues to how Mo offered to help me battle Crispin Dunne in more legal, and less lethal ways. We talk about mundane things, about how we need a rainy weekend to finally tackle cleaning out the garage and how Craig wants to convert an unused bedroom into a "listening den" where he can play old albums with concert-level sound.

It's when I pour a second glass of wine, likely something I'll regret tomorrow, after the earlier martini, that Craig brings up a more serious topic.

Our wedding.

"Is it weird that we've done more planning for our honeymoon than the wedding?" he asks. His hazel eyes aren't on me, but instead he's gazing at the first few pinpricks of stars popping out overhead.

"Not to someone who eats dessert first?" From the forensic research of my life, I know that just a few days after our wedding we're jetting off to the Maldives for two weeks. I can completely understand why future me chose to focus more on that than the boring part of actually getting married.

"I know we talked about something low-key, but, don't get mad, I made an appointment with a wedding planner at the venue for next weekend," Craig says, still studying the sky, as if he's afraid to meet my eyes. "Think of it as someone who will do all the things that make you break into hives."

Like marrying a complete stranger?

The thought wanted to fly out of my mouth like a caged bird spotting a window to freedom, but I drowned in a large gulp of wine.

This man loves me. It's evident in how when given a night off, Craig immediately wanted to spend time with me. How he knows how I like my steak cooked, and my favorite wine. How he knows planning the honeymoon is more important to me than the wedding, and even with that, he took the steps to have someone help.

It's obvious I feel something in return. How relaxed I feel in his presence. How in the two times we've kissed since I woke up thirty years in the future, my body responds to him like a chocoholic in a candy store. More, more, more. I can't stop with just one kiss.

"Thank you," I say, standing and gathering our plates. "It's better to let a professional handle the wedding planning anyway. I'd likely forget something important, like chairs or the officiant. I'll take care of the clean up since you cooked."

"You sure? Thanks Em, I have a bit of work to do." His smile glows like one of the stars overhead.

While I rinse the dishes and load the dishwasher, my mind goes back to the kisses Craig and I've shared, how there was more passion in those kisses than anything I felt with Wick.

Wick wasn't the first guy I slept with, but he was the one I'd slept with the most. Who I had an opportunity to learn his body as well as I knew my own.

I was surprised the first time we'd slept together, that Wick seemed to know instinctively what I'd like. As I rinse my wine glass and load it into the dishwasher, it hit me how he never progressed. Like writing a hit song, he found the one thing the masses loved and just rewrote that song over and over and over. Never tried to play something new.

My gaze goes down the hall toward our bedroom, toward where Craig padded off with his laptop in hand. Something tells me he didn't just know my body, but he'd never stop trying to learn more. Never stop trying to make beautiful music.

With a strong martini and two glasses of wine flowing through my bloodstream, I follow the path he'd taken earlier to see if my body, my heart, knows something my brain doesn't.

He's stretched out on the bed, back propped up against the headboard. Craig studies his laptop with dark frame glasses perched on the bridge of his nose, awakening my deeply buried Clark Kent crush.

I stalk across the room in what I hope is more sexy than predatory. Straddling him, I close his computer and place it on the nightstand, purposely leaning across him, drawing inspiration from all the romance novels that Jo, Sof and I read lounging by the pool during our teenage summers. Twenty-year-olds aren't exactly the masters of seduction.

"Hi there," Craig says, his hands running up my thighs and resting at my hips, holding me in place. "What if that was something important?" Despite the question, his hazel eyes are a cross between playful and aroused.

"Was it?" I straighten, but he tightens his grip on me.

"Not at all, just checking basketball scores."

Emboldened by the fact I didn't inadvertently cause harm to any of his patients, I lean in, slowly pulling his glasses from his face. "Would you like to go back to your basketball scores?" I breathe, just inches from his mouth.

"Actually, yeah, now that you mention it," he deadpans.

I freeze, my heart stumbling. "What?" Did I completely misread the situation? I should have brushed my teeth or at least sniffed my pits before trying to put the moves on him.

In my hesitation, Craig flips me over, boxing me in between his forearms, his weight more comforting than crushing.

"You have to admit, you sorta walked into that one," he says, his mouth tugging into a wry smile before dipping down to my neck.

Like before, electricity radiates across my body from the places where his lips trail, up my neck to a little spot just behind my ear, a spot I never knew existed until he gently nips at it. From there his mouth travels across my jaw line, taking a slow, lazy route to my lips.

Finally, as if he could taunt me no more, his mouth meets mine and my body levitates off the bed, possessed not by a demon, but by this insatiable need for him. I'm asphyxiating and he's my breath. I'm starving and he's my nourishment.

I'm lost and he's my lighthouse.

Fingers pull at clothes. His. Mine. It's hard to tell who is who at this point.

"Emily," he murmurs my name, as if it's a prayer.

I want to say his, or to at least some sort of affirmation of how I feel, but the words are buried below this primal need for him.

Time ceases to exist as our mouths and fingers explore each other, sometimes working in tandem, other times almost in competition.

My breath catches as he starts kissing my stomach, causing a ringing in my ears from lack of oxygen.

Or...

A curse tumbles from his mouth, as bawdry as the fantasy playing in my mind.

He sits up and grabs his phone. "Shit, it's my resident, hang on."

Craig takes a deep steadying breath before answering. He listens intently, inhaling another sharp breath before sliding his gaze toward me. "Okay, you were right to call. Keep him stable and I'll be at the hospital in thirty." He ends the call and drops his head. "I'm so sorry."

"It's—" My voice comes out husky, less sex kitten, more chain-smoking grandma. I clear my throat and try again. "It's fine, you're saving lives and all." I sit up and place a chaste kiss on his lips. "Be careful heading down there, okay?"

Five minutes later, he's dressed and out the door, off to do whatever he needs to do for his patient.

I lie back on the bed and stare at the ceiling. The endorphins fade into darkness like the most brilliant sunset fades into the night sky.

It's obvious that my body is a flag-waving member of Team Craig.

I just don't know if my heart can join the team before I walk down the aisle to him.

CHAPTER 14

If there is one thing I've learned in my time thirty years into the future, it's that middle aged people sit a lot.

Commuting through horrendous traffic twice a day.

Sitting.

Meeting with clients.

Sitting.

Doing paperwork.

Sitting.

Even just chit chatting with Monique between clients, we start standing but after a few minutes my knees, ankles and back start begging for the comfort of a chair.

When Saturday rolls around, the last thing I want to do is sit some more. I need movement. I need to work out this anxious energy.

I need to figure out why I was flung halfway through my life and missed so much, including falling in love with an incredibly hot and attentive man I'm marrying in two months.

What if I don't really like him?

What if he realizes I'm not the Emily he fell in love with, because I'm not. I'm a twenty-year-old college junior who can't find a purpose in my life, who loved a boy way more than he loved her and whose dad was one bad mood away from cutting her off.

That's who I am, a girl who shaved her head and fell through time.

Craig is out running errands when I decide to check out the few pieces of workout equipment we have tucked into a third garage. A weight rack sits to one side, perpendicular to a machine with various weights and pulleys, and on the other side of that is a stationary bike with a computer between the handlebars.

Can we not do *anything* in the twenty-first century without a computer?

I study the bike. Sure, my bike in college was as much about getting around campus and town as it was about getting exercise.

Where Josie's a runner who found solace pounding the pavement but give me wheels and some hills to fly down with the wind whipping in my face, and I can solve all the world's problems.

Then I see it. A glint of muted red metal wedged behind two suitcases and a box with clothes erupting from the top.

Like a kid on Christmas morning, I shove the box and suitcases aside and unearth her. My beloved college bike emerges like a relic from the past.

My past.

The once bright red is now more of a faded cinnamon with spots of rust spread across the frame. Dust coats the seat like a layer of fine snow. A tiny spider skitters away from the spokes of one tire, no doubt annoyed that her haven has been disturbed by the very person who put this bike into exile.

I grip the tires, expecting them to be soft from both age and lost air, but instead they're both firm, solid.

There's no plan when I hop on and start those few tentative pedals. Even though my mind rode as recently as a week ago, it's obvious by the clumsy wobbling of the handlebars that this body hasn't needed the balance or the core strength to stay upright in a while.

I ride down the street, hugging close to the right side, not quite confident I can swerve to avoid moving or parked cars.

At the end of the street, I take a right, letting gravity do most of the work as I glide down a hill as gentle as a lover's caress.

The weather is perfect. The sky is that crisp blue of early spring, before the Texas summer heat scalds its beauty. Marshmallowy clouds float by, granting just a moment of shade before moving on to cast their benevolent shadows on someone else. A northerly breeze kisses the sweat off my brow, leaving the same goosebumps in its wake as Craig's lips.

It could've been worse. I could've woken up thirty years from that freak out to find myself homeless, or still living in that college apartment, having majored in every course of study—twice. Or, I could have woken up next to someone who absolutely disgusts me or abuses me.

Somewhere along the way, I got my shit together and made some good choices.

So why do I feel so…cheated? Like reading the last chapter of a book and having no clue who any of the characters are, or what's at stake.

How did I go from free-spirited, lovable fuck up Em Murray, to *Dr.* Emily Murray?

A person who doesn't create problems, but who solves them.

Maybe that's what I'm missing.

That evolution to becoming…*me*.

The bike path I'm on follows the road heading west out of Austin. What'd been flat now starts to swell to hills. Instinctively, I flick the gears on the bike and stand on the pedals, readying myself for the climb.

Halfway up, fire spreads from my legs to my lungs. That's the thing about hills. They're deceptive. When you're coming up to it, it may not look like anything more than a bump in the road. It's only when you're halfway up you realize you're scaling Everest on wheels.

Kinda like my relationship with Wick. His desire to make it big didn't seem all that daunting when we started dating. Standing there in the street, watching him load all of his belongings into the back of a moving van felt very much like a sheer rock face. He had momentum to push past the steepest part and I slid back to the bottom.

Now, all of that felt…inevitable. As if he was always going to make that journey without me. As if I was always going to be left behind.

Then become just some girl who may or may not have a song written about her.

I glide to a stop, where an off-road trail runs into this paved one. The packed-dirt path is rocky, cutting across a gently rising hill with squat bushes and cacti lining the path.

It looks wild, feral, and considering I'm riding a road bike instead of a mountain bike, it looks very much like a bad idea.

So of course, I'm in.

I start off fine enough. Then again, the Gates of Hell never really advertise themselves as the Gates of Hell.

The tires of my bike fall into ruts made by wider wheels. I drift downward, following a well-worn path and meandering the way down to the shores of Lake Travis.

I hardly pedal, no need to add to what gravity is already doing. Instead, I focus on the path, making sure I avoid rocks and anything that might bite or sting. Anything that might turn this from a morning on the trails getting some exercise into a trip to something I'll regret.

Maybe that's why I do it. Take off down this path I'm incredibly unprepared and unskilled for. Somehow over the last few years, I've gone from the Queen of Bad Decisions to making some pretty badass decisions.

I picked a profession that I'm good at, and until Crispy Dung showed up on my literal doorstep, I was pretty successful. I live in a nice house in a nice neighborhood. I drive a bitchin' car, and a gorgeous, successful man wants to marry me.

Am I even still capable of making bad decisions?

Is the old me still here? The one who jumped and worried about sticking the landing later.

There's only one way to find out. If I can make it down this path and back up again without a broken neck, then maybe this is all real.

My career. The future.

Craig's love. The love I must've given him in return.

After another thirty feet, the path jags back to the left. *Sharply.*

I hit the brakes, and…nothing. No slowing, no stopping. Nothing but the brake pulling effortlessly against the handlebars.

"Oh shit."

My options were bad and worse.

I could steer uphill and land in a beautiful, flowering cactus, or downhill and tumble to my death.

Instead, I choose what's behind door number three.

My body instinctively leans to my left side, and I tilt the bike just enough to plant my foot, hoping that digging my heel into the packed dirt will slow the momentum.

Which it does. A little too much.

As my left foot drags, the back tire skids to the right, making my already precarious balance precarious-er.

Just when I think I can save the last shred of my dignity, the shoelaces in my right sneaker snag in the pedal. Such a rookie move.

With nowhere else to go but down, I land hard on my left shoulder. Rocks dig into the side of my shin on the ground, the teeth of the bike pedal bite the other side, and stars explode behind my eyes as my head hits something hard. The pain is all-consuming, swallowing me whole like a monster snake from deep in the Amazon.

I curse again and lie still, chest pounding from adrenaline and exertion.

"Well, glad to know I'm still capable of bad decisions," I say to the mocking clouds passing by.

After a quick scan to make sure nothing's broken, I untangle myself from my bike. A fresh wave of pain supernovas across my body. Once we're both upright, the front wheel's new dent glares at me like the spill is my fault.

Well, it's not wrong.

I half drag and half roll the bike back up the way I'd come. I've probably only gone a couple of miles, but two miles on a bike, going downhill, is nothing compared to walking those same two miles uphill with blood running down my leg.

Because I can once again reclaim my title of Queen of Bad Decisions, my cell phone is sitting exactly where I left it.

On the kitchen counter. Doing me a hell of a lot of good.

Tears prick behind my eyes with such ferocity I suspect I also went face-first into a cactus. I hold tight to the emotion, to the pain in my heart competing with the pain in my shoulder and leg. Two hurts battling it out, the pain of skipping ahead and missing so much of my life versus the pain of crashing my bike.

Why me? What did I do to fast forward through my life?

Did something traumatic happen, more traumatic than Wick leaving me, and Astrid's Spirits are saving me from experiencing it?

If that's the case, what of the Emily I was before?

The woman who'd gone to bed with Craig the night before he was leaving for a conference and I woke up in this foreign life.

Is she back in 1996 buying a shit ton of hats and sunscreen for our now bald head?

I make it back to the top of the bike path, back to the paved trail that'll take me back home.

The tears I held on to with a mental fist fall like a summer rainstorm. Furious, hot and heavy.

This is tiring.

The walk dragging a broken bike with a sore body.

Pretending I belong in this time. In this life.

Questioning why a man like Craig loves me. Waiting for him to wake up one day and realize he can do better.

That I'll hold him back.

The levee holding back the tears breaks and I'm full-on bawling. Like heaving sobs, snot flooding from my nose, face heated.

Maybe if I go inside and shave my head, I can wake back up in my crappy college apartment. I can face the heartbreak I know is waiting for me instead of waiting for one lurking around the corner.

I can make the mistakes that get me to this place. I can even meet Craig for the first time and decide he'll just be a fling instead of someone who can get inside my most guarded possession.

My heart.

The storm of tears tapers off to a drizzle by the time my house comes into view.

Unfortunately, I'm not going to be able to sneak inside and clean up before anyone has to know what happened.

The back of Craig's SUV sits open in the garage, the back loaded down with potting soil, mulch and plants. He comes around the corner from the backyard as I limp up the driveway.

His eyes widen as he takes me in and I feel another tear-storm on the horizon.

"Baby, what happened?" He rushes over, thumbing the tears and dirt from my face. "I saw your phone on the counter, but couldn't find you. I was starting to worry."

"Wasn't kidnapped, if that's what you were worrying about. And if I was, you know they'd pay you to take me off their hands." My chin wobbles at the feeble attempt at humor.

His hands feel around my head, pulling back when I hiss at the spot on my temple where my head hit the ground.

"Where is your helmet?" His voice is stern.

Dare I say, *doctorly*.

"Umm…" I absolutely did not wear a helmet. Just like I absolutely did not check to make sure the brakes worked on this old bike.

"Em, really? I see people with brain damage every day. All it takes is hitting the wrong place, and…" he swallows, his voice breaking. "And I won't have you anymore, and just thinking that scares the shit out of me, okay?"

I nod, dislodging one last tear. Maybe he's more afraid of me leaving him than I am of him tiring of me.

Craig's gaze finally leaves my face and travels down my body, checking my shoulders, arms, legs. "Come on," he said, bending to hook one arm under my knees. "Let's get you cleaned up. And, just for that scare, you're getting straight alcohol in those cuts." Even though his voice was warm with humor, I'm pretty sure he's not kidding about the alcohol.

"I can walk. I made it this far, a few more feet won't matter."

He looks down at me, worry and love dueling in his hazel eyes. "I know you can, but Em, I'll always be there to carry you those last few feet."

CHAPTER 15

That's the other thing I learned about being nearly fifty. You don't heal as fast as in your teens or early twenties, and even though my left side got the brunt of the fall, my right side seemed to want an invitation to the pain party.

After a weekend of Craig following me around the house like a codependent puppy, he handed his babysitter duties off to Monique for the work week.

"Let me guess," Mo says, slowing stirring her coffee. "Crispin unleashed some sort of midlife crisis, so you decided to skip the Peloton and see if you can cascade down a rocky hill just for the hell of it?"

I blink.

She's not that far off, except it's not exactly a midlife crisis. More like missed-most-of-my-life crisis.

"You've obviously been hanging out with me too long," I say before a sip of Mo's special jet fuel coffee concoction. I wasn't going to admit anything that would quickly make its way back to Craig, but not only does my body feel like it's been hit by a truck, my head feels like the losing end of a trashcan punch hangover.

It doesn't help that a shadow of a bruise showed up Sunday morning on my left temple.

The chime at the front door echoes around the lobby.

Mo puts her coffee down, mumbling that the delivery guy is coming earlier and earlier every week.

It's only a second later when her lilting voice calls me.

There was a delivery guy, but his retreating back doesn't hold the logo of an office supply company. Instead, it's an ornate floral design, as ornate as the vase now sitting on Mo's desk.

"Wow, Craig must be really worried about me." No matter how much I used to grumble that flowers were a waste of time and money, it was really to give Wick permission to never send me flowers.

Not that he had the money to. Or the notion. Or, even the motivation.

However, standing here with an arrangement taking up half of Monique's desk, it hits me just how much I really, truly love getting flowers.

"Not from Craig,"my friend forces out between gritted teeth.

I grab the card from her hand.

Dr. Murray, Thank you for making sure my clinic kicks off with a strong launch. I truly appreciate all those client referrals. — Dr. Dunne

The little prick didn't just underline 'all' once, but twice.

"We didn't refer any clients," I mumble numbly. The warm blush of getting flowers fades like a scorched rose. "Have we had any cancellations?"

Mo shakes her head. "None over the weekend." She leans over her computer, hitting a few keys before straightening. "Oh, five just came in..."

I relax the breath that's been locked away in my lungs. "Five total? Okay, that's not too bad."

"No boss, five for this week. We have..." She clicks her mouse. "Another eight that cancelled for the rest of the month."

Thirteen, plus the two I lost last week. Fifteen clients. Future me is going to come back to her life and be so pissed at, well, *me*.

Staring at the flowers, at the colorful arrangement of pink lilies, orange and red roses, plum-colored daisies and lavender carnations, a gesture that should've been a birthday greeting or cause for celebration, the still very-fresh memory of Wick taunts me.

I rub at the silvery scar on my palm. The colors in front of me morph into Wick onstage, singing our song to the appropriately named Fleur, to them walking shoulder to shoulder. Would he have left her behind?

Likely not, because unlike me, Fleur was so cool she would've been offended to have been called cool.

I bet if she and I traded lives, Crispin would be begging her to teach him everything she knows instead of trying to siphon it away.

The heartache, the anger, starts at a low simmer, deep down, below the protective cage around my heart. It spirals up, filling in the fissures left in the wake of never being enough. Never being smart or motivated enough for my dad. Never being pretty enough to bond with my beauty queen mom over the shared experience of pageants. For not being cool enough for Wick, or even talented to get a sincere compliment from my art teacher.

The only people who accepted me; my faults, my attributes, my strengths and my weaknesses, are Josie and Sofia.

Well, Jo, Sof, Monique and…

Craig.

I look up at Mo, a woman I only just met but already feel like I've known her my entire life.

Maybe I have. Maybe as the stubble started to itch on my bald head, I met this powerhouse of a woman and we've walked through the past thirty years together.

It's because of her I choose to fight, completely unsure of what I have in my arsenal, but it doesn't matter. If she believes in me enough stand by me when my clients are jumping like rats off the *Titanic*, then I can at least do my damnedest to keep the ship afloat.

"Oh, no," Mo says. "I know that look. That look usually ends up with you having to eat an extra-large helping of humble pie."

Without a word, I swipe the heavy vase off her desk and march out my front door, not even bothering to close the door behind me.

My wedges clap against the pavement, like an army's heavy footsteps heading into battle. Left arm swinging in step, my right curled around the insulting floral arrangement like a soldier holding a bayonet.

I don't look both ways when I cross the street. The only acknowledgment that anyone, anything, lies between Crispin and me is the annoyed beep of a car horn.

My pounding footsteps follow me up the path, my heart beating with each determined step.

I've not yet been to the converted home with Crispin's clinic, but it took me no time to find the door. Zenith Therapy, the lettering on the door says with a logo of a sweeping mountain peak.

I grip the doorknob, intending to turn it and push my way into his office in a dramatic flair befitting a woman heading into battle.

Instead, I'm met with a locked door, the flowers crushing into me and water sloshing out of the vase, coating my shirt.

Unperturbed, I try again, trying the knob in a different direction. Even more water flows out of the top.

Before going up against the door for a third time, it swings open, revealing Crispin and a softly lit room behind him.

"Dr. Murray," he says, his blue eyes lighting up at the floral arrangement cradled against me. "You got my flowers! But you didn't have to bring them down here to show me. You could have sent a text, or better yet, post a photo on Instagram and tag me."

"You really think I am here to *thank* you? I know exactly what you're doing. You're trying to be all sweet and benevolent when deep down, you're a hyena lurking outside my office, pouncing on my clients."

His eyes flatten and he leans against the doorframe, crossing ankles that end in soft leather loafers. They're probably Italian. Or made with unicorn hides.

Crispin's gaze flits down to my chest. "Dr. Murray, you seem like you might be having an anxiety attack. I'd help you through it, but I'm with—"

"Seem?" I cut him off. Heat flares through my body like a supernova. It wouldn't shock me if steam rose off my body where the water from the vase soaked my shirt.

His gaze once again travels down to my chest.

"Quit staring at my boobs!" Everything is shaking now. I hate confrontation. I hate the rush of anger. I hate the aftermath when I feel both exhausted and embarrassed.

When I know I have to apologize, to admit someone got under my skin, and I absolutely lost my shit because of it.

One side of his mouth tugs into a cat-eating-the-canary grin. "I'm not staring at your *boobs*. Your anatomy does nothing for me, but that lily pollen you've smeared all over that fabulous shirt pains me."

I move the vase away and glance down. Sure enough, orange pollen is smudged all over the front of my crisp, perfectly tailored white shirt.

"You'll want to soak it in cold water," he drawls. "Half an hour should do, then treat it with a stain remover and then wash it in cold water."

My temper evaporates, as if the remaining water is dumped on my head. "What?"

"I worked for a florist while in college," Crispin says with a shrug. "I used to trim the stamens off before we delivered them. Guess not everyone is as thoughtful as me. Next time, I'll ask them to do that. Oh, and you'll want to use a yellow concealer for that bruise, maybe go for stage makeup. Your regular under-eye concealer isn't cutting it. Now, if you'll excuse me—"

I shove the vase into his chest, startling the twerp and forcing him to take a step back. When he wraps his arms around the arrangement, I take the opportunity to peer around his shoulder.

His office is much smaller than mine. Instead of a lobby, it opens directly into a seating area with a small couch and two mis-matched but complementary chairs.

Seated in one of those chairs is a wide-eyed Olivia. The first client I saw when I woke up in this strange new world. The girl who came to me to help with a toxic boss but ended up leaving when I gave her the advice she needed to hear.

Holding up a mirror to someone is terrifying, they might hate what they see, and instead of blaming themselves, they blame the mirror.

Or, in my case, the person holding it.

I blink twice and back away. Maybe Crispin is the better therapist. The more mature one, at least at this moment.

"Stop. Poaching. My. Clients." My voice is low and key-your-car menacing.

I don't wait for a response. Instead, I hurry down the steps, catching up to Monique who stood halfway down the front walk, her face a mix of pride and apology.

"So, what are we going to do, doc?" she asks, falling in step with me as we make our way back to my office.

"Well, first I'm going to change shirts and soak this one in cold water." I equally hate and appreciate him for that tip. I really do love this shirt. "Then buy some yellow concealer. After that we're going to fight fire with gasoline."

CHAPTER 16

Thankfully, I lose no more clients for the rest of the week. I half expected Crispin or Olivia to post something about my tantrum, but if they did, Mo and I never stumble upon it.

The future sucks if people can't have a bad day without fear of it being posted online like some sort of public shaming. Then again, there are people out there who *should* think twice before speaking, so maybe it's not so bad after all.

Mo, true to her promise, sat me down with a plan to up my social media presence and try my hand at content creation. Whatever that means.

We decide to wait a few more days, to allow the shiner from that disastrous bike ride to fully fade away.

With no clients for the afternoon, and all our paperwork caught up for the week, Mo and I close up the office early. A part of me feels like I'm playing hooky by knocking off work at one on a Friday afternoon, but the adult in me whispers that no clients also means no income, and I'm most likely off my dad's payroll by now.

The one thing that hasn't changed in three decades is Friday afternoon Austin traffic. It's equal parts everyone getting out of Dodge, and everyone heading into town to party. Which basically means you're screwed whether you're coming or going.

Halfway home, Craig texts me that he has a few more patients and he'll be heading home. Considering he's coming from downtown; I'll be lucky if I see him a week from Tuesday.

Nearly an hour later, I pull into the garage, exhausted, battle-weary and needing a drink. My body, still sore from the bike accident, is tense from gripping the steering wheel in the stop-and-go traffic.

After dropping my bag and abandoning my shoes just inside the house, I gravitate out to the pool. I roll up my jeans and step onto the top step. The water is cool, but in a good way, not in a painful, hypothermia way.

Maybe that's what I need. A dip in the pool with a glass of wine. It'll help with the swelling, both from my bike accident and the fall through time.

If I own a swimsuit, it's nowhere to be found. I rummage through the drawers in the bedroom. Nothing. The built-in drawers in the closet still don't produce a swimsuit.

"This is my damn house," I murmur. "If I can't skinny-dip here, I can't skinny-dip anywhere."

I strip off my clothes and grab a bath towel. Not out of modesty, but because I'll need one later and there's no guarantee there's beach towels anywhere near the pool.

With a plastic wine glass filled to the top with rosé—at least we practice glass safety around the pool—I ease into the cool water.

At first, the chill steals my breath, but then I glide over to a patch of sunlight, and the warmth loosens my lungs and everything relaxes. A large drink of wine and whatever muscles still clinging to tension give up the fight.

It's been two weeks since I woke up in this strange world.

Assuming I'm awake. I'm still not fully convinced this isn't a dream, or that I'm not dead. Did I even make it back home from brunch with my dad?

What if I flipped my Jeep trying to hurry home to Wick? Instead of leaving me for his rock and roll dreams, he waited for me, giving up on the career he could've had because his girlfriend—his muse—the one who'd supported him through it all never showed up.

I drown that thought-spiral in another large gulp of wine.

There's no way that happened.

For many reasons, but mainly, as romantic as it sounds that Wick would've sat on his crumbling, crooked front porch with his head in his hands waiting for a girlfriend who'd never return, I know deep down he would've just left.

I glance down at my body, partially distorted by the water flowing around it. The goose pimples from the cold water feel real. The fall from the bike with the resulting bruises all feel real. The first-drop-of-a-roller-coaster whenever Craig kisses me feels more than real.

It feels natural.

As if I'd waited my whole life for it. Being with Craig is like finally, for the first time in my life, being able to fill up my lungs with a deep breath. I want more. Half breaths just won't do it.

A trilling sound cuts through the quiet of my backyard oasis. My first thought is to ignore it, but at the second ring, some sort of Pavlovian response kicks in. I push out of the pool to grab my cell off the outdoor dining table.

I see Craig's name on the screen just as the call goes to voicemail. It's becoming abundantly clear that these devices were not made for talking, or else it would ring more than three times.

I press on Craig's name to call him back.

"Hey," he says, picking up on the first ring. His voice is quiet, as if he stepped away to take the call.

Whatever he says next is lost, as a lawnmower and its evil twin the leaf blower start growling at the exact same time at the house next door.

"What was that?" I ask, plugging my free ear in an attempt to cut out the noise of the lawn equipment.

Nope.

It does nothing.

"Hold on, let me go inside," I say. Forgetting the towel, I hurry inside to the kitchen. The chill of the AC attacks my wet skin, causing it to erupt in a terminal case of goose pimples. "Okay, say that again," I say, the offending growl of the lawn crew is now just a muffled grumble.

"I was just saying, Aiden got in early, so he'll beat me home."

Aiden? Who the heck is Aiden?

Before my brain can shuffle through the pieces of my life I've shoved in it like cramming for a forgotten exam, a key turns in the front door, popping it open.

Something falls in the foyer, and two seconds later a tall, gangly teenager does what all teenagers do—heads straight for the fridge.

I scream, and drop the phone to the counter.

The teenager skids to a stop and also screams. "What the shit, Emily?" He covers his eyes.

Craig's tinny voice floats up from the counter. "Em, Aiden? What's happening?"

The boy, Aiden, speaks first. "Dad, your girlfriend is running around the house naked!"

Thoughts fly into me like arrows.

Craig has a son.

His son is named Aiden.

Aiden is standing in my kitchen, covering his eyes.

He's covering his eyes because I am standing here buck-ass naked.

What the shit is right.

"Sorry!" I come alive and crouch down so the cabinets cover me. "I forgot." Hopefully Craig and Aiden will think I forgot he was coming over, and not that he *existed*. "And I couldn't find a swimsuit."

"I'm blinded, Dad," Aiden's voice is pained, but also laced with teenage snark. "I need to go wash my eyes with bleach or something."

I glance down at my body. "Oh, come on, I'm not that bad."

"Have you seriously never seen the sun, Emily? Dad, my hockey career is over, and it's your girlfriend's fault. I can't play right wing blind!"

A chuckle comes through the phone. "Aiden, why don't you go up to the guest room and give Em some privacy? By the way, she's my fiancée, but you can skip ahead and just call her my wife. Em, you going to be okay?"

"Has anyone ever died of embarrassment?" I ask.

He *is* a doctor after all.

"I'll do some research and let you know," Craig says, his words riding on a tide of laughter. "But no, I don't think it's been listed as any cause of death. Sorry to say it, but you'll live to face Aiden another day."

Great.

Just great.

CHAPTER 17

Thankfully, Aiden slips away upstairs. His heavy footsteps overhead are my signal that I can sprint down the hall and put on fourteen layers of clothes. Even though Craig doesn't direct me to, I stay in our room until he comes home.

I shouldn't be all that surprised that he has a son. It's absolutely likely that the me I was before two weeks ago had a long conversation with Craig about his son staying with them—us. She—me—likely happily agreed to Aiden's visit, maybe even planned activities, like spray painting overpasses or whatever the hell teenagers do these days for delinquent fun.

Hidden away in our closet, I go back through the messages between Craig and me. Six months back, I see it, a picture he sent me of him and Aiden in the middle of a crowd, surrounded by a sea of green and black jerseys. The accompanying words, *'Stars win!'* mean nothing to me.

I tap on the picture to make it bigger and study it. When I first saw it, I assumed this was his nephew. After a closer look, I see the stronger familial resemblance. Their faces are the same square shape, but Aiden's eyes are a bit more wide set. Craig's hazel eyes weren't passed down to his son who sports a deep ocean blue color made even more startling against his dark brown hair, the same color my fiancé must've had in his younger days. While their eyes are different, everything from the nose down is the same.

I don't study the similarity in their faces, but rather their differences, trying to piece together what Aiden's mom looks like.

Who was the woman Craig loved first?

I'm guessing they are divorced. If Craig were a widower, his son would live with us full-time and not just show up at spring break, right?

Did she leave him, or the other way around?

I think about Aiden's blue eyes. Does she look like me? Does Craig have a type?

A knock at the door startles me, and I fumble with the phone, quickly trying to swipe away from the photo like I'd just gotten caught with my mom's bodice ripper romance novel.

"Em?" Craig calls out into the room.

"In here."

He chuckles when he finds me. "It's nearly ninety out."

Maybe I didn't actually put on fourteen layers of clothes, but I did pull on the baggiest sweatsuit I could find, with a scarf wrapped around my neck. There's no way Aiden's going to see another inch of my skin.

"Honestly," he continues, sitting down on the ottoman next to me. "It could've been worse. When Aiden was about eight, he walked in on Diane and I, well you know…" He clears his throat and squirms.

"Doing it?" I don't need to say it; I know exactly what he meant. I just felt the need to help alleviate the instant tension that struck his body.

It works.

Craig huffs out a laugh and his shoulder bumps into mine as he relaxes.

So, his ex is Diane and there's still something raw there. Something that causes a visceral reaction just by bringing up her name and the fact that they had a physical relationship.

Does he still love her? Hate her? Something in between?

Even though I've exchanged less than ten words with Aiden, I've *been* him.

The kid shuttling between homes. The kid tethering two people together who want nothing more than to be rid of the other. The kid reminding any future love interests that the ex is still in the picture.

"Anyway, he'll forget about it soon enough," he says.

I want to interject, to tell him I have the most recent experience with teenage boys and while I seriously hope he shoves this whole interaction into a box and buries it so deep it will take years of therapy to draw it out of him, I have a feeling seeing his future stepmom naked is not something he will forget.

Ever.

"Perhaps, but I'm pretty sure I'm going to have night terrors about it for the rest of my life." I rub my hands over my face, feeling the flush under my fingertips.

"Sorry," Craig says, bumping his shoulder against mine again. "I should've reminded you he'd be here later today."

"It's okay, it's been a busy couple of weeks." It's been a busy couple of weeks of me trying to figure out what the hell's going on with my life, and learning lines to this world I fell into like an understudy suddenly thrust into the spotlight.

He straightens and looks down at his hands. "Even though he's going to be in and out with the hockey tournament, I think this weekend might be good for you guys to try to find some common ground."

His words sink in.

Do Aiden and I not have a good relationship?

It was hard to tell in our brief interaction, mostly because I was naked and trying to hide from him.

I've never *not* been liked.

Sure, I might not always be someone's cup of tea, but I always considered myself to be more of someone's cup of trashcan punch. There's a lot that goes into making me *me*, but people can usually find the flavor they like.

"Is it that bad?"

"He's seventeen, everything is more dramatic with hormones. You know that," Craig says.

I know he means that clinically, but I can't help but think about how just a few short years ago, I was also that age and everything *was* that much more dramatic.

"Anyway," he continues. "I guess it could be any number of reasons that teenagers act like assholes to their parent's new partner. Although I don't seem to remember him giving Diane grief when she and Veronica got married."

That little nugget of information settles the worry churning in my stomach. His ex is married and not just married but married to a woman.

Somehow that makes me feel like I'm going to be instant best friends with her. Perhaps we already are.

"Maybe he doesn't want a third mom?" I ask.

Craig barks out a laugh. "That's probably closer to the truth than you know. Will you be mad if he and I grab some dinner tonight? Just the two of us so we can catch up?"

I shake my head. "Not at all. Put in a good word for me, will you?"

My fiancé stands and pulls me up with him. "Okay, I'll see what I can do to dispel the myth that you're part of a nudist cult trying to recruit new members. But, I think he's already posted a half dozen videos about it."

The twinkle in his eye tells me he's joking.

The sinking in my heart worries that he's not.

CHAPTER 18

When Saturday rolls around, I groan at the pattering of rain against the skylight in the bathroom and patio outside.

Craig's side of the bed is empty, cool to the touch. He didn't get home too late from dinner out with Aiden, but rather than come to bed, they stayed up playing video games.

There's something endearing about hearing the good-natured trash-talking they'd lobbed back and forth. As if the meaning behind those words were the complete opposite of what was said.

What would it have been like to have had that kind of relationship with either of my parents?

To have a foundation so strong that insults are really declarations of love.

I grab my phone and see a text from Craig.

CRAIG "MCFINE ASS" HARRISON

At the gym.

Despite some late shifts most nights this week, he was back up before dawn to hit the gym on the way back to the hospital. Deep down, I understood that the early workouts were more about preparing himself to see patients who may not make it, or if they do, may end up changed for the rest of their lives. It didn't take a fancy degree to know that sweating out the concern was his therapy. However, knowing his son and I don't have a great relationship, I can't help but worry I'm part of the concern he's sweating out.

I roll over and stare at the ceiling. These feelings for him are somehow foreign yet comfortable. As if awakening from a long sleep and realizing I can speak and understand another language perfectly.

Loving Craig, being loved by him, is as natural as breathing.

No, not natural.

Necessary.

Half an hour into searching the ceiling for any clue as to what to do with this gaping hole in my life or how to fling myself back to 1996, Craig swoops in, smelling of sweat, freshly cut grass in the rain, and, sexily, coffee.

"Good morning, gorgeous," he says, sweetly, planting a chaste kiss on my lips and handing me one of the cups. "If we didn't have the meeting with the wedding planner, I'd suggest we stay in bed and take advantage of the rainy day and Aiden spending most of the day down at the rink."

Something about those words, the promise behind them, makes my stomach drop like those first few moments of skydiving, plunging out of a plane, falling, but also knowing, hoping, a chute would open and save me.

"Need to leave in an hour," he adds, before peeling off his shirt and heading into the shower.

My body jerks, as if wanting to follow him, but my heart holds back. Is this purely physical?

There's no doubt I'm drawn to him, but what if he wakes up one day, tomorrow, next week, next year, and realizes that *I'm* not the woman he met? The woman he fell in love with and asked to marry?

As precise as a surgeon's blade, an hour later, we're in Craig's car heading west toward our Hill Country wedding venue. The rain hasn't let up, instead vacillating between torrential downpour and heavier, start-collecting-two-of-everything Biblical flood.

He drives carefully, as if he's seen enough of the aftermath of bad car accidents to do whatever he can to avoid one.

It appears, through all of the searching of my life before I woke up out of time, one of my biggest weaknesses is still fully intact.

Procrastination.

Aside from booking this venue and sending out save the dates, I've done absolutely nothing to plan our wedding.

I glance down at the gorgeous ring on my left hand. Was the other me having second thoughts?

If so, she never expressed it to Josie or Monique, neither of them so much as hinted at our relationship being anything other than ironclad.

As if feeling my thoughts, Craig's warm right hand grips the hand I was studying before bringing my knuckles to his lips.

"It's okay to call in some help with this." His voice is soft, understanding. "We've both got a lot going on, so let someone else worry over the details."

The traffic slows to a stop and he finally takes his eyes off the wet road.

"I don't care what color the flowers are, what songs are played and what the cake looks like, I just want to be married to you." He flashes a smile that stops my heart like the traffic around us.

I meet his eyes and nearly crumble at what stares back at me. Love, unending, as vast as the universe, as if it had always been there between us, just waiting for our lives, souls, to get close enough to collide into each other.

Words form a traffic jam in my throat. Everything I want to say bumps together. Tell him I'm secretly twenty years old. I'm still nursing a broken heart over a boy who left me thirty years ago, but in truth it was just weeks ago.

I'm not the put together successful therapist he fell in love with, but instead someone more afraid of committing to a major than a boy in a band.

Thankfully, my body knows better than to let any of that out.

We pull into a driveway, leading us to the venue we've chosen for our wedding. Even in the rain and gloom, I can see why we picked it.

The car climbs a winding road, freshly budded trees line the road, offering a peekaboo glimpse of the glass, stone and iron building on the hilltop. We finally crest the hill and I gasp.

The limestone fades into the craggy hillside, not wanting to interrupt the beauty of the surrounding Hill Country. While closed up against the elements, the glass is all doors, able to open up the venue on all four sides. To the right is a large patio with an equally large pergola, wisteria climbing and twisting up the beams, draping over the top like a bride's veil.

This place is unassuming, yet breathtaking. A place for families and friends to gather, to dance beneath the Texas night sky to a chorus of stars.

We park and jog inside. Even though the hardest rain has stopped, it's steady enough to soak us.

Workers are setting up tables and chairs inside, rounds for guests, and long buffet tables for food. Diligently working to ready the venue for tonight's event.

"Emily, Craig?" A woman's voice pulls me away as I'm studying the space, trying to imagine it on a bright, sunny day.

She's wearing black pants and shirt, her blonde hair in a flawless bob. From the perfect cut and dark clothes, to the designer flats and overflowing clipboard, it's obvious this is a woman who gets shit done.

"I'm Farrah, it's nice to meet you." She shakes both of our hands and takes a deep breath, also studying the space around us. "I've done several events here, and you booked it at the perfect time." Farrah waves a hand at the fields of green flowing around the patio. "The lavender should be blooming at your wedding; it'll be gorgeous at sunset. Shall we sit?"

We follow her to a seating area off to the side, Craig and I taking the sofa and she perches on the edge of an adjacent armchair.

"All right, let's go over what you've done to date," the wedding planner says, pen poised in her hand to take down a long list of…well, nothing. "Venue, obviously." She makes a check. "What are your colors?"

Colors? Red has always been my color, but how would that look against a field of light purple?

The confusion on my face must've been answer enough as she makes a note on her clipboard.

"That's okay, we can come back to that. What about your dress, can you describe it?"

"Umm, I haven't bought one yet, technically," I squeak out. "But I'm going shopping with my best friend and her daughter soon."

This time the woman's blue eyes cartoonishly bug out. "Your wedding is in two months!" Farrah clears her throat and gathers herself before placing a patient smile on her face. "But you are lucky enough to have a perfect figure, so off the rack will look great on you."

Craig squeezes my hand, a small gesture to let me know I don't suck.

"Let's talk wedding party," Farrah says. "You'll have a best man and maid of honor, how many other groomsmen and bridesmaids?"

"Four each," he jumps in, saving me from yet another failure in Farrah's eyes.

Thank goodness past me made some decision and shared it with her fiancé.

"Em's best friend's Josie will be maid of honor; my son will be the best man," he continues. "Then she'll have Josie's daughter, another close friend she grew up with, and her work colleague. Josie's husband Daniel will be one of my groomsmen alongside two of my close friends."

Warmth blooms from my heart. Somehow, having Daniel as part of my wedding fits puzzle-piece perfectly. I've secretly cheered him and Josie toward a relationship through high school, and when that didn't happen, helped her pick up the broken pieces of her heart, always feeling it was just a matter of time for them.

That was one of the best parts of waking up thirty years into the future. To see that my best friend got her happily ever after.

It's what romance novels are made for.

"Oh perfect," she says, making a flourish with her check mark, like we're two delinquents who finally got something right. "Let's see, we need to talk about number of guests, food and drink, deejay versus band and any special traditions, father-daughter, mother-son dances. What would you like to walk down the aisle to? Preferences on an officiant? My guess is this isn't your first trips down the aisle, so we can skip through some of the traditional parts."

Heat flushes through my body, either from embarrassment or a hot flash. Don't they sell weddings-in-a-bag, like those bedroom-in-a-bag sets everyone in the dorm had?

"I don't...It's just that, I don't know really," I stumble over what I really want to say. *Don't ask me, I just woke up here.* "Isn't that what we hired you to figure out?" The words come out harsher than intended.

I take a deep breath, hoping it'll calm my rising temper, not toward the woman who was simply doing her job, but at past me for not having her shit together.

Craig clears his throat. "This is Em's first—hopefully, only—wedding, so if she wants the full traditional experience, we'll do it." He turns toward me, his hazel eyes unreadable. "Or if we just say 'I do' and dash, that's fine too."

I hold his stare, hoping my face is as steady as a high-stakes poker player's. All I know about this man is what I've gleaned from the two weeks I've been in the future, or from scraps of our life pieced together like trying to read a torn-up letter. I know some of the basics, enough to fake it, but the holes are bigger.

What if I *had* said yes to the father-daughter and mother-son dances, only to find out later his mom has been long gone.

I must have given away the hand I'm playing.

Craig drops my hand and turns back to the woman next to us. "We'll do open bar, let us get back to you on the food," he says, making the decisions I'm too paralyzed to make. "Guest list will be under a hundred."

"And," my voice is weak and watery. "I'll let you know my colors, but it'll probably be lavender, something that won't clash with the scenery here."

Even though the rain has moved off, the drive back is as tense as earlier. Thoughts rumble through my head like rolling thunder.

"If this is too much," Craig says, his soft voice slicing into the growing storm in my mind. "We can keep it simple, a few close friends in our backyard."

I nod.

"That's," he swallows audibly. "That's if you still want to get married."

CHAPTER 19

Craig and I go our separate ways when we get home.

Not in the handing him back this gorgeous engagement ring sort of way. Not him telling me I'm a commitment-phobic, irrational failure of a human being way either.

No, nothing that dramatic. I simply cleared my throat and told him I need to run errands and he responded that he had some paperwork to do before catching up with Aiden at the hockey rink.

The parking lot of Astrid's shop was more rain-filled potholes than concrete. The rain washed away some of the dreariness of the building, clearing off dust and pollen and crushed hopes and dreams.

As always, the psychic's shop is quiet. The heady scent of a burning incense stick wafts through the empty lobby.

I study the various crystals and tins, the glass containers and plastic pouches of what looks like freeze-dried leaves. Thumb through the books and New Age CD's, hoping the answer is somewhere on these shelves.

"Wasn't expecting you today," a gruff voice calls out from the back.

The beads clang together, and the woman appears in the doorway.

Astrid rolls her eyes after her gaze lands on me. "Will you ever tell me when she's coming?"

The question isn't for me. To be honest, I'm kinda liking that the Spirits keep her on her toes. Even if I feel like they're conspiring against me.

The older woman narrows her eyes and purses her thins lips, the wrinkles forming even deeper lines around her mouth. "You're still here."

"Yeah, still in the right place, just wrong time." I fall into the faded zebra print chair, dust plumes up like a volcanic eruption. "The Spirits haven't given away any secrets on how I can get back to the right spot in my life, have they? Don't get me wrong, there's some upside to being here, my badass car, cool house, a full head of hair…" I twirl my finger around a loose curl.

Astrid shuffles behind the crooked checkout desk and leans on her forearms. "Ha!" she scoffs. "In case you haven't noticed, the Spirits are like bored, naughty children. Eternity is a very long time, so they get their kicks any way they can."

I tilt my head. "Who are these Spirits anyway?" Not that I believe any of this, but if this is what the afterlife has to offer, then I can totally get behind messing with psychics.

She shrugs. "It's like a chorus. Some are my ancestors, other seers who guide me from the Beyond. Some are souls who lived on other planes of existence, places that still believe in magic." Astrid huffs a laugh. "And others just like to drop in and stir metaphysical shit up."

I tilt my head and narrow my eyes. "Which ones are behind this?" I wave a hand around my head. "The ones from another plane? I can't imagine there's anyone else in this world dealing with…this level of metaphysical shit." Not that I can put words around exactly what I'm dealing with.

My mom always complained about hot flashes. Is this a bad case of the flash forwards?

"You'd be surprised. So, are you here to torment me alongside these insufferable Spirits?"

I take a deep breath of incense-filled air and push myself out of the chair. "I need something and figured this would be the best place to come."

Astrid quirks an eyebrow.

"A love potion."

A guttural laugh spews from her mouth. "A love potion? Girl, you've been watching too much TV."

I cross the small shop and lean on the counter, matching her posture. "Okay, maybe not a *potion*, but..." I wave my hands around the shop. "Something in here has to invoke or manifest love."

"No." It was delivered simply, no nonsense. No budging.

"What do you mean *no*?"

"I mean exactly what it means. No. Nope. *Nada*. Ain't going to happen."

"Because you can't do it?"

"I didn't say that." The older woman blows out another breath and shakes her head. "Because it's unethical. It robs someone of their free will."

"What if...what if I told you it's for *me*? I'm the one who would take it." My eyes sting at the admission. As if something deep down inside of me awakens. A monster guarding my heart like a dragon protecting precious jewels. At the mere mention of letting someone into the protective cage it grumbles its disapproval.

"And why would you need a love potion?"

I take a deep, fortifying breath. "I'm engaged to get married."

"Yes, I know."

"Because you're a psychic?"

Astrid arches a white eyebrow. "Because that rock on your finger is blinding me."

"It's just..." More furious tears poke behind my eyes. All angry, stabby little needles. "He loves me, and I think I can love him. I *will* love him. It's just not there yet. At least for me. I don't know. I'm twenty, and the one time I thought I loved someone, it turned out he loved himself much, much more. I need it because I want to love Craig. I just don't know how to yet."

Her sharp gaze softens. She shakes her head softly, resolutely. "Still no. Because it robs the other person, the one you're supposed to love, of your heart. Your sincerity."

"What do I do then?" I throw my hands up, hoping all those meddling Spirits see my desperation.

"It may not feel like it, but you *are* still you." Astrid waves a ring-filled hand. "Maybe old you is less of a pain in the ass. Regardless, the face may age and boobs may sag, but the heart doesn't change."

"So, I...what?"

The woman rolls her eyes. "What is it that most couples do when they are interested in someone? Go on a date. *That's* your love potion. Ask that man of yours out on a date. Get to know him and you'll find out why you fell in love with him in the first place."

CHAPTER 20

Back in my car, I stare at the open text thread with Craig. Astrid makes it seem so easy, asking someone I'm engaged to out on a date. What would middle-aged me want to do?

I'm not even sure I know what twenty-year-old me likes doing on a date.

I've had plenty of boyfriends, but none that ever started with a first date. The guys in high school I dated I grew up with, so there was none of that awkward getting-to-know-you conversation. Same for college, really.

Poor college students don't have the money for wining and dining. We're wooed by quarter beer night and a cheap slice of greasy pizza.

Before I can find a way to inconspicuously ask Craig out, my phone vibrates in my hand while simultaneously ringing through my car's speakers.

Mom.

I hit the green button.

"Hey, Mom." The screen on my car pops up a new notification.

Would you like to drive to Aiden's hockey game?

I hit 'yes' and a map fills the screen.

God, I love the future. It's like having a keeper at all times.

"Emily Marie," the exasperation in my mom's voice fills my car. "You may not give a flip what you wear to your wedding, but I care about what *I'm* going to wear."

I should've known as soon as she used my first and middle name together I'm in trouble.

It seems that's one thing that doesn't change with time.

Parental disappointment.

"Okay, well just pick something. I'm sure you'll look beautiful no matter what." I back out of the parking spot at Astrid's shop and follow the prompts on the map.

"I can't just pick *something*," she says.

I can almost see her throwing her hands up in the air.

"I need to make sure our necklines don't clash. And I need to complement the bridesmaid dresses, without looking too matchy-matchy. Did you even *look* at some of the options I sent you?" she demands.

"Can you resend them? I, uh, must have deleted them." If she sent me anything, it must've been before I'd taken a face plant into the future. "And I'm thinking a muted lavender for the bridesmaid dresses," I add, imagining it would look great on Josie, Monique, Sofia and Aubrey. "You should go with a champagne color for your dress. It'll look great on you and won't clash with the girls."

Look at that decision making. I'd say it made my momma proud, but she keeps right on talking.

"Oh, but honey, that color is no good on me. And at my age bronzer just looks fake."

So everything else in the world got more advanced, except bronzer?

The car tells me I've arrived, so I need to cut this conversation off like a drunk sorority girl at the bar. "Okay, so how about this, you can wear whatever color you want as long as it's not white." The edge is my voice is a sharp shard of broken glass, but I soften it through my rock tumbler heart. "Mom, I just want you to feel comfortable and have fun. You can wear a rainbow-colored ballgown for all I care."

"Well, since you put it that way, I *do* have my eye on a full taffeta skirted rainbow dress…"

I catch the sarcasm in her voice before it trails off, and roll my eyes.

"I'll be in Austin in a little over a week. Maybe we can work in a shopping trip between appointments," she says.

Someone who didn't have near daily conversations with my mom might've missed the wobble on that last word. She's the most self-assured person I know. She had to be. Going from a stay-at-home mom to a divorcée almost overnight, Mom worked as a secretary while studying for her real estate license at night. Then, before the ink was even fully dry on her license, we moved back to her hometown so she could build her business from scratch. There's nothing my mom is afraid of.

Except for whatever those appointments were for.

"What appointments do you have?" I try to make my voice light and airy, but the words feel heavy on my tongue.

"Oh, some doctors."

"Are there not any doctors where you are?"

Where did she live again? New Mexico? Colorado? Surely, they have doctors there.

"What aren't you telling me?" I ask.

"It's probably nothing."

"Mom, what is *it*?" Was this what it's like parenting me? Asking a direct question and getting barely a tenth of a response. "Because right now my mind is going to the worst-case scenario, so if that's not *it*, please tell me what is going on."

There's a long beat of silence before my mom finally speaks. "I'm not sure exactly when it started. A word would be just out of reach when I needed it." Her voice is small, freezing my heart more than what she's saying. "And then I didn't recognize a couple at the club-house. I told Geoff it was because they'd just come back from the South of France and had no business being that tanned at our age, and I simply didn't recognize them. But he wants me to see a specialist, just in case."

My mom, who memorized minute details of homes she was selling or filed away that the hard-to-please couple could be won over by a view and a sunken tub, was losing her memory. If it started with a misplaced word and forgotten friends, what would go next?

Would she forget where she lives, or who she lives with?

Would she forget me?

I don't know the man my mom married, but hopefully he'd take care of her through whatever diagnosis she receives.

"I'll go with you. To the doctor."

"Emily, sweetheart," she sighs my name. "I truly don't think this is anything more than old age and bad facial recognition. How about this, let's do dress shopping and champagne brunch together. I'll do the boring thing with Geoff, and if there is something to worry about, I won't hide it from you. I promise."

My throat closes up, neither letting me swallow the growing lump or speak around it. I look out the windshield and see Craig pacing at the door, his eyes down on his phone.

Will there come a time when he can't pull up a simple word, or recognize an old friend? Recognize me?

If so, will I have enough memory for both of us?

I finally find my voice. "Okay, if you promise you'll tell me everything. I gotta go, I'm running late for Aiden's hockey match."

There's a long pause that makes me look to make sure I didn't accidentally hang up.

"Didn't you always correct me that it's a game, not a match?" She laughs softly. "Now who's using the wrong words? I always found it funny how you just woke up one day and decided to be a hockey fan. I guess it's something you picked up from a college boyfriend that just stuck."

Am I a hockey fan?

Sports were never my thing. Call it a side effect of being raised by a single mom and a workaholic dad, but I just never got the point of balls of various shapes and sizes being lobbed at holes of various shapes and sizes. It's amazing more people don't lose an eye each year because of sports.

"Er, yes, that's right." I laugh, but it's hollow. "Just making sure you're listening. Love you, Mom!"

I end the call and rest my forehead on my steering wheel, squeezing my eyes shut while everything from the last day soaks in.

Craig has a son and I've embarrassed myself in front of him.

We're really doing this 'til death do us part thing. Then, turns out my mom and I are both having a case of the forgetfuls.

My phone dings with a text from my fiancé.

CRAIG "MCFINE ASS" HARRISON

You here?

Oh, and now I have to go be a fan of a sport I know nothing about.

Maybe I should tell Mom I'm coming with her to the appointment after all and see if the doctor offers a family discount.

CHAPTER 21

Craig's waiting for me as soon as I step into the lobby.

"Hey," he says, his voice is quiet, almost lost beneath the clicking and whooshing sounds coming from the ice rink. "About earlier…"

I cut him off with a hug so tight if he were a pimple he'd pop. "I talked to my mom and told her what to wear for the wedding. Of course, she didn't like it, but I made a decision."

He squeezes me back. "That's the thing about decisions, you're guaranteed to piss someone off when you make one, but once you get used to the fact that you won't please everyone, it's quite liberating." He flashes me a smile.

"Well, I feel absolutely liberated." I look up at my fiancé. "We should celebrate, maybe grab a drink or something tonight. Unless you and Aiden have plans."

"Nope, he's going out with the team afterwards, so you're stuck with me tonight." He kisses me on the temple and grabs my hand. "Come on, they're going to drop the puck soon and Aiden is on the first line."

None of those words make sense to me, but I follow him inside.

It's amazing to think how much a person can change in thirty years, and not just in a physical sense. New likes, passions, and things I thought I'd love deeply until the day I die are less important. Is that what maturity is? Recognizing I can change and evolve just as much in adulthood as I did in childhood? Instead of outgrowing my favorite outfit from Esprit, I've outgrown my love for seeing live music every night of the week.

Is it as subtle as how kids grow? Every day they get a little bit taller. Every day parts of me evolve. Neither is really noticeable, until you run into the kid you used to babysit on a trip home from college and need his help getting something off the top shelf at the grocery store.

Or, until you wake up thirty years in the future and suddenly find you're a therapist who's engaged to a hot doctor, with a mother who might be losing her memory, and now, you're a die-hard hockey fan.

Maybe these were changes that happened subtly, but I'm going to need someone to help me reach the new top shelf of my life.

We slip into our seats as the players from both teams glide effortlessly around the ice. It's easy to spot Aiden, even covered up in bulky hockey gear and a helmet that covers his face like a cage.

Exactly how dangerous is this sport? How many eyes have been lost to it?

A buzzer sounds and the players skid to a stop with Aiden heading to one side of a giant circle in the middle of the rink.

The referee drops the puck, and the players start skating around each other like they've choreographed a haphazard dance. Whistles blow.

The puck zips around the ice with a dozen teenage boys chasing after it. My head whips back and forth, trying to follow the action so fast that a zing of pain races up my neck.

A whistle blows and the players immediately shift their momentum and skate back to the circle.

None of this makes sense, yet I'm absolutely fascinated by the athleticism, by the speed of the sport, heck, I'm even mystified by how the goalies can deflect this tiny piece of black plastic flying at them at a million miles an hour.

Craig chuckles next to me. "You're usually yelling your head off. Sure you're okay?"

Mom's words wash over me like the spray of ice off Aiden's skates at a hard stop. I'm supposed to be this hockey super-fan.

"Oh yeah, sorry, just running through wedding plans in my head." It was the lamest thing I could say. Well, next to *I've never seen a hockey match—excuse, me, game—before in my life and I'm supposed to not only know what's going on but to respond appropriately.*

He knocks my knee with his. "Forget about the wedding for a bit, blow off some steam and enjoy the game."

I flash a tight-lipped smile. I want to confide in him what my mom shared, to tell him I, too, am having memory problems. Instead of not calling up the name of too-tanned people, I can't recall thirty years of my life. But, like me, I get the feeling Craig needs to blow off some steam, so instead of burdening him with my problems, I lock them away.

The first twenty minutes of the game ends with no score. Players skate off the ice and my fiancé stands, stretching.

"They finally started to get their rhythm down toward the end of the first period," he says to me.

Honestly, if there was a rhythm it was as foreign to me as anything recorded after 1960 was to my Great Uncle Melvin.

In the second period, the other team snuck the puck past the goalie, resulting in half the small arena erupting into cheers, while the half where we sat stayed as quiet as a funeral.

It's in the third—and final period, according to a quick search on my phone during a bathroom break—that I finally start to feel like I'm understanding the game. Or at least understand the cues of the people around me.

I jump up when Craig jumps. I jeer when the people in front of us boo. I even tell the ref he needs glasses for no reason other than I think he'd look good with glasses. Everyone around us seems supportive of that.

With ten minutes left, a player on Aiden's team ties up the game. The arena goes quiet. The other team's fans now no longer confident this game is theirs; our team's section holds its collective breath.

I can see why future-me became a fan of the game. It's fast paced and thrilling with just the right amount of violence.

The players square off at center ice again with less than two minutes left. This time, instead of being in the middle of the circle, Aiden is off to the side of the circle. The puck hits the ice and the player on Aiden's team whips the black disc in his direction. He responds, slapping the puck toward another team member but when he does, his stick flies up and strikes his opponent in the face mask.

The ref blows his whistle and lifts one arm up while using the other to point at Aiden. Like calling him out.

An attaboy?

"Woohoo, go get 'em Aiden!" I launch out of my seat, but instead of being in the middle of an eruption of cheers, everyone around us stays seated.

And, looks…upset?

"It's a penalty, Em," Craig murmurs. "He's going into the box."

His son skates by us, his deep blue eyes boring into me across ten feet of ice and through the cage of his face mask. Boring into me and judging. Calling bullshit.

"Oh."

"Our penalty kill is awful," Craig adds, mostly to himself.

A quick headcount of the players tells me why this is such a big deal. We're one person short. The only sound in the entire arena is the slashing of skates on ice and the slap of the puck against sticks. The players don't talk, don't call out to each other. The coaches are quiet.

Even though it's a digital board overhead, the ticking down of time reverberates in my chest. With only two seconds left, a player on the other team hammers the puck toward the goalie, the black disc flies right over his shoulder and into the net as the buzzer sounds.

Half the players on the ice hop into each other's arms in celebration. The other half glide back to their bench, heads down.

Aiden sits in the penalty box until the ice clears. He doesn't stare at his hands. Instead, his bright blue gaze is laser focused across the ice. In our direction.

At me.

I feel more naked than when we first met.

CHAPTER 22

Aiden and I manage to avoid each other for the rest of the weekend. It really isn't that hard. Him, being a teenager who stays up until the wee hours of the morning doing whatever teens do in this weird digital world, and, me getting up at the crack of dawn because that's what grown-ass adults do on a Sunday morning. Even if they had too much to drink the night before.

Anytime I think about the look he gave me at the end of his hockey game icy fear flashes through my veins. I'm not afraid that he'll rat me out to some secret government agency. I'm only the tiniest bit worried he'll say something to Craig.

What worries me, is if Aiden, someone who's spent a whopping one hour with me—well, an hour and ten minutes if you count the time I was naked and hiding behind a kitchen counter—could sense I don't belong in my life, how likely is it that others will see that?

Will I say something so out of character that Craig will question who I am? Or will I slip up at the office and have Monique calling that little twerp Crispy, not just begging for a job, but also suggesting that maybe I need to have my head checked.

Then there's Josie. She knows me better than anyone else, in the past or present. For her, it's not just my words. It's my actions. Or better yet, *reactions*.

Josie knows what I'll say before I say it. And, vice versa. Is she expecting the words of twenty-year-old Emily or the nearly fifty-year-old version of me?

I hop up from the stool on the long edge of the kitchen island and refill my coffee. As long as I have my phone nearby I can do this. I've been studying my text messages, a catalog of the words I've used, a script for the role of Adult Emily, a woman who somehow has her shit together.

Rather than perch back on the stool, I stand at the counter, scrolling down a text thread with my mom. Unfortunately, it's not especially insightful for what I've shared with her.

Instead, I read her long missives about how her new husband's children are always coming to him with their hands out, or how their retirement community is thinking about lowering the age requirement to fifty-five and how all these young people are going to throw loud parties all hours of the night.

I don't know how to break it to her, but I barely see the back side of ten p.m. most days. My responses back to my mom are short, vague, a written version of a distracted agreement.

"Hey."

The sudden sleep-grumpy teenage voice startles me. Even though it's perfectly natural to have a phone in one's hands at all times these days, I fumble to pretend like I wasn't pouring over old text messages to get caught up on everything I've missed over the last three decades, dropping my phone face down on the counter.

"What? No!" I shout nonsense at Aiden, for no other reason than those are the first words I manage to grab from my vocabulary.

He gives me world class side eye as he fills a coffee cup. "Are you cheating on my dad?"

"What? No!" I say again. Am I psychic now? Did I know he was going to make this accusation? "Why would you ask something me like that?"

I might not know much about this current version of myself, but I do know I am *not* a cheater. Never have been, never will be. There is nothing more cruel than to shatter someone's trust, someone's heart, like that.

Aiden nodded toward my phone. "You acted like you were doing something wrong."

Well, I was trying to read up on my life. Not like a seventeen-year-old would understand that.

"No, just catching up on messages. You startled me, that's all."

He shrugs and pulls out the stool furthest from me and starts staring at his own phone.

How do parents of teenagers not tear that thing from their hands?

I pick up my phone and bring it back to life. The screen looks different. I swipe to the next screen, and then the next and back to the Home Screen again. Where my messaging app had been sits a gaping hole.

"Oh, shit." I look on the counter, as if it fell out of my phone and was lying there.

It wasn't.

Panic slithers up my spine, leaving a slimy wetness where my semi-calm once resided. How am I going to communicate with... anyone?

What am I going to do if Craig asks me about my last sushi order? Or, if my mom mentions her new husband and I have to go back to my text history to remember that his name is Geoff, not Jeff? Or maybe it is Jeff. I have no clue because I have no way of checking.

What if Josie brings up a photo she texted me three years ago and I have no clue what she's talking about?

A strangled gasp escapes my lips.

"Dude, I can feel your panic attack all the way over here," Aiden says between slurps of coffee. "Did you like forget to take your fiber or something?"

I cut a razor-sharp look in his direction. "No, my fiber consumption is just fine, thank-you-very-much." I swipe through the screen again. *Nada.* "It's just that I lost something on my phone."

The boy disappears into the pantry and reemerges with an open box of cereal, tossing handfuls of, yep, fiber clusters, into his mouth. "What, like an email? You can go to your trash you know." He says through a mouthful of old-people cereal.

"No, bigger than that."

Aiden leans over the counter and studies my phone. "You didn't break the screen," he says with a shrug. "Not sure what all the drama is about then."

I inhale a deep breath, begging the patron saint of stepmothers for patience. "My text messages, they're all gone."

He narrows his eyes, a move that makes him look remarkably like his father. This time, he plucks my phone from my hands and holds it up to my face. "Your text messages aren't gone. You just deleted the app."

"Can you—can you get it back?" My voice comes out wobbly, weak. Like I'm begging him to do whatever he can to save my favorite stuffed bunny after an unfortunate run-in with a Doberman.

"Yeah, but so can you," Aiden says, one eyebrow lifting.

"I'm not very good with technology." Which is absolutely true, but hopefully not so out of the realm of possibility.

"Huh."

"Why 'huh'? What's that 'huh' about?"

Aiden shrugs and his fingers fly across my phone screen. "The 'huh' is because Dad always said you helped him when he had trouble with his iPad, because before you, he'd FaceTime me to see if I could help him." He tosses my phone back on the counter, the little green box back in its rightful place. "So yeah, that 'huh' is because you look like you, you talk like you, but there's just a little something that's off." He stands and grabs the box of cereal, tossing another handful in his mouth. "Even for you," Aiden adds over his shoulder as he walks out of the room.

CHAPTER 23

Monday slams into us like a tsunami, bringing with it the debris of my failing business, and the realization that I'm starting my third week in the future. I'm no closer to figuring out how to get back to 1996. Not only that, but my fiancé's teenage son is on to me like a red wine on white pants.

I had the perfect explanation prepared, in case Aiden made his suspicions known to Craig. No, I'm not cheating on him. Of course, I still want to marry him. Why do I seem to have forgotten…everything?

Easy; I hit my head harder than I thought during that tumble on my bike.

Aiden hit the road back to Dallas after lunch Sunday, with barely another glance in my direction. If anything had been said to my fiancé, it was never brought up to me.

I don't think I've been let off the hook. More like left hanging just to see how much I'd squirm.

This morning, I'd eyed Craig's electric razor, curious; what if what'd sent me here in the first place would propel me back?

I banished that thought. If it doesn't work, instead of getting back to where I belong, I'd just be a bald-headed bride.

I'm on my computer at work, going down a rabbit hole of searching for ways to go back in time that doesn't require black magic, secret government agencies or major changes to my appearance, and my phone dings with a text.

CRAIG "MCFINE ASS" HARRISON

Plans tonight?

Two simple words that somehow take me too long to answer.

After Aiden left Sunday, Craig holed up in his home office getting caught up on work, then he was outside getting caught up on yard work. After that, it was getting caught up on errands. I was starting to understand that adulthood was ninety percent catching up.

Deep down I know, the truth whispered. The truth accused.

This is more than that.

It didn't take all those diplomas on my wall to know what he's doing. Laying the foundation around his heart to shield whatever hurt I might wield in his direction. It's what I should've done decades—months—ago with Wick.

I slow my galloping heart enough to type back a response.

Nope. Maybe watching Seinfeld, but that's about it.

When I'd found my favorite show was on a streaming service, I watched it anytime I could. Not just the seasons that aired after I skipped forward in time, but I watched the earlier shows as much as possible. Like visiting an old friend that reminds me of home.

CRAIG "MCFINE ASS" HARRISON

Want to go out instead? I know Mondays aren't the typical date night...

My insides go gooey at the words that appear on my screen. Like a forgotten candy bar inside my car on a hot summer day. I want to scream yes, but I'm also afraid that if I do, like peeling open that wrapper, I'll just make a mess all over myself.

And, others.

However, this is exactly what Astrid had suggested when she refused to help a sister out with a love potion. I'd been wanting to ask him all weekend, but he'd been just so busy catching up, which felt an awful lot like another way of saying *'avoiding his potentially unstable fiancée.'*

A tug from my stomach, and something lower, and before I could stop myself, I'm typing back.

> Sure, I've always thought Mondays were sexy as hell.

Seems I've got no willpower when it comes to my fiancé and melted chocolate.

When the little *'haha'* pops up next to my words, my heart does a stutter. Laughter is an aphrodisiac, and it always gave me a little thrill when I made Wick laugh. Same the three or four times he'd—whether on purpose or by accident—made me laugh.

I frown when the clarity that can only come with distance, three weeks or thirty years, creeps over me. Wick was always so serious. Took himself so seriously, which at the time I'd thought was due to his sensitive artist soul and that deep drive to make his dreams a reality.

Who says that ambition has to be humorless? If you can't laugh at yourself, or a clever joke, then why even bother?

Life is hard enough as it is, even without skipping three decades ahead. Life without laughter is just a drab colorless existence.

I have no interest in existing. No matter how many years I've skipped. I want to live. Even if that comes with tears and frustration, it will also come with laughter and light.

> See you tonight

I text back, even though I was already going to see him tonight. Just now I'll be in something other than PJs. With makeup on. Maybe even with my hair fixed.

One of the biggest downsides to Crispin coming in and luring away —okay, stealing—my clients is there's not enough to keep me busy. By busy, I mean out of Monique's way.

I rearranged the four cabinets in our tiny kitchen last week. Unfortunately, all of our files are digital now, or I would've spent an afternoon with the blissful growl of a paper shredder.

The only task that's left to do—that I'm allowed to do—is clean out my junk drawer in my desk.

I pull it open and study it. A junk drawer can tell you a lot about a person. Mine oddly looks like the bottom of my college backpack. So much so, I wonder if perhaps I held on to it for all these years to just dump it into a drawer.

Various flavors of gum. Paperclips of all sizes. Hair ties. A toothbrush and small toothpaste. Tampons. Various pain and stomach meds that, yep, expired eight years ago. Pens, some boring and utilitarian and others with flowers on the barrel or a little flourish on top. Post-It Notes. Stain sticks. Yes, multiples because I'm me and a magnet for random stains showing up on my clothes. That hasn't seemed to change in three decades.

I'm midway through testing the plethora of pens in my possession when Mo pops her head in to let me know my first client for the day has arrived.

Callie is a recent divorcée. A quick perusal of her file tells a tale as old as time. He left her for a younger woman. To rub a block of salt into that gaping wound, she'd just learned from their eleven year old that the new wife is now pregnant, a shock considering that she'd been eager to have another, but her ex had put his foot down and said his baby making days were over.

Jerk.

Instead of being a therapist, maybe I'm better suited to be a hired assassin. Sure, it might suck for the new wife, but from where I'm sitting, it'll end up saving her in the long run.

"You won't believe his latest crap," Callie says by way of greeting as she's sitting down. "He wants to move to California to buy a winery, *and* he still wants the same custody arrangement. So, he sees nothing wrong with putting an unaccompanied minor on a plane every other weekend." She shakes her head, blonde curls responding dramatically.

Yep, definitely opening a side business as an assassin.

I lean forward and drop my voice. "I can make it look like an accident."

Callie's mouth forms a small O in surprise before tiny lines flare from her eyes, and she lets out a cackling laugh. "Oh, you really are the best therapist in town."

The shift in her mood is remarkable. When she sat down, she was so tense I was afraid she'd strain every muscle in her body. By the time our hour is nearly up, Callie is leaning back in her chair, one arm across the back, propping up her head in her palm.

"I've been replaying the last year of our marriage a lot lately," she says. "Trying to understand what broke us. This might sound silly, but I think we stopped having fun together. We stopped playing. Laughing. Is there something to that?"

I study my client and let her words sink in. Psychology books might have a totally different answer, but I know what sits in my heart. "Maybe, but relationships are unique and complicated," I say, worrying that while my intention might be good, my actual words may miss the mark. "And, it's easy to fall into a trap of dissecting everything you did or said. Sure, maybe you stopped laughing together because of something you each were feeling. Or maybe because he quit trying to make you laugh."

Callie drops her gaze and studies her nails, her chin quivering slightly, like leaves rustling in a gentle breeze.

If I weren't watching for it, I'd almost miss it. I lean forward and grip her hand. "Regardless, all of that is in the past. Just don't let it change your future. He doesn't get to take up space there."

She smiles, her eyes shining with tears. "For real, you're the best," she says, her voice as watery as her eyes. "I never feel like I'm being talked down with you. It just feels so…natural."

It's funny, this doesn't feel much different from all the times I'd given Josie and Sofia advice. Maybe this has been inside me all along, counseling people, helping them find their way through the quagmire of emotions, or even giving them the tough love they need, even if they don't want it. All of the majors, from accounting to art, were just part of the long road to get me to my true life's calling.

Our time up, Callie stands and leans in for a hug. "You have no idea how good you are at this," she says in my ear. "You are a gift to everyone you touch."

After she leaves, I fall back into my chair, letting her words soak in like the balm my soul needs.

In just the three weeks I've known him, when I'm not giving him heart attacks or making him question our future together, we spend our time together making easy jokes, funny observations that leave the other snorting, and, my personal favorite, quiet little puns that cause Craig's gorgeous mouth to pull up on one side.

I grab my phone and open up the messenger app.

Mind if I pick tonight's activity?

The three dots appear and disappear. Appear again and then words materialize like magic.

CRAIG "MCFINE ASS" HARRISON

Should I be scared?

I smirk down at the screen.

Very.

CHAPTER 24

The tinny cacophony of music, bells, cheers, dings and disembodied voices growling *'Finish him,'* wrap around us as we stand at the entrance.

"When was the last time you actually came to an arcade?" Craig asks, raising his voice over the din of game noise.

"High school?" It comes out as a question because I honestly don't know if I ever stepped foot in one since August 23, 1996. "What about you?"

His brow wrinkles in concentration. "Eighth grade? So you have more recent experience."

I follow him to a machine that itself could've been an arcade game back in the day.

"How much should we start with?" He pulls his wallet from his pocket, but I put my hand on his wrist.

"This was my idea, I'll treat." I say, sliding my debit card into the gaping maw of the machine and purchasing us each play cards, putting way more credits on them than we could probably use this evening. "Know how this is going to be much cooler than the arcades of our youth?"

He lifts his brows in a silent question.

"We don't have to talk some older kid into buying booze for us. I'll get a tab started."

My fiancé chuckles.

With drinks in hand, a beer for Craig since he's driving and responsible, and an extra large margarita for me because no one cards me anymore, we survey the large hall in front of us.

There's the standbys I could play with my eyes closed, Skee-ball, the basketball game that only looks easy, even a few throwback arcade games that I don't have to throw that far back in my past. There's also plenty of games I've never seen before, including one that looks more like a workout than a game.

"What do you think?" Craig asks before taking a long sip of his beer. "Should we start with something we know?"

I nod toward a line of eighties era arcade games. "Better ease into it. We'd hate to hurt ourselves."

We swipe our cards into side-by-side machines, which I have to admit is much more convenient than having a stack of quarters, and get to work killing pixelated ghosts that only come faster and faster.

Out of the corner of my eye, I watch my fiancé play. He's tentative at first, moving his joystick with jerky, halting jabs.

Can't say I'm much better. After losing a life because of a dead-end move, muscle memory kicks in and I'm coasting through the levels like any good latchkey kid who spent most of her afternoons pouring quarter after quarter into the arcade.

At one point, Craig quits playing and just watches me, sometimes mumbling under his breath when one of the villains gets a little too close. When I finally get knocked out, sweat trails down the back of my neck and my margarita is more slush than frozen.

"Dr. Murray, I had no clue you had such dexterity," Craig says, finishing his beer. "Fresh round?"

We're at the bar, waiting for the next round of drinks when he speaks again. "So you've played that game more than a few times, huh?"

I take a long enough slurp of my margarita that pain spikes behind my eyes. "Yeah," I say once the brain freeze subsides. "When your choice after school is to go home to an empty house or spend your allowance at the arcade, you choose the latter."

His hazel eyes narrow as they study me. "You've never told me that before."

"Really? Surely you knew my mom worked her ass off after my dad left." Did I really not tell him this part of my history?

"Of course I know that. I just didn't you know you were so… lonely."

A flare of icy heat flashes from my heart, stiffening my spine and locking my jaw tight enough to hold in a snarky retort. Or a sob.

Loneliness is not something I talk about. Never in all those afternoons playing game after game until Mom came home.

Or on the weekends spent with Dad's housekeeper because he forgot it was his weekend to have me and had a big trial coming up. It was only when I'd found Josie and Sofia and our friendship was solidified enough that my spending every afternoon, and some evenings, at their houses was the norm, not something to call Child Protective Services about, that I felt like I found where I belonged.

No, we never talk about my loneliness because even though I don't have the knowledge to go with the degrees on my wall, I know that facing it head on will force me to confront feelings I shoved in the far back of my emotional closet.

"Sorry, that came out all wrong. It's just, you're the most magnetic person I've ever met, and I can't imagine a young Emily spending hours in an arcade." He downs half his beer. "Okay, this just took a turn. Want to go see what muscles we pull with one of the dancing games?"

Words clog in my throat, so I just nod, and follow him.

We approach the game with the trepidation of the middle-aged, our brains telling us we can absolutely master dance steps on a slippery light up board while our bodies scream *'Danger, Will Robinson!'*.

A teenager on the next game over flies through the dance moves, his feet seemingly acting on their own as he stares ahead with glassy-eyed concentration.

I turn to Craig before we hurt either our prides or our asses. "Did I ever tell you about Marta?"

His brow narrows in a question. "Is she a friend?"

"Dad's housekeeper." I stir my melting margarita with my straw, wishing I could recall just what I've shared and how much of the ugly bits I've kept hidden away. "But really, she was more like an aunt. Actually, I called her Tía Marta. If Dad was tied up on the weekends I went to Houston, I'd usually go to her house. Her sons were like my big brothers." My heart spins wondering where Marta, Tony and Felipe are today. "Anyway, loneliness only hurts when you let it. You can choose to let it wrap its darkness around you, or you can find your own light to get away from it."

We stand there in clashing sounds of games, sugared up kids drunk on autonomy running past us, but none of it matters as our gazes fall deeper into each other.

"Tell me something I don't know about you." My words come out as soft as a kitten.

His hold on my gaze is pure gravity. I couldn't look away if I wanted to, and something tells me he feels the same. We're two stars locked in a gravitational force that won't let go.

Can't let go.

"The first time I saw you, it felt like you were the final piece in a puzzle I'd been constructing my whole life." The clashing sounds of the arcade fall away as he speaks. "A final puzzle piece I didn't know I was missing. And now—" The sound of a digital explosion beside us pulls our gazes away from each other. "And now, I'm afraid that without you none of it can fit together anymore."

Eight-year-old Emily, the little girl with a step stool and a stack of quarters spending afternoons in the company of pixelated heroes and villains, melts like my forgotten frozen margarita.

Isn't that what we all want?

To be the one who doesn't just fit into someone's life seamlessly but fills a hole.

"You've never told me that," I whisper the words, low and breathy under the din of arcade noise. Even though I've only known this man for a few weeks, I somehow *know* in my bones he's never opened up like this.

By giving me these words, Craig's doing something that goes

against every self-preservation mechanism screaming at him to stay silent.

He may be an expert in the brain, but he's turned over control of his heart to me.

I can't help but wonder if he knows me well enough to entrust something so precious with me.

Do I know myself well enough to bear this responsibility?

CHAPTER 25

"I don't know how you're going to do it." Josie crosses her arms and shakes her head.

I wrinkle my nose. "And there's no chance of getting out of it?"

"Nope. You're committed to this, Em. Would you really want to let your goddaughter down?"

Aubrey, the red-headed menace my best friend had given birth to, was absolutely giddy in the bridal boutique.

When I froze in fear of all the dresses of various shades of white, those cut slim and close to the body or voluminous and otherworldly, all the lace, the beading, the trains that went for miles, the tulle—so much tulle—Aubrey stepped in and offered to pick out some options for me to try on.

Thus, why I'm standing with my best friend in a dressing room trying to figure out how to get into a wedding dress with a skirt of so much tulle, the thing can stand up on its own.

Despite the fact the wedding planner declared that because of my procrastination—which I'd like to point out was the doing of future me—I'll have to order a ready-to-wear dress, I kept the wedding dress shopping date with Josie and Aubrey. I approached it with the same childish glee of the time last year—thirty-ish years ago—when Jo and I ditched class to spend an afternoon playing dress up at a local costume shop.

No matter how old we get, it's still fun to make-believe a little bit.

To make-believe I'm a deliriously happy bride, and not just delirious.

To make-believe I'm not scared shitless to be marrying a total stranger.

To make-believe I'm not still heartbroken over a boy who chose a dream over me.

Who am I kidding? He would've chosen a cheeseburger over me. So why does it hurt so bad?

Why has Wick burrowed under my skin like a stubborn splinter, festering instead of coming out.

"I think," Josie says, pulling me out of my internal freak out. "You're going to have to come up from the bottom. Think of it as spelunking, but in tulle."

After a few attempts ending in a mouthful of fabric, I finally emerge through the bodice, like a newborn entering the world.

Victorious, if not a bit ridiculous.

I turn to the mirror, while Jo closes up the back with binder clips.

Correction, *a lot* ridiculous.

I'm more dress than human. The skirt billows out with a force field, keeping away any wandering hands of dirty old great uncles twice removed. The sleek, strapless bodice tapering into the skirt makes me look like a human cake topper.

"This is awful," I whisper, hoping the dressing room isn't bugged and a judgy sales lady isn't going to burst in and rip it off me.

"I know," Jo agrees. "Aubrey is going to love it." She emphasizes the point by dramatically opening the dressing room door.

Squeals fill the room as an over-caffeinated sixteen-year-old hops up and down. "Yes, Aunt Em, that's the *one!*"

"It's definitely an option." That's a lie. Based on the fact I waited too long for a special order dress, the sales associate pulled only the dresses I could get immediately. However, that didn't stop Aubrey from adding to the selection with the most ridiculous dresses she could find. "I'll keep this in the possibly, maybe, pile."

My next options were much more practical. I pull on a simple white satin dress with tank straps with an A-line skirt that brushes the floor with the gentleness of a kiss on a newborn's head.

"Hmm…" Josie cocks her head.

"That one screams fifth wedding, don't care," Aubrey says. "You can do better."

That's how the next four dresses go. Too boring. Too lacy. Not enough sex appeal. Too much boob, which, to my knowledge, I've never been accused of.

The next to last one, a dress that could also double as a nightgown with it's slinky, body-skimming fit, spaghetti straps and draping neckline, was declared to be 'not on brand' for me.

Whatever that means.

With each dress I step into, with each button that Josie closes and then opens again, I feel the funnel of my life narrowing.

Meeting Craig, the flirtatious glances, nervous first date, tentative kisses that turn into passion, all of it feels like the pages ripped from a novel leaving me just the final few chapters to read. To live. He had the benefit of falling in love. I woke up and the world thinks I feel the same.

There's one last dress hanging expectantly in the dressing room. I sigh as I slip it off the hanger and step into it, pulling it over my hips, sliding my arms through straps that hang sexily off my shoulder. Once the bodice is in place, I meet my gaze in the mirror.

This dress is beautiful, but not in a showy way. It's an antique white, with light-silver embroidered flowers on the corset-style bodice and scattered throughout the skirt. The skirt, while layered, it's a softer effect, swishing, inviting instead of overpowering, with just enough of a train to remind people I'm a bride.

Straight out of a period romance novel, this is the dress a heroine wears as her lover rides in from some far-off battle, hops off his horse and whisks her into his arms.

It's not just the perfect dress.

It's the perfect dress for *me*.

My allergic-to-the-sun pale skin looks luminous. Soft curls graze my shoulders. The more intricate wedding dresses wore me, overpowering my petite frame with fabric and decor.

Not this dress. We were made for each other.

Which, I guess, is the point of finding the perfect wedding dress, for when you pledge to love and honor the person who was made for you.

Tears flood my vision, making me look even more like a ghostly Victorian portrait. Should I have waited to find this dress with my mom?

If she is losing her memories, should I have waited to give her, me, this moment?

She's never been sentimental in shared mother-daughter moments. Maybe I am?

A knock sounds at the door and I swipe at my eyes.

"Em?" Josie opens the door a crack and gasps. "Oh, honey."

"Is it that bad?"

She shakes her head, her eyes shining with tears, too. "It's that *good*." It's her turn to dab at her eyes. "Stupid hormones. Can't shed a tear at a funeral, but a commercial for homeless pets and seeing my best friend about to marry the love of her life, and I'm a puddle of tears." Josie laughs. "All those hospital bills were worth it, to see you this happy."

Hospital bills? Did something happen to Josie?

Is there a way I can nonchalantly ask her to tell me the story of how Craig and I met, without sounding like I've lost my mind?

"I wanna see!" Aubrey's voice slices into my musings.

Jo rolls her eyes. "So demanding," she says, but the smile on her face is nothing but fierce love and pride.

I'm a tad bit jealous of the other me, the one who was there when Aubrey grew inside my best friend, who watched Josie parent Aubrey and her brother, Ben, to become these incredible kids who would grow up to be even more incredible adults.

I step through the dressing room door and Aubrey squeals. Modern teenage speak for 'Hell yeah!'?

I study my reflection in the three-way mirror. This dress really is perfect. It's not hard to imagine Craig's reaction when he sees me. The love and admiration etched on his face. How he'll murmur he loves me as we stand in front of our friends and family pledging to have and to hold.

It's also not hard to imagine Wick throwing open the doors and racing down the aisle to stop the wedding because it took him three decades to come to his senses.

"What's wrong?" Josie asks, the line between her brow even more pronounced with her frown.

That's the curse of having a best friend who's known you since the beginning of time. They notice the little things. A gaze that shifts away, as if unable to see the reflection of what's supposed to be happiness. The barely perceptible dimming of the bridal glow. The quiet inhale of a shuddering breath.

I meet my best friend's eyes in the mirror and contemplate telling her everything. However, if there's no going back, if I skipped through life like a VHS stuck on fast-forward then I can't have my best friend looking at me like I've lost more than half my life but my grip on reality.

"Am I rushing into this?" My voice is as weak as my conviction. "I mean, I went all in with Wick and see where that got me."

Josie's eyes narrow and she purses her lips. "Wick? What's that asshat got to do with…" She pauses, takes a deep breath and folds her arms across her chest. "Em, don't do it. Not now. Not with Craig."

"Don't do what?"

"What you do with every relationship you've been in *since* Wick. You bail. You stay long enough to have fun and not be alone on the weekends, then you toss them aside the minute it gets serious." She drops her arms. "You always said none of them were the one. And I believe you." Her voice softens. "From the moment I saw you and Craig together, I *knew* this was different. That you've waited your whole life for him. For this. It's okay to have nerves. Just don't let them control your happily ever after."

I let her words wash over me, hoping that somewhere deep down they'll hitch on a truth if my mind doesn't know my heart will.

The words float by, leaving more doubt in their wake.

CHAPTER 26

I'm fidgety as I pace the lobby of Mom's hotel. The coffee cup in my hand crinkles, and the lid pops off, sloshing sticky, lukewarm coffee across my hand.

I canceled my morning appointments, well, *appointment*, singular. Deep down, a voice whispers that I should hold on to every appointment like the precious diamond it is, but I wanted to be available in case my mother needs me.

She refused to let me accompany her to her doctor's appointment earlier this morning, instead providing a buffet of excuses. *You have work. There won't be room for all of us in there. This is really just a basic exam, they won't have a diagnosis.*

Closing with, *Honey, I just don't want you to worry until there's something to worry about.*

The truth, at last.

I get it. I didn't tell Mom about the time my sophomore year I thought I could cure myself of a bladder infection with cranberry juice and an over-the-counter herbal remedy. A week later, I found myself spending the night in the hospital with a kidney infection.

It was for the exact same reasons. She was busy with work.

I didn't want her to worry about my ability to function as an adult on my own.

So yeah, there's something achingly poignant about the fact I was less than forthcoming about my health then, just as my mom is in her seventies.

It's funny that loving someone usually means not wanting to burden them, when all they want to do is help carry some of that weight for you. Love is about carrying and being carried. Why is that so hard for us to understand?

Just as I start to make a mental list of everything that could possibly be going on with my mom's health, the elevator dings and there she is.

Even though I came from her body, I barely got any of her genetics. As a kid, I remember thinking my mom was a real-life Barbie doll. Tall, thin with blonde hair and blue eyes. Always perfectly tanned, never too pale or sunburned.

I'm like some experimental, limited production of a friend of Barbie's. Short, pale and brunette; my purpose to show that not all California girls look the same.

Thirty years later, Mom's still got that doll-like wonder. Her blonde hair is a little shorter now, and doesn't glow like it's lit from within. Her face is smooth and taut, but almost a little too smooth and taut. While she's still thin, the loose fit of her pants and top indicates the softness that comes with age.

"Momma." My voice breaks on the word. Hopefully she'll think it's just the worry festering inside of me and not the fact I'm a traveler adrift on the sea of time.

She wraps me in a tight hug.

One thing that will always stand the test of time is a mother's love.

"Hi, baby girl. Have you been that worried about me?"

For so many years, it was just Mom and me. The dinners she burned, the rare weekends she had off, and we'd hit the road for a day trip. All the times I laid my head in her lap, silent tears falling down my face, and she just stroked my head. I'm sure there's more that came after August 23, 1996.

What if I never get back to that time?

If Mom loses her memories and I never made them, does that mean our relationship has holes in it?

That there's parts of our shared history that doesn't existence?

I nod into her shoulder. "And I've missed you, too." It's so true. Even though my school was barely an hour away from home, once I went off to college, I might as well have been on the other side of the country.

It wasn't that I didn't want to see my mom, it was just that once I spread my wings it was hard to tuck them back in.

"What did the doctor say?" I launch right in as soon as we pull apart.

Mom waves a hand, swatting away my question like it's an annoying fly. "They gave me two different cognitive tests, and I passed them both with flying colors, of course."

"So...?" I prompt, leading us out of the hotel lobby and to my waiting car.

My mother waits until we're in my car and both buckled in before speaking again. "It's likely just normal decline that comes with age, those moments when it's hard to pull up someone's name." She smoothes her pants.

I study her hands. Her nails are still immaculate, painted a ballet slipper pink and shaped modestly. Beyond that, her hands are thinner, the knuckles a bit swollen, veins prominent. It's the one place, beside her mind, that shows age on her body.

"So," she continues. "He told me to do some puzzles every day to keep my mind active, keep a journal of times I can't recall something and to follow up with him if it gets worse."

I exhale a long breath I didn't know I was holding. "You're going to be okay?"

"Well, I won't be if we sit here all day and I end up with an awful dress for my only daughter's wedding." One side of her mouth pulls up into a wicked grin; the kind she'd give me when I was a kid just before we'd open a pint of ice cream and huddle on the couch watching cheesy action movies.

We went back to the shop where I'd found my dress and the saleslady was kind enough to let me try it on again for my mom.

"I'm sorry I didn't save the dress shopping for when you were here," I say, opening the fitting room door.

Mom's eyes grow wide and her lower lip trembles. "It's fine," she says. "I get to see you in it now. And it is perfect."

Once I'm back in my jeans and T-shirt, the dress shopping isn't really all that excruciating. I expected her to pick apart every option the salesperson or I present her, but instead, she gleefully tries them all on. Eight dresses in, she emerges and my breath catches in my throat.

The dress is a muted lavender, but somehow she makes it sparkle. The skirt is pleated and nips in at the waist. The top is simple lavender chiffon with cap sleeves, and a beaded silver and lavender wrap drapes across the top of her shoulders.

"Wow," I whisper.

Mom looks in the mirror. "I am happily married, and have been divorced from your father longer than we were together, so is it wrong that I want him to look at me and realize he messed up...even all these years later?"

I can't help but laugh. "Nope, you have every right to always make your ex jealous." I might be speaking from recent experience. "There is no statute of limitations on that."

With the dress and complementary shoes in hand, I turn to my mom. "Where to next?" The time with her is a homecoming, and I'm in no hurry to have it end.

"You know what I'm craving?" Mom asks once we're back in my car.

"Willa's?" It was really the only answer. A small mom and pop place on the square of our little town an hour west in the Hill Country. It was only open for breakfast and lunch, but it was the kind of place where the staff knew everyone by name and by their order.

Where regulars would have to tell the staff if they would be out of town because if someone missed a usual Saturday breakfast, they were known to call the local police for a wellness check. It's the kind of place I would happily drive an hour each way to have their famous grilled cheese and tomato soup.

"You don't mind, do you? I haven't been back home in ages," she says. "Maybe we can even go by the old house. See how the new owners are taking care of her."

We make it out there in record time, and even though Willa's would be closing in half an hour, the waitress said it would be no problem to serve us lunch.

"You know," Mom says, sipping on her freshly poured champagne. "I thought marriage was just not for you."

"Oh yeah?" I take my own sip. "Why is that?"

My mother looks out the window, her gaze tracking a mother with a teenage daughter walking down the street. "Sometimes we pass along more than genetics."

I snort. "Honestly, if I didn't know my father, I'd think you'd brought the wrong baby home."

She gives me the patient smile of someone who'd heard the same joke so many times its humor is as thin as a worn sweater.

"I was afraid I passed along my trauma from a failed marriage." She pauses and glances out the window again.

The mother and daughter had stopped to look inside the shop next door, them looking inside as we look out.

I study her, waiting for her to finish her thought.

"Not failed, because we have you, but not successful. Not lasting." Mom meets my eyes, and reaches for my hand. "Emily, I worried for so many years I scared you off of the idea of spending your life with someone, but who am I to tell you that love is worth it? It will be hard. It will be scary and, while I hope this never happens, there will be times when you just want to give up and walk away." She releases my hand and takes a longer sip of her champagne. "But giving up and walking away doesn't make the love end, it just opens a wound where it lived. And sometimes that wound never fully heals."

It's my turn to take a long drink. Is that why it took she so long to remarry and why my dad never did?

Did their love turn into a festering wound for both of them?

"And if that wound does heal, the scar tissue it leaves behind is just too hard to penetrate," Mom says, her voice barely above a whisper.

CHAPTER 27

I 've grown so accustomed to Astrid's shop being empty, I skid to a stop when I fling open the door and find a woman who looks like she'd be more at home on a golf course instead of a psychic's shop.

She's at that age where the cosmetic surgery only just fills in the cracks, but the foundation beneath is still crumbling. Her hair is that indeterminable shade of blonde. Or was it white?

Judging by the size of the rocks on her finger and gracing her ear lobes, whatever voodoo she wielded either through a surgeon's expertise or Astrid's spirits, is working.

They stop their conversation, and two pairs of eyes rake over me. Red splotches creep up the woman's neck and she ducks her head, moving her face out of my line of sight. I might have Rip Van Winkled for the past thirty years, but I know enough about body language to know this lady is *someone*.

"Just leave these crystals where you feel like you need the most protection, and they'll absorb all the negative energy," Astrid says, her voice softer than she's ever used with me.

The woman nods.

"Call me if you feel anything…off," the psychic adds, squeezing the woman's arm.

I busy myself with studying various teas and homeopathic books while the lady finishes her transaction and leaves. It's only after the tinkling of the bells above the door die away that Astrid acknowledges my presence.

"You say anything to anyone about the governor's wife being here and I'll put a hex on you."

My eyes widen, not at the *who*, but the *what*. "You can do hexes? Why are you just telling me this?"

The psychic rolls her eyes and leans her forearms on the glass counter. "You guys really should give me some warning," she says, in what's become my favorite part of my visits. Her Spirits fucking with her. "I take it you're still immature beyond your years."

"Yep, about as juvenile as I can get," I pause, glancing over my shoulder to make sure the governor's wife isn't about to walk in on something that would have her clutching her literal pearls. "No chance the Spirits feel like telling you how to get rid of me, huh?"

Astrid closes her eyes and takes a deep breath. "Nope, seems like I am very unfortunately stuck with you. Do you have a reason for being here, or is this some sort of Karmic punishment?"

"What do you know about hypnosis?"

The psychic narrows her eyes. "You don't look like you need to quit smoking or lose weight."

"But I do need to remember my fiancé, and I know that hypnosis can unlock what's hidden inside the brain."

"No." With that one word, Astrid moves from behind the counter toward the back of her shop.

"No, you don't know how to?" I ask, following her down the dark hallway.

"I didn't say that," she huffs over her shoulder.

"You just said 'no,' so you didn't say a lot of anything." I blink, to make my point.

Astrid stops in the small room where she'd done my reading thirty years ago. "No, I won't do it. Not because I can't, but because there's nothing there. There're no memories to retrieve, and it'll do more harm than good."

"But if my body has aged thirty years, then surely my brain has, which means this information is somewhere, it's just not...accessible. I didn't just come out of nowhere."

Even though my mom's fine, her memory scare made me realize if there's a diagnosis coming further down the road, then it stands to reason I could be facing the same fate. If that's the case, what happens to my memories when I'm starting at a disadvantage?

Astrid straightens and gives me a sympathetic look. "Remembering someone doesn't instantly make you love them," she says, like the psychic she is, practically reading my mind. "Love is not in a memory, it's what comes in the moment. Love is fought for. Earned. You won't find that in a download of information."

I shake my head. "You're right but you're also wrong. Love is many things, and one of them is shared memories. I owe it to Craig to remember, otherwise..." My voice trails off; the rest of the words lodged behind a tangle of emotion. "Otherwise, our relationship is nothing but a lie, and I can't let him believe that. He deserves so much more."

Like the governor's wife, Astrid pats me on the arm. "I wish I understood what's happening to you. All I know is that when you asked, the Spirits said no. They're not telling me why *not*, just that it's not the way."

I take a deep breath and press my lips together, banishing the sob that so desperately wants to erupt from my throat. "Well," I clear my throat. "Please tell the Spirits they can, respectfully, bite me."

She flashes a smile that's both wry and understanding. "They don't really give a damn, my dear."

Frustration smolders through my veins, as I drive to my office. Every other car on the road has the sole purpose of pissing me off. Rolling through stop signs. Not using blinkers.

Simply existing.

All of that fans the embers of my anger. Anger at myself. Anger at Astrid and her damn Spirits.

Even anger at Craig for loving me.

Because I'm getting to my office later than usual, the street is packed bumper to bumper with parked cars.

More than halfway down the block, in front of Crispin's office, I finally find a parking spot that, after about ten minutes of effort, I manage to fit my car into.

The high-pitched purr of a motor comes up behind me when I'm getting out of my car.

A scooter pulls in the tiny space behind my car, its front wheel touching the curb.

Despite the driver's helmet, it's no mystery who I'm looking at. The loafers, dark jeans, blazer and messenger bag slung across his chest seal his identity.

I turn, hoping to rush toward my office before he shuts off his stupid scooter.

"Dr. Murray, what're you doing this far down the block?" Crispin calls, after killing the hum of the tiny motor.

"Seeing how the other half lives," I toss back to him. Maybe I'm also experiencing some sort of Karmic punishment.

He takes off his helmet and shakes out his mullet. "Oh yeah, street's busy this morning. Figured people of your generation followed the more conventional work hours. You know, early bird gets the worm kind of mentality."

I smile sweetly to hide the sneer twitching at my lips. "I think you're thinking of my Nana's generation. Haven't you heard? Gen X is the slacker generation." I know damn well we're not, but I say it anyway. A thought bubbles up from the abyss of my mind. "Professional question, what do you know about hypnosis?"

Crispin cocks his head and shuffles, shoving the helmet under one arm. "I mean, I know some therapists use it as a short-cut to changing behavior rather than getting to the root cause of said behavior."

"Do you know how to do it?"

His eyes narrow, and he purses his lips.

Is he doing it now?

I self-consciously scratch my head, trying to see if I can feel him getting inside it.

"I took a seminar on it, a few years back. But I wouldn't say I'm an expert. Like I said, it feels like cheating in a way." Crispin shuffles the helmet to his other arm. "Dr. Murray, is there a reason you're asking about this?"

I take a deep breath. There's no way I'm going to tell him the actual truth. However, I also happen to be the worst liar on the planet. "A client of mine asked about it, and I've never done it." Hopefully the side of honesty balances out the big fat lie. "Just wanted another, you know, professional opinion."

He nods and a smile brightens his face. "Dr. Murray, Emily, it means so much that you see us as equals." He pushes a palm against his chest. "I'm truly, truly honored."

"Well, okay then, thank you for your time." I hitch my bag further up my shoulder and head down the street toward my office. "Crispin, if I—my client—I mean, wants to try it, would you feel comfortable doing it? Like you wouldn't do something to make me, them, act like a monkey when they hear a certain word, right?"

He pauses halfway up the walk toward his office. An indecipherable look passes his face.

"I'm kidding!" I say on the most fakest laugh I've ever laughed. "You know, professional humor, right?"

"Right."

Two hours later, I'm elbows deep into an internet search on self-hypnosis with a random side trip into manifestation and positive thinking, when Mo gently knocks at my open door.

"Emily, got a sec?" Her voice is soft, hesitant and her usually lyrical accent is flat, almost like she's holding it back. "There's something I think you need to see."

She crosses my office; her phone cradled against her chest. Concern and fear cloud her usually warm eyes. With a deep breath and another glance at her phone, she hands it to me. "Click play," she says quietly.

There's a frozen image of Crispin.

I hit the play icon.

He springs to life, standing outside a yellow house. Not just any yellow house, the yellow house that's been converted into a duplex of businesses with a yoga studio on one side and my therapy practice on the other.

"Hi y'all, earlier today a professional colleague, one who might be a bit old school in her way of thinking, but a colleague nonetheless, came to me with an unusual request." He points over his shoulder.

My gaze dances around the scene behind him. Positioned perfectly to where he's pointing is the sign with my name.

"She was asking about hypnosis, for a client. I know at one point last century—"

Heat curdles in my stomach, like an angry lava flow churning to get out of its lair.

"This was an acceptable form of treatment, but all it does is put a band-aid on the problem. It doesn't solve for anything."

Crispin pauses, readjusting the phone to ensure my name is still positioned behind him. "I normally wouldn't call out a colleague like this, especially one who comes from a generation where this was an acceptable form of treatment. But, I feel it's in the best interest of the public to remind everyone that at Zenith Therapy, we take time to help you be a better version of yourself, without the use of junk science. Hit the link in the bio to schedule your free fifteen-minute consultation to find out how I can help you reach your zenith. No shortcuts. No junk therapy. Just *you*...at your best."

The video stops on his smug, punchable face.

Everything in the world turns red before my eyes.

My grip tightens on Mo's phone, hand trembling so hard I'm afraid it'll fly across the room and smash against the wall without me even trying.

"This has gone too far," she says.

I shake my head and gently hand her phone back to her. "This hasn't gone far enough." I race out of my office, through the small lobby, out my front door and down the three steps.

Something in my knee pops, but I ignore it as I look for that stupid brown mullet.

Crispin is nowhere to be seen.

It would've been too easy to find him outside doing one of those livestream things. Chances are, he snuck down the street to film while I was doing my research and Monique was busy keeping my life together.

The anger—self-loathing really—in the pit of my stomach shifts, threatens to consume me. For the first time in the weeks I've been in this cruel and unknown future, I feel homesick.

I miss my tiny old apartment I share with Josie. I miss my Jeep, with its cranky clutch and even crankier AC. I miss days where skipping class wouldn't inconvenience everyone in my world. I miss the freedom of not having a phone literally in my back pocket.

Hell, I even miss Fleur and that awful art class, and Wick, and his dreams of stardom I'd adopted as my own.

I miss everything in between. Things I never experienced. Graduating college, my first job. Making mistakes, and right calls. Setting goals and achieving them. Or completely falling face-first.

I miss growing to this more mature version of myself, even though I never experienced it the first time.

Needing to get away, to do whatever it takes to find my way back to 1996, I glance down the street to where I parked my car.

Mo's shouts of my name are faint under the blood rushing through my ears.

I sprint half a block, ignoring the little stabs of pain in my knee. My gaze falls on the scooter still parked behind Ruby. The car that had been behind Crispin's stupid scooter is gone behind me. Just Ruby, my beautiful red BMW, and a robin's egg blue scooter.

Before rational thoughts could outweigh visions of vengeance, I hop in my car and start it in one fluid move, throwing it in reverse and gunning it.

My car jerks.

The satisfying sound of popping plastic fills my ears.

I put the car in drive and edge it forward, only to stop and reverse it again. In addition to the screeching of metal under my tires, shouts of my name reverberate around the quiet street.

"Em, what are you doing? Stop!" Monique stands in the street, trying to get my attention, while smartly staying out of my way.

"My scooter!" Crispin is running down the front walk to his office; his phone plastered to his ear.

At least he's not filming it.

After one more cycle of drive and reverse, a siren peels in the distance before I see the red and blue lights racing toward me.

I coast the car forward to get the scooter out from under it, calmly turn it off and get out just as the police cruiser pulls up beside me.

Crispin's face is awash in utter devastation. As if I'd run over his favorite bunny instead of his scooter.

With a deep breath, I push the hair out of my eyes and take three steps toward him.

He has the good sense to take three steps back, his arms flinching like they may have to block a blow.

"Getting out of these tight parking spots are hell," I say with dead calm. "You shouldn't park so close."

CHAPTER 28

I'd always thought if I was going to get arrested, it'd be for underage drinking or getting caught pulling off some elaborate prank. In my delinquency daydreams, Josie was always right by my side. My loyal best friend never missing an opportunity to try to save me from my bad ideas, but who'll also go down with the ship.

The officer was kinder than he needed to be. Maybe it was because as soon as he got out of his cruiser, I was already waiting, hands behind my back, wrists together, eager for the bite of cold metal.

Instead, he just opens his back door and says, "Ma'am, why don't you just have a seat and take a break for a moment. Collect yourself."

Shut inside his car, I can't make out what Monique and Crispin are saying, but their body language gives me a good idea.

Mo gestures down the street, toward our office and shows the officer her phone. His brow furrows as he watches.

While their heads are ducked over her phone, Crispin's face reddens and he gestures toward the broken remains of his scooter.

Now that adrenaline ebbs from my blood, empathy leaks in. What if this was an heirloom from his long-dead grandfather?

Or his only mode of transportation and now he's going to be stuck walking or waiting for the bus? Worse, walking in those expensive, soft leather loafers. They probably have awful arch support.

Crispin says something, his face tight, and whatever it is causes Monique to stride across the sidewalk and stick a well-manicured—and sharp—finger in his face.

The officer steps between them just as another patrol car pulls up.

After several minutes of conferring with the new cop, the first officer pops open my back door.

"Well, Dr. Murray, seems Mr. Dunne here would like to press charges, so I guess that means you're coming with me." He seems almost relieved to be able to get out of there. "Your office manager will meet us down there."

"Are you going to handcuff me?"

He arches an eyebrow. "Do I need to handcuff you?"

"Not really…I just feel like if this is my one time to get arrested, I should get the full experience, you know? Handcuffs, prison stripes, soap on a rope. What about my one phone call?"

This time, he heaves out a heavy sigh. "You realize you'll be home by supper, right?"

"Hey, doc," Mo appears over his shoulder. Her Caribbean lilt is back in place, and I feel like everything will be right in the world. "I'll cancel your appointments for this afternoon and be right there."

"Can you do me a favor? Don't tell Craig, but can you call my dad?" I cringe as the words leave my mouth.

Somehow, I feel like my dad has waited for this call his entire life. So, like me getting the full arrest experience, he should get the experience of getting his only daughter out of jail.

The cop doesn't even take me downtown. Instead, he takes me to a substation a few blocks away. No fingerprinting. No mug shot. He even had the nerve to ask if I wanted any coffee before settling me into a cozy conference room. The coffee was actually not bad.

An hour later—and I know this because they leave me with my cell phone—the door opens and my dad peeks in.

The last time I saw him, he was younger than I am now, and still had a full head of dark, wavy hair. The seventy-something-year-old version of my father still has a full head of hair, but it's shockingly white now.

He was never a tall man, something that I've attributed to his viciousness in the courtroom and unrelenting parenting skills, but thirty years of life seems to have diminished him, just enough that I barely have to look up to meet the disappointment in his eyes.

"Hi, Dad," I muster brightness into my voice that has no business being there.

"Funny how I'm the first person you call when you get arrested," he says, his voice sharp with reprimand. "Yet I find out about your engagement from my housekeeper," he adds, his gaze dropping to the ring on my left hand.

Parents are parents no matter if you're ten, twenty or fifty. If their parenting style is lifting you up on a platform, they'll still do it.

Or, if in my father's case, it's chastisement and questioning my life choices, it's still there no matter how much of an adult I seem to be.

He pulls out a chair across from me and sits, slowly, grimacing as if something hurts. "Pulled something teeing off this morning," Dad grumbles, reading my watchful gaze. "Lucky for you, I was in town for a golf tournament."

"I figured you would've just called one of your young associates to deal with this." I lean back in the chair and cross my arms over my chest, the classic teen move.

"Did you want someone to get you out of this mess or a drinking buddy?" My father mirrors my posture.

Our relationship has never been warm and fuzzy. Where Josie's dad could be stern when we deserved it, he was mostly loving, telling silly jokes to make us laugh despite ourselves. However, my dad saw me less as someone to love and more as someone to mold in his likeness. Whether I wanted it or not.

"You're welcome by the way," he says.

"Thank you for skipping the nineteenth hole?"

His razor-sharp eyes force me to shrink in my chair, as if I'm still a petulant teenager in his mind. Which isn't wrong. "Why do you always do that?"

"Do what?"

"Assume that you're an inconvenience." His face softens, starting with his light blue eyes, the same as mine, all the way down to his jaw. "I get that you were angry growing up, but I somehow expected you to…outgrow it once you fell out of love with someone. You'd understand." He sighs, revealing a weariness that I've never seen before settling on his shoulders. "There are no victors in heartbreak, Emily. I know that, your mom knows that. And while we made a lot of mistakes we never wanted you to feel like one of them. Unfortunately, we—I—was unsuccessful in that." He clears his throat. "Back to the issue at hand. I explained to Mr. Dunne that we won't press charges against his cyberbullying if he agrees to likewise against your…*automobile accident*. Your insurance will have to cover damages, of course." A slow smile spreads across his lined face. A shark's smile. The smile of someone who just outsmarted his opponent. "He realized rather quickly accusations of that nature would be detrimental to his business, considering he brands himself as a positive mental health advocate, so he happily deleted the video."

I sit there, dumbfounded. I expected my dad to get a reduced bail, maybe even talk them into allowing me to do some community service to get this off any record. I didn't realize he'd not only sniffed blood in the water but went for the kill as well.

For me.

"Wow, thanks, Dad. I, uh, thank you." There's so much more I should say. I want to say, but the words are shy, unsure of how to navigate this version of my father.

My father nods and presses on the table to stand. "I know I haven't said this enough, but I really am proud of you. You fought back against the life I tried to push you into and came into a career where you make a real difference." Dad's mouth turns down. "I just make rich people richer. You're the better person."

I stare. Words evaporate. If I didn't know what to say a few heartbeats ago, I sure as hell don't now.

He reaches for the door, pulling it open before closing it again. "One last thing. Take it from someone who spent his career fighting off every new generation nipping at his heels. Fighting time is like fighting a rip tide. The more you struggle, the more it pulls you under.

Time is a gift, and of course that's only something people like me come to realize. If there's nothing else you learn from me, learn *this*, don't worry about trying to stay young and relevant. Just worry about living. And, loving."

With that, this man I thought I knew, thought I'd had pegged as the hard ass, absent father disappears out the door.

His words eddy around me, sparking as if they're made of magic.

A second later, the door opens again. This time the warm face of my office manager fills the space. "All right, Doc, we're free to go. I can give you a ride."

I look up at her and suddenly everything clears. Angels singing and all that shit.

It's time for a therapy session of my own.

CHAPTER 29

We don't go back to my house. Or even the office. When I tell Monique where I'd like to go instead, she simply presses her brightly painted lips together and drives.

An hour later, we find a parking place on a side street, and I wordlessly lead Mo to my favorite place on campus. A spot Josie and I spent time studying, daydreaming and philosophizing in the way that those straddling adolescence and adulthood can.

A place where Josie confided that she made a mistake letting Daniel go, but she also knew they'd find their way back to each other. A place where I shared with Jo that I felt lost, as if in this great big over-populated world there wasn't a spot for me.

A purpose for me.

The banks of the river running through campus are crowded, but I've seen worse. Mo and I find a quiet patch in the shade, and we watch the river go by, the students go by, for several minutes before she speaks.

"I should've asked this before, but are you okay?" Her voice is as soft as the new green grass under my fingertips. "Ever since you missed work a few weeks ago, things have been…off."

It's no surprise she's noticed. In just the few weeks I've known her,

Monique has picked up on things that fly right by me. In truth, she'd be a better therapist than me.

"Is it something with Craig? The wedding?" She twists a piece of grass around her finger before letting it fall back to the ground. "Or, is it something else? Are you *sick* sick?"

I lean back on my elbows and study the college kids around us. Unlike Jo and me thirty years—just weeks—ago most of them are on their phones, a few have their laptops open. My generation had to rely on the information in our books and notes, these guys can find anything anywhere, at any time.

A few things haven't changed. The trio tossing a frisbee over the heads of classmates. The guy threatening to throw a squealing girl into the river. The promise of the future. The carefree spirit of the present. The smell of pot...

"Would you believe me that just a few weeks ago I was one of them?" I nod toward the co-eds around us.

Mo glances at me from the side of her oversized sunglasses. "I think we all feel that way sometimes. With Jaden, I swear it was yesterday I was holding him for the first time, and now he barely gives me a goodbye before hopping out of the car."

I fall all the way to my back and shield my eyes with my forearm. "It's more than that. I don't *feel* that I was one of them. I *was* one of them."

She hitches her sunglasses on top of her head and narrows her gaze in my direction. Her brown eyes bore into mine, likely looking for any sign of humor, of some sort of psycho-therapy BS.

"You know about what happened at the start of my junior year, right? How I had a freak out and shaved my head."

"Yeah, a really traumatic breakup and that prompted you to be a therapist, right?" Mo says.

I nod. "But first I had a detour thirty years into the future."

Everything around us freezes. The sounds of the college kids. The tinkling of the river. Even my friend's breathing.

"You mean like a premonition?"

"I mean, like, a life. I'm still leading. On August 23, 1996, I had a terrible brunch with my dad where he basically threatened to cut me off. I stopped by a psychic shop where this woman told me I was going on a journey. And, when I got back here, I find Wick packing up to move to L.A. Without me. Turns out, my journey wasn't to the West Coast but to the future."

My friend blows out a long breath. "Did she curse you? This psychic? Or hypnotize you into thinking you went forward in time? Is that why you were asking Crispin about that?" The questions tumble out of her like an overpacked suitcase bursting open.

"I don't think Astrid cursed me. But I'm sure if I go back to her shop one more time looking for a way back she might." I shrug. "And yeah, I mean, I didn't tell him why I was asking about hypnosis. I was thinking if someone could, maybe I'll remember falling in love with Craig."

At the mention of my fiancé's name Mo's face softens. "Does he know? Or, Josie?"

"Not officially. I think he might suspect something's up. Like I'm having second thoughts about the wedding. Seems I haven't outgrown my massive procrastination streak. And if I tell Jo, she'll have me in Craig's office for a thorough neuro exam so fast, you'll think I got swept up in a tornado. But..." I let my voice trail off. "I think Aiden thinks something is up. I didn't know how to get something back on my phone that apparently was the first thing we all learn when we get the damn things. But he probably just thinks I'm old."

Mo lets out a low whistle. "So, wait, you don't know me then?"

The sadness in her voice is a dull knife to my heart. For these past few weeks, she's been thinking I'm someone I'm not. That she's someone to me. More than an office manager, but a dear friend. The thing is, I sensed the minute I met her that she was *someone*. I just didn't know who at that time.

Until now.

"I didn't, but would it be weird to say that when you came by my house that morning, I felt like I knew you? That you're someone very dear to me."

"Any weirder than you saying you skipped thirty years of your life?" She arches a manicured eyebrow.

"Fair enough."

"So, Craig…"

"Well, when I first met him, I thought he was a sex dream."

Mo laughs. "That man is a sex dream all right."

"Isn't he," I say on a sigh. "That's been the hardest part. Technically, I'm still nursing a shattered heart from Wick, but I'm a month away from marrying this amazing man."

"That you have no memory of falling in love with," she finishes for me. Saving me from having to say those treacherous words aloud.

"Right. And it's not to say I won't love him. I just feel like I missed all the firsts. You know, first date, first kiss, when we first told each other I love you. I don't even know how we met. It's like reading a book. I read the first few chapters, and everything else in between is blank. Now I'm at the happily ever after, but I'm missing all the big moments." I suck in a deep breath. "My life would be the world's shittiest romance novel."

Mo reaches over and grabs my hand. "I'd still read that novel. Mostly for the comedy. But, seriously, this is real?"

I stare at our joined hands. "Yeah, unless I'm in a coma and you're my spirit guide or something."

My friend straightens and tosses her braids. "I think I'd make a rather fabulous spirit guide."

I rest my head on her shoulder. How did I meet this amazing woman? Were we friends first and I talked her into working with me? Or, did the Universe bring us together in the form of a job opening?

We sit in silence for several minutes. Mo likely absorbing my revelation or mentally calculating if she can carry me back to her car and drop me off somewhere to get some serious help.

"Do you believe me?" My voice is barely a whisper.

She chuckles. "I actually do. Because something has been off. You're you, just…"

"Immature. Inadequate. A hot damn mess."

"I was going to say free. Like you're not trying to follow any rules."

It's my turn to laugh. "Probably because I don't know any rules."

"But you also seem a bit lost, like it's your first day on this planet."

"Well, it kinda is," I shoot back.

"And even a bit…*lonely*," she whispers.

The word circles around my heart before finding a little spot I hadn't fortified, plunging in deep. The thing about loneliness is that it only needs the smallest opening to infiltrate.

A tiny crevice and then it expands, taking over like a virus. Loneliness can be in your heart, your soul, even when surrounded by friends. It hides, waiting to attack when self-doubt rears its ugly head.

Yes, I've been lonely these last few weeks. However, loneliness and I are old friends. Enemies. Loneliness was there when my parents weren't. Rather than let it take over, I let it make me stronger. Self-reliant.

"But then again, I guess I'd feel alone if I was suddenly thrust into the future," Mo continues, almost speaking to herself. She eyes me, surveying me once again. "I have to hand it to you; you figured things out. How did you do it?"

"Seems that in the future we feel the need to post every single thought and action on social media." I shrug. "There were a couple of sleepless nights, but I think I got pretty caught up."

"What about work? Have you even taken any psychology classes yet?"

"Uh, no. At the time I…*whatevered*, I was an art major. I've just been going with my gut."

My office manager nods. "Well, for what it's worth, you're a natural."

"Except for Olivia." I cringe when I think about the first patient I saw after my time warp.

"That girl needed to hear that." Mo's expression softens. "Anyway, even seasoned professionals make mistakes. What can I do to help?"

I snort. "Will you save me from myself? Keep me from burning all this down. I might not remember building this life, but so far, I like it and think I want to keep it."

CHAPTER 30

The other thing about loneliness is it hides from friends.

After telling Mo, the weight of my loneliness drops away. There's nothing this strange new world can throw in my direction that I can't handle. Can't handle with my friends.

I even feel so bold I contemplate telling Craig. However, not long after he got home, he got called back to the hospital. That boldness rushed out the door with him.

My office is quiet the next morning. Mo is at her son's school, helping out with a field trip. The street outside is mostly empty, as if everyone else heard about yesterday's...incident.

I pause with my key in the door, glancing down toward Crispin's office. My heart plunges, recalling how I destroyed his scooter. Sure, it's a thing, a thing that my bank account says I can replace for him if I need to, especially now that my dad ensured I won't be doing any hard time.

What I can't replace is the shard of my dignity sliced away as I backed over his scooter again and again and again.

A car drives down the street slowly, brakes flaring in front of the building housing Crispin's practice. He emerges from the back seat, and even from halfway down the block I can almost make out his gaze sliding in my direction, just briefly enough to grab that shard of my lost dignity to dig into my heart.

With a deep fortifying breath, I open my door and flip on lights, waking up my dying business.

My first appointment isn't until eleven, so I spend my morning reading up on the clients on my schedule for the day, and rest of the week. Now that the time traveler's out of the bag, I feel the need to prove to myself even more—and maybe even to Monique—that I can be a fully functioning adult.

I'm not using something as trivial as falling forward three decades in time as an excuse for not having my shit together. Okay, maybe not *together*, but I should at least have my shit in the same *vicinity*.

I'm pouring my second cup of coffee when the bell at front door chimes.

A man dressed in matching brown shorts and short-sleeved shirt stands in the small lobby. He's studying a box in his grip. His face in profile, a muscle ticks in his jaw.

There's something eerily familiar about him, even though I don't have a full view of him.

"Can I help you?" I ask, the words almost afraid to leave my throat.

That's when he looks up, his ice blue eyes colliding into mine.

That's when the last of the breath in my lungs whooshes out of me.

That's when I see the man Wick Tanner became.

"It really is you," he says. His voice is a little rougher than the last time he spoke to me. The lightness of youth gone, replaced by the heaviness of disappointment. "I saw this name on my route, and thought there's got to be more than one Emily Murray out there. It can't be you. But…wow, so you look great."

It's my cue to return the compliment, but I can't find it in me to shake myself out of shock.

He's still tall and lean, face and arms tan but his legs are a shade lighter. His hair, more dirty than blonde, is pulled back into a low, tight ponytail, but I can just make out the waves throughout.

"Yeah, likewise." I finally find a way to make words, despite the fact my heart and stomach have swapped places in my body. I'm fairly certain my heart is about to puke all over my shoes. "So, how long has it been?"

Maybe he's actually the regular delivery guy, but something about the way he keeps staring tells me that's not the case.

His cheeks puff as he blows out a breath. "Gosh, I mean, like maybe not since I went to L.A.?"

I tighten my grip on the coffee cup, almost feeling the groan of the ceramic. "Yeah, L.A., so you're…" A delivery guy. "Back?"

A slight wince flutters across Wick's face. "Been back for a few years now. We got close, Em, really close. Had that deal inked, was working on some new songs, had time blocked in the studio to start laying tracks. Our manager was even talking with some really big names about us opening for them and then…" He shuffles the box from one hip to the next and shrugs. "Boy bands."

"Boy bands?"

"They exploded." Wick makes an explosion sound with his mouth, his free hand fanning out. "We were too late. But hey, *Firefly Sky* got into several big radio markets, got some airplay even."

The sadness in his eyes drags my heart into an abyss. Here was a man I once loved, maybe even still love, who had a dream. A dream so big that many were afraid to pursue it, but not him. He threw everything into making it big.

Well, almost everything.

I somehow didn't fit, so I got thrown out.

My eyes warmed, like they were gearing up to unleash hot, angry tears, but I blinked, hoping to cool them instead of fanning the flames. I didn't let him see me cry then, and he sure as hell isn't going to see it now.

"I'm sorry." My voice is thick and gooey. "That must've been… honestly, that must've been just shitty."

Wick chuckles and I can almost feel it echo through my body like a phantom limb.

I remember lying on his chest, feeling his heart beating under my ear, how his body would shake when he laughed.

"Would you believe they asked us if we'd consider being a boy band instead? Like have they ever seen Micah dance?"

It's my turn to laugh when I think of the bass player who had surprisingly awful rhythm on the dance floor.

"But it's all good," he says. "I'm still playing, writing a few new songs here and there. I'm actually playing tonight, at Acoustic Pour, it's a wine bar that has a little stage. You should come check it out; I might even pull out some oldies. I've stripped down *'Be You'* and I think you'll really dig it."

Our song. The song he wrote for me.

Would usually sing to me, until that last show.

"Sure, I'll see what I can do."

"Cool." Wick grins and suddenly I'm back to the crappy, falling down house he shared with his bandmates. Back to smokey nightclubs and Xs on my hand from getting carded.

I'm back to being curled up next to him as he mindlessly strums his guitar, trying to find a riff for his next hit song.

"Cool," I say.

"Cool," Wick repeats, then blushes.

He's older but the boyish good looks are still there. The charm that drew me to him in a crowded lecture hall of two hundred students cuts through the discomfort of the moment and tugs at my center.

Wick turns to leave.

"Aren't you forgetting something?" I call out.

He glances over his shoulder; confusion crosses his still handsome face.

I nod down to the box under his arm.

"Oh, yeah, sorry." He shoves a tablet toward me. "Can you sign for it?"

I reach for it with my left hand. My engagement ring flashes like a solar flare between us.

Wick's gaze drops to my hand. One side of his mouth twitches.

For some reason, embarrassment rocks through me. Like I've been caught cheating.

"For what it's worth, I've always been chasing your ghost," he says, his voice low and serious. "I'm happy for you. Really."

His words settle between us like fallen ash, and my mouth goes dry again. No way I can speak, even if I knew what to say—and I don't.

"Anyway, it was good seeing you, Em. Hope to see you around."

He's halfway down the front steps when I call him again. "Hey, Wick, whatever happened to Fleur?"

He pauses, one foot on the ground, the other the first step. "Who? Oh, that French girl, right? No clue."

I close the door and lean my back against it. My heart has climbed back into its usual space and bangs against my ribcage, like a beast begging to be set free.

Only after I hear the growl of the delivery truck outside start, then taper off as it drives down the street do I push myself off and set the package on Monique's desk, opening drawers until I find a pair of scissors.

Two smaller cream boxes stare up. I lift one out and pull the lid off.

I slide a finger down the soft paper, gliding over words that split my heart in two.

You are cordially invited to the wedding of Dr. Emily Murray and Dr. Craig Harrison.

CHAPTER 31

The visit with Wick plays through my mind for the rest of the day like a VHS tape stuck on a loop. The light that'd drawn me to him was still there, but there's a dullness to it. Like a sexy red convertible that'd been left out in the elements, the sun robbing it of its glean and rust settling into the cracks.

I have to stay late tonight to accommodate two clients with after work appointments. After the second one leaves—a young woman who doesn't want her new husband to know that she's struggling to adjust to married life—I sit at my desk, and stare at the two boxes of wedding invitations.

I might've asked my last client more questions than necessary. What was she struggling with? Was it the idea of forever? The realization that the rest of her life is now set on a clear path?

Or, did she have any regrets? Was there someone who broke her heart?

In that case, did he happen to walk right back into her life delivering a box of her wedding invitations?

I should visit Astrid and grill the woman to see if she *did* put a hex on me. Because if so, *bravo*, this was a perfect way to get back at me.

The boxes continue to taunt me. Tell me, as soon as they're

addressed, stamped and mailed, I'll be one step closer to marrying a man I'm still getting to know.

Still trying to love.

Before I could talk myself out of it, I grab my phone and call Josie.

"Hey," she answers on the third ring.

"What's up?"

"Oh, you know, feeding children. Did you know that you have to feed them more than once a day, and, like, every day?"

I smile into the phone. She's always a balm to my sore heart. Even when she doesn't know it. "What? That's crazy! What happens if you don't?"

"Well, the red head gets mean as a snake, bites even." I hear Aubrey say something in the background. "And Ben starts asking if I overdrew the checking account again, and offers to get a job to help with bills."

"Do they hire fourteen-year-olds to be CEOs these days?"

Jo laughs. "He's more qualified to run my company than I am, so maybe I should. What are you up to?"

"Procrastinating. Wanna have an impromptu girls' night?"

"Sure, hang on." Her voice is muffled but I hear her say something about meeting me out. "All right, Daniel says hi, and that he might call Craig to see if he wants to come over to watch the game."

My heart squeezes. This was how it was supposed to be. Our partners would become as close as Jo and I.

"I'm sure he'll love that." I pause, my finger tracing over my name on an invitation. "So, I heard about this wine bar that has live music, Acoustic Pour. Wanna meet there?"

"Sure, that sounds fun. See you in an hour?"

I chicken out of calling Craig and send him a text instead.

> Meeting Jo for a glass of wine. Daniel might
> call you to hang.

A second after I hit send his reply pops up.

CRAIG "MCFINE ASS" HARRISON

> Sounds good. And yeah, after this day I'd be
> up for a beer or 12 with Daniel.

Guilt creeps over me. A good partner would cancel her plans and be there for him. Especially, when her plans include covertly dragging her best friend to a wine bar where her ex-boyfriend will be playing.

Inviting Josie was more than the desire to see her. I need her to be my conscience. The breaker of whatever spell I might fall under at hearing Wick's voice, the velvety growl that could have me dropping my panties faster than gravity. I need Jo to keep my panties firmly in place.

An hour later, I snag the second to last parking spot in the lot beside Acoustic Pour. It's a cute place. A forest green building that has a wide front porch lined with Christmas lights. On either side of the door is a seating area with mismatched-on-purpose rattan furniture.

Inside, a bar lines one side of the room, and directly opposite is floor to ceiling bookshelves, filled with random books and seen-better-days board games. At the very back is a small stage, just large enough to accommodate maybe two people, but no more than that.

The stage is empty except for a wooden chair atop an old Oriental rug and a mic stand. Part of me secretly hopes I misheard Wick. That maybe this isn't the bar he'll be playing, or this isn't the night.

I snag a table a few rows back from the stage, intentionally grabbing the chair facing the stage. As if I can keep Josie from knowing it's Wick up there.

"Hi, sorry," Jo says, leaning in for a quick hug. "Aubrey chose the exact moment I was walking out to ask if she can—get this—not just go on a cruise with her boyfriend's family this summer, but also to share a room with him."

"What? We would never be that bold."

"Right?" Jo pauses when the waitress approaches to take our wine orders. "We just wouldn't have told our parents we were sharing the room. Honestly, my mom doesn't know how lucky she is that we didn't tell her the half of it. This generation and their over-sharing."

I laugh, thinking of Josie's sometimes-prim and trying-to-be-proper mom's reaction at that kind of request.

"So, what did you say?" Maybe I can snag some pointers for how to handle Aiden and whatever he decides to share with me as the hated stepmother.

She leans in, her blue-green eyes sparkling. "Well, since Peter has classic divorced-dad syndrome and would say yes to anything to make her happy, I told her, if she can convince Daniel then she can do it. We'll see if she can find a crack, but the dude has top secret security clearance, so good luck with that." Josie raises her just dropped off glass of wine to mine. "I wish I could be a fly on the wall for that conversation," she adds with a laugh. "I don't know who will break first, but it would be worth the price of admission."

This was exactly what I needed. A welcome distraction from the disaster swirling in my gut.

"What's new with you?" she asks.

"Wedding invitations got delivered today," I say. In some alternate universe I'd tell her *who* dropped them off, then we'd snicker about how he'd never actually made it, and how I'm so much better off with Craig.

We're not in that world. We're in the one where I know an ex who dumped me thirty years ago better than the man I'm marrying in less than two months.

"It's getting real. You're excited, right?" Jo says in that loaded way only someone who's known me for most of my life would ask. "That reminds me, your bachelorette party. Sof is coming in early for it. I'll come up with an itinerary for the evening."

I open my mouth to answer, but movement at the stage steals my attention.

Wick is there, having come in from a back door. He's dressed in jeans with worn cowboy boots. The sleeves of his flannel shirt are rolled up, and the front is unbuttoned, revealing a faded Nirvana T-shirt underneath. Unlike this morning, his hair is loose, hanging down to shoulders.

What I didn't realize when he'd had his hair pulled into the tight ponytail is how much less of it there is. Thirty years ago, I'd run my fingers through those thick, wavy locks. If I did that now, how many of those precious strands would I come away with?

Josie's chatter about possible bachelorette party plans fades away, as I watch Wick pull his guitar from the case. He fiddles with the tuning pegs, strums, and fiddles again.

I scoot my chair, moving myself out of his line of sight. This is a terrible idea. I shouldn't be here. Not when my heart is straddled between the love I'd felt for this man, but who obviously chose his dream over me, and the man I left at home, the man who sparks something in my soul even if my brain is malfunctioning.

Heat flares throughout my body and a bead of sweat runs down my forehead.

I need to flee. To run to my car.

To Craig.

Where I should be.

"Em? You okay?"

I fan myself. "Hot flash," I say. My mom wasn't wrong; these things are hell.

Before Josie could say anything else, the first few chords of Wick's guitar fills the air and he launches into a song I don't know.

I hold myself taut, studying my best friend's face for any recognition of the voice singing behind her, but she continues talking about ideas she, Sofia and Monique have tossed around for my bachelorette party.

While he plays his first song, I keep my head angled toward my friend, so I can hear her better, but also hoping if he were to look our way, he'll just see a strawberry-blond head and not my face lurking behind it.

Midway through his third song, Josie's phone rings. Aubrey's pretty face filling the screen.

"Lordy, this should be good," she says, standing. "I'll be right back and fill you in on all the gory details."

My best friend hustles out the front door, and in her absence, nothing blocks my view of Wick on stage.

Blocks his view of me in the audience.

At first his eyes are closed, but as if sensing a shift in the audience they fly open and land squarely on me. Slowly, seductively, one side of his mouth pulls up into a smile.

Damn. Him.

Josie slides back into her seat. If she noticed it was Wick on stage, she says nothing.

I sit frozen. That earlier hot flash is replaced by a glacial cold radiating from my heart.

"Daniel won the battle, but it remains to be seen if he wins the war," she's saying, setting the phone back on the table. "He said we'd consider it if his entire family's report comes back clean after—" She stops, her eyes narrowing at me. "What's wrong?"

Before I can answer, to lie to her that I just realized Wick was on stage, his voice fills the air.

"Thank you, this next song is an oldie, written for someone right here tonight."

Jo's eyes widen, as if noticing for the first time that she *does* recognize the voice.

"Someone I should never have let go," Wick continues. "Someone I had the good fortune of running into just this very morning. Em, babe, this is for you."

The first chords of *'Be You'* play throughout the hushed crowd, but I barely hear them.

"What, and I cannot emphasize this enough, *the fuck*," Josie seethes. I swear actual steam is coming from her flared nostrils.

"I—" But whatever excuse I was going to fling at her dies on my tongue.

Jo leans over the small table, nearly toppling her glass of wine, but she pays it no attention. "Outside. Now."

Like one of her children about to get the ripping of a new one, I follow her to the front porch. My gaze sticks to the worn wooden floor, watching our feet hurry outside and away from lyrics written about a long-gone girl.

"Are you sleeping with him?"

I jerk my head back like she slapped me. "What? No, I really did just run into him today. When he delivered my wedding invitations."

"And you just happen to suggest a new place for us to meet for an impromptu girl's night?"

"Okay, so yeah, he might have mentioned he plays here," I say, intentionally vague with the details.

"So, what is this then? Cold feet, self-sabotaging? You tell me, *you're* the therapist."

I have no response and just give her a half-hearted shrug. Part of me wants to come clean; tell her everything I told Monique, but sometimes it's too hard to tell the people closest to you the truth.

She softens. "Em, I love you, you're my person. You know that, right? It's just…You with Craig is different than you with anyone else. It's like you've waited your whole life for him." Jo glances through the window toward Wick still strumming a stripped-down version of the song he'd written for me. "I picked up the pieces when Wick broke your heart, and I'm afraid of what it will do to you if you and Craig fall apart."

I follow her gaze and it all comes back. Everything I did for Wick, for his band, that was never reciprocated. The girls. Did he only just flirt with them, or was my side of the bed filled when I wasn't there?

"Thirty years is a long time to hold on to a broken heart," my best friend says, softly and thick with emotion. "I know that, but you have a good thing with Craig."

I fold in my lips, barricading the words so eager to come out. *It hasn't been thirty years. It's not even been thirty days. I didn't sign up for this.*

I might not yet love Craig, not in the way he deserves to be loved, but I *know* I'm it for him. That when I'm not there my side of the bed remains cold.

If I'm not there, I also know my place in his heart will also remain cold.

Empty.

CHAPTER 32

I live in utter fear for the week after seeing Wick. Not fear that Josie would rat me out. She's put enough fear in me she didn't even need to, plus, that's not what we do.

I fear once the door is open to Wick he'll pop back up in my life again. However, when the next delivery comes to my office, our regular guy is back, tanned and refreshed from his week in Mexico.

It was only after hearing that I could take a deep breath.

Of course, that deep breath is short-lived, as I contort myself into a pretzel, trying to zip up the black formal for Craig's hospital foundation's fundraiser.

"Here, let me before you pull your shoulder out of joint," he says, coming to my rescue. His fingers are warm, electrifying, as they trace my spine bringing the zipper up to my neckline.

The dress I chose is exactly what a doctor's fiancée should wear to a hospital fundraiser. A black halter, with a bodice fitted through my hips and thighs and a light flare at my knees. It's sassy enough to show some of the younger doctors Craig has a hot fiancée, but nothing that will scandalize the older donors.

"I much prefer the zipper going the other way," he murmured, sending another wave of electricity through my body.

This time I can't control it, and Craig laughs at the shiver he caused.

"You look beautiful, as always," he adds, before planting a chaste kiss on my temple.

Back at the mirror, I study a reflection that's getting more familiar each day. So much so, I barely remember the long hair that'd flowed to the middle of my back. I'm beginning to forget the youthful face that was part ingenue and part cynic.

The girl with wide blue eyes, eager to take it all in, but also wary of the fact no matter how many people she surrounds herself with, ultimately she's alone in the world. *That* absolutely terrifies her.

Terrifies me.

I sweep my hair up, pinning it into a French twist. A dusting of powder, another sweep of mascara. The whole time I'm getting ready, Craig's gaze is on me in the wall length mirror.

He disappears into the closet and comes back out with a light blue box in his hand.

"I was saving this for our wedding day," he says before handing it to me. "You know, your something new. And I guess this close to the day, they'll still be new."

I stare at the box for a second before it clicks. *Something old, something new. Something borrowed, something blue.*

My breath comes out in a gasp after I pull the lid off and flip open the interior black box. A pair of teardrop sapphire earrings encircled by two rows of diamonds sit nestled inside. These earrings must've cost as much as my entire college education.

"It can also be your something blue," Craig adds quietly. "When I saw them, they instantly reminded me of your eyes."

Eyes that now burned with tears. It's not the fact that they look like he spent a year's salary on them, or that they're likely too precious to wear on a daily basis.

It's that he thought of me. That when I was not with him, I was still on his mind.

Is that what love is?

That even when the person isn't with you, they're still your first, second, third or fourth thought. It's buying them a present then being so excited about it, you give it right away.

Love is someone who moves into your heart, taking up space that doesn't squeeze you out, but makes you feel whole.

"You like them, right?" His voice is tinged in apprehension.

Words aren't adequate enough, so I answer him with my mouth on his. I don't care if I have to redo my makeup. I don't care if my hair's a mess.

All I want at this moment is him.

All of him.

Even the parts I should know but don't.

When I start to undo the buttons on his shirt he stops me. "Trust me, I want nothing more than to see you in these earrings and nothing else, but the foundation president will have my head if we're not there."

I give one more chaste kiss. "Fine, but later you'll have your wish of me and the earrings."

The event is a casino night theme, transforming a downtown Austin hotel's ballroom into a mini-Vegas. One part of the ballroom is the casino floor, with various dealer tables scattered throughout. The other part is set up for dinner for at least a thousand guests.

"So, we'll be seated with the board president and her husband," he says, his voice low and close to my ear, his warm hand on my lower back leading me through the crowd of people.

Anxiety wrenches my stomach. How many of these people do I know? Is someone going to talk about something I should have intimate knowledge of? Twenty-year-old me would have bee-lined to the bar for as many vodka tonics as I could down before someone noticed I was underage. Middle-aged me needs to have all her wits about her.

Craig grabs two champagne flutes off a passing tray, handing me one.

"Remind me, have I met them before?" I decide to feign a bad memory instead of embarrass myself later.

"No, they've spread all the medical staff out, so it'll just be us with some board members and donors."

The little knowledge I don't have to pretend calms the butterflies with chainsaw wings in my stomach.

We find our table and sit in our assigned places. After a few words from the foundation president, salads appear, and conversation at our table begins in earnest.

I'm seated next to an older gentleman, the owner of a chain of car dealerships throughout the Hill Country. We engage in polite chit chat of two people with nothing in common.

Midway through our entrees, the board president addresses Craig from across the table.

"Dr. Harrison, a little bird told me you and Dr. Murray have a wedding in your future," she says, her voice drawing a hush over the table.

My fiancé sets down his fork and clears his throat. "We do, Mrs. Bridges, on May 16."

The woman leans forward, her diamond collar necklace dangling dangerously close to her beef filet. "Please, call me Grace. And that's so exciting." The woman turns her attention to me. "How did you two meet?"

The steak in my mouth turns to ash. Despite all my forensic research into my life for the past thirty years, I never found exactly how Craig and I met. I always assumed it must've been some shared professional association.

Maybe an intramural baseball team of brain surgeons versus shrinks, doctors who mess with the brain in very different ways.

"Well, it's a funny story, actually." I start, pausing to take a sip of wine to wash down my filet.

Craig cover my hand with his much larger one, likely sensing the panic flaring through my body.

"Allow me, I always love telling our story." He turns his attention back to Grace, but the rest of the table is focused on my fiancé. "Two years ago, her best friend came into the ED. On the surface, it appeared to be a panic attack, except she wasn't waking up. Her friend's ex-husband called Emily. And here comes this fireball." His gaze slides from across the table to me. "She was fierce and determined and when I came out to give the family an update, the look she gave me…It was like she was thinking, *'Finally, I found you.'"* He squeezes my hand, his hazel eyes glistening. "And I have to say I felt the very same thing when I saw her. Finally, I found you."

My face warms, and wetness coats my cheeks.

Craig thumbs my tears away. "Don't hit me, but you really are a big softie."

I laugh, but it does little to keep the emotion threatening to overtake me.

Here is this charming, sweet, sexy man who cared for my best friend during some unknown-to-me medical scare. He saved her. My sister in every sense of the word. That version of me, it was as if she'd waited her whole life for that moment. I can almost feel it, the warmth of coming home.

It's not my memory, but something stolen from him.

I'm the thief, robbing him of the woman he should love.

CHAPTER 33

I park in what's starting to feel like my home away from home. It's a Saturday afternoon, and the parking lot of Astrid's is busier than usual.

The governor's wife isn't inside this time, but instead, it's crowded with at least a dozen twenty-somethings all dressed in high heels and short, tight dresses, including one in a white dress with a veil attached to her over-teased hair.

Great, the last thing I need today is an obnoxious reminder of what looms in my future. I don't even need a damn psychic to tell me that.

There's a younger woman behind the counter. A beautiful girl with dyed blue hair that nearly matches the cornflower blue of her eyes. An intricate tattoo encircles one of her biceps and a diamond stud clings to one side of her nose.

This must be Astrid's mythical niece.

As if sensing my presence, the psychic comes from the back, pushing aside the beads in the doorway. She studies the giggling gaggle of girls, chattering over the various crystals, taking kissy-faced selfies, then her gaze slides to me.

I raise an eyebrow. A card on the table.

She matches, with her own raised eyebrow.

"Oh good, my two o'clock is here," Astrid says to the room, inclining her head for me to follow her down the hall. Meets my card and raises.

I wait until we're in her reading room, until the door clicks shut behind me and silences the noise of the bachelorette party, to speak. "Did the Spirits warn you?"

"Actually, they did." She winces as she sits in her chair. "They said you'll... You'll need a friend today." Gone is the usual annoyance shining in Astrid's rheumy eyes. The I-don't-get-paid-enough-for-this exasperation I've grown accustomed to.

In its place is compassion, sadness.

My chest hitches, stumbling over a breath. I've seen so many sides of the psychic, but this is new. This is…concerning?

"Are they feeling like sending me back today, by any chance?"

She shakes her head. "No, sweetie. They said you're not done here, but they also said there's something wrong with your heart."

A brittle laugh escapes my throat. "Should I go straight to the hospital?"

"I think we all know which heart they're talking about." The older woman reaches for my hands and turns my palms upright, a finger tracing the faded scar from the last night in my past timeline. "I remember your reading like it was yesterday. You're special, Emily. Not everyone has a front row seat to what their future holds. Most of us have to make our decisions and hope we stay on our paths. But you still have your battle ahead of you."

"Are you sure? Because I had a fight with a scooter. Pretty sure I won that one." I fall to my defense mechanism of sarcasm, but the words feel as listless as a deflating balloon.

Her grip tightens. "I can't say what it is, it's not clear. But what I can tell you, as a friend, is sometimes the hardest battles of our lives is with ourselves."

I stare down at our hands. "I just—" My throat closes on the words. "I have no doubt I'll love Craig. I might already. But he deserves someone who knows him, not someone who feels like it's the first time every time he tells the story about how we met. Or every time he touches me."

The room warms and suddenly I feel a presence behind me. Not a ghost, but more like a…companion.

"I'm not the person Craig fell in love with. I'm not the person my clients entrust their lives with. I'm not even the person my best friend knows. It's not fair for any of them to have this version of me. To not be there when my best friend got married, had her children. I wasn't there when she got divorced, then reconnected with the love of her life." I push out of the chair and cross the room, wrapping my arms around my stomach. "I'm not the person who healed from her first heartbreak. Who spent her lifetime growing and traveling, building a life, having flings.

"Who are we but the sum of our lives? I'm not the person that any of them know. And it's not fair." I glance around the room, hoping the Spirits are there, then silently chastising myself for actually believing in this. "I beg all of you, please send me back. Please give me the opportunity to become who all the people I love deserve in their lives. Who Craig deserves. Because I'm not the woman he loves, and I—" the words won't push out, even if I'm speaking to a mostly empty room save for an octogenarian psychic, I can't say I love Craig too much to let him marry a lie.

"I feel cheated. Like I'm cheating. Even if it means I'm missing nothing but shitty times, they are *my* shitty times. So please, I beg you, please send me back." The sobs take over before I can stop them. Flowing from deep inside me, the tears are fast and furious, hot as lava. I cry for the girl who'd given all her love to someone who chose a wild dream over me. I cry for the mistakes I never had a chance to make. For the love affairs I never had. I cry for the people in my life who are no longer alive, for the goodbyes I never got to say.

At some point my knees must've given out. It's only when I'm kneeling, my arms around Astrid's middle and I'm crying into her skirts that, it hits me, I'm on the floor.

She'd come to stand beside me. Comfort me.

To be the friend the Spirits told her I'd need.

Astrid's stroking my head, whispering soft encouraging words, when the tears finally subside.

"I wish I could send you back, baby girl. The Spirits are sympathetic, they hurt for you, but even they cannot change your destiny," she pauses. "But Emily, know this, even if you are able to go back, this path is only one journey. A single decision can change everything, so you'll still be able to experience it all. Nothing is set in stone. Not even this life you're currently in."

CHAPTER 34

The dandelion is seriously pissing me off. The flowery yellow weed is at least six inches tall with twelve feet of fight in it. And teeth. I jerk back my hand, the sneaky razor edges of the leaves burning my palm.

When I got home from Astrid's, I couldn't sit still. But, I couldn't do anything constructive. The only way to relieve my frustration is through destruction. Since I have absolutely zero know-how in home renovation, taking a sledgehammer to a wall was out of the question.

So, weeding it is.

"*Fuck* you," I seethe at a particularly strong weed. "Fucking die, you fucking fucker."

"Wow, remind me to never get on your bad side."

I didn't hear Craig come home from wherever he was, but he's sitting on one of the lounge chairs on our back patio, dressed in basketball shorts and a T-shirt cut into a tank top, with a baseball cap turned backwards.

There's something youthful about his appearance, as if I'm seeing a twenty-something version of himself.

That pisses me off even more.

"What's up?" he asks, his eyes on his phone, pecking out some message.

I gesture to the path of destruction behind me. "What does it look like? I'm weeding."

"Are you sure all of those are weeds? Some look like the grass we planted last spring." He nods at one of the plant carcasses. "I think that one is a caladium." His words are light, playful. Likely still riding high on me making good on my promise to wear nothing but the sapphire and diamond earrings for him last night.

I can't blame him. It's still playing through my mind, too. How we started making out in the back of the Uber. How we managed to pull apart long enough to unlock the front door and make it down the hall to the bedroom. How our clothes came off in a mess of fabric. How we came together in a tumble of legs and arms. Of sighs and whispered promises.

"Really?" I ask, sitting up and pointing the spade in his direction. "You really want to go there, cowboy?"

He chuckles and looks down at himself, as if calling out that he's the furthest thing from a cowboy. "You're spicy today. Wanna take it inside?"

There's a world in which I would've heard his words and would've absolutely taken it inside.

We're not in that world.

We're in the world where I belong thirty years in the past and he belongs with a version of me that doesn't yet exist.

"Is that all I am to you?" I snap.

The shock on his face melts me. Tells me that's absolutely not what he thinks.

It also fires up my fuse that's been smoldering since I left Astrid's.

I love this man.

I don't deserve this man.

He can do so much better than me.

He can marry a woman who actually remembers. Remembers the first moment she laid eyes on him. Remembers our first kiss.

A woman who said yes when he asked her to marry him.

"What are you talking about?" Craig asks, dropping the phone onto the lounger beside him, turning his full attention to me.

"Sex object. That's what I'm talk about."

"Em, I'm sorry, I was just flirting," he says.

It's the right answer. Of course it's the right answer, because this is the man I chose to spend my life with.

"I swear, I'm not objectifying you. I worship you. All of you. You know that right?" The earnestness in his words both break my heart and fan the flames of my temper.

I throw down the spade and stand. "You know, maybe this isn't working."

Craig stands and crosses the patio, his chest just inches from mine.

The same chest I explored recklessly last night.

"You just came to that conclusion after what, last night?" He doesn't have to say it.

My mind is already flashing to him exploring my body, to his mouth on my neck. His gaze burrowing into mine.

"No, it's, just, it's too much," I bow up against him. Hoping that my five-foot-three frame doesn't betray too much of what I'm really feeling. That I really want him to swoop me up and take me back to bed. To hold on to me like my life depends on it.

That I also really want him to walk away from me and never look back. Because his life depends on it.

"Emily, what's going on, talk to me." Craig's words are patient, understanding.

Way more than I deserve.

I shake my head. "Maybe we're moving too fast."

"Moving too fast," he repeats. His voice is flat, as if not buying what I'm selling. "This argument is what's moving too fast."

I shake my head. "You don't want me, trust me. I'm broken."

"You are the least broken person I know."

"We're not good for each other. *I'm* not good for you." I'm throwing everything I have at Craig, begging him to make the decision for us.

For me.

"Did I do something?" His eyes darken. "Did *you* do something?"

I know seeing Wick play three and a half songs at the wine bar isn't technically cheating, but it feels that way.

"I saw an ex," I admit, quietly.

"Saw?"

"Yeah, ran into him when he was playing at a wine bar a few weeks ago." Admitting that I sought out Wick feels…embarrassing.

"Playing? Like music? Was this the guy from college? The musician?"

At least past me was open about my relationship history. "Yeah."

His face tightens, guarding himself against what he might hear next. "And?"

"I left after three songs. Came back home." Even though I should tell him the full story, I just can't find it into me to lob that truth bomb in his direction. To tell him that some part of me was drawn to Wick. Because it's only *was*. The love I once felt for him has hallowed out, and that evening the remaining shell of it crumbled away.

"That's it?" Craig's shoulders loosen. "Of course we have exes. I have an ex-wife and you've never had a problem when she and I talk or see each for Aiden. You said yourself, you came back home."

"You don't understand," I say, the fight in my blood is starting to cool and my gaze dropping to the ground. "I'm not who you think I am. Who you think you love."

He tips my chin up, forcing me to meet his hazel eyes. "I know exactly who you are. I knew it the minute I saw you. You're the woman I'm going to spend the rest of my life with. So, if you're having some sort of anxiety attack, I'm here for you. I love whoever you think you are. But remember, I *know* you, Emily."

I take a step back, out of his grip. "I think you should leave."

"Okay, I'll go inside and get cleaned up and let you finish out here. We could use a cool-off period."

I take a deep breath, inhaling the light scent of his sweat. That's right, he was going to the gym to play his weekly basketball game. The smell of grass tickles my nose. Chlorine from the pool mingles with it, making me a bit heady.

I lift my chin and level my gaze at him. "No, I think you need to go somewhere else. I'm not good for you."

He pauses for a minute. "No." A simple word spoken firmly, yet gently.

"Yes."

A muscle ticks in his jaw, and he glances back toward our house. Our shared bedroom, just off the patio.

Finally, he nods. "All right. I know the stress of the wedding planning has been a lot. I'll give you that." Craig sniffs. Is he holding back tears? "I'll go for a few days. Give you some space. But this isn't over. *We're* not over."

I stay frozen in that spot, watching through the windows as he goes into our bedroom, into the bathroom. Several minutes later he emerges with a duffle bag hanging from his shoulder.

The sound of the garage door rumbling open growls over the tinkling of the pool. His car tires squelch on the pavement. Then the engine builds as he accelerates down the street.

Away from me.

I strain to hear his car as it merges onto the main road, but it's lost to me.

He's lost to me.

CHAPTER 35

I spend the rest of the weekend in the quietude of a convent. It's as if all sound had left with Craig.

The murmuring of the TV tuned to whatever sport was being played.

Gone.

The shuffling of paper and keyboard tapping from his office.

Gone.

The bustle of the kitchen coming alive as he pulled out ingredients and cookware for dinner.

Gone.

The only sound left is the metronomic ticking of the mantle clock, marking off the minutes since I told my fiancé to leave.

My phone never rings.

No ding from an incoming text message.

From the shared location app, I can see he's staying at his old condo near the hospital. The one we had a conversation about just a week ago whether to keep for when he's on call or to put it on the market.

I expect Josie to show up. Maybe Craig had called Daniel to tell him I'm losing it. Maybe even to ask advice, since Daniel's also known me since high school. Not so much. It's as if the world has forgotten me.

As if Craig has forgotten me.

His side of the bed is frozen to my touch. Saturday night I leave it untouched, secretly hoping he'll come home in the middle of the night. That he'll reach for me and pull me across the chasm of our bed—our life—and hold me, tell me it'll be okay, even if he doesn't know what *it* is.

By the time I crawl into bed Sunday night, even more emotionally exhausted by the silence that's enveloped every aspect of my soul, I lay my head on his pillow, letting his scent comfort me.

My reflection isn't kind to me as I dress for work Monday morning. Dark shadows cushion my puffy eyes; the usual vibrant blue is muted. My complexion is even paler than usual and waxy, as if I'm fighting off an infection. I don't have the energy to do more than pull my hair into a low ponytail and dust some powder over my face.

"What have you done?" Monique barrels out of the small kitchen of our office as soon as I pop open the front door.

Seems Craig did make at least one phone call.

"What did he say?" My voice is hoarse, strained. It's the first time I've spoken since I told Craig to leave.

She hitches her hands on her hips. "He asked me to keep an eye on you." Mo softens. "He didn't say much more than that, but I know what heartbreak sounds like."

I fall into the chair in our lobby and let my bag drop, the contents tumbling out. "I couldn't let him do it. Marry someone I'm not."

She takes the seat next to me. "Look, I get that you're not...you, but that doesn't give you the right to ruin things for...you." She throws up her hands. "Good lord, this is a mess. You being you, but not *you*."

A sad laugh escapes my lips. "Yeah, welcome to my world."

Mo grips my hand. "Want to tell me what happened?"

"He told the story of how we met, and...it sounded like this magical moment that shifted everything for both of us." I glance down at the ring on my left hand. "I haven't felt that shift. I felt a different shift. He's marrying someone who doesn't exist anymore. And he loves her so much. She's everything to him."

My friend's brown eyes soften and her full lips pull down into a frown. "Emily, *you're* her. He loves *you*. *You're* everything to him."

I close my eyes and shake my head. That all too familiar burn of tears heats my face. "I'm an impulsive, irresponsible college student who can't get her shit together. I can pretend to be an adult and give people advice, but it's all fake. I'm fake."

We sit in silence for several minutes before she speaks again. "Did you end it?"

I sigh. "I tried, but he only thinks I need a break. That this is all wedding stress."

"What would happen if you told him what you told me?"

My mind chews on her words. He'd listen. He'd be concerned, worried that something neurological happened to me, because that's what he does. He fixes people with broken brains. Or maybe, he'd think this is more of a mental health crisis, so he'd find the best psychiatrist in Austin to dissect what caused this break with reality.

Part of me thinks this is what I need.

Part of me knows this would only shift our relationship to a place we couldn't come back from. Craig becomes my caregiver. He loses a partner.

"I can't, as much as I wish that's an option."

Mo squeezes my hand before letting go and standing. "You trust him, right?"

"Of course." Since I first woke up in this strange world, *that* has never been a question. I trust Craig fully, even when I thought he was a dream.

"Maybe you should trust the reason he loves you," she whispers.

I sleepwalk through the rest of the day. Luckily, the exodus of clients to Crispin's practice slows to a trickle, and even a few new clients pop up on my schedule.

My last client has just left when Monique pops her head into my office. "How you doing?"

"I'm okay," I say, clearing off the files from my desk and shoving my laptop back in my bag. "To be honest, it's been great to focus on other people's problems instead of my own. I might even come back tomorrow and do it all over again." My laugh is as thin as a supermodel's thigh.

"You got time for a walk-in?"

My heart lifts out of my ribcage, buoyed on hope I didn't know had taken root. That maybe it's Craig and I can tell him I take it all back. I miss him and this is nothing more than pre-wedding jitters.

"Sure." My voice sounds lighter than it's been in days.

Mo nods and backs down the hall.

I stand, smoothing my hair, making my sure skirt isn't caught in my butt crack. Do I jump into Craig's arms, or fall to my knees to beg him to forgive me?

My hope deflates when a familiar figure walks down the hall. Tall and waif-like, with white-blonde hair.

Olivia.

My first disaster.

"Hi, Dr. Murray," she says, ducking her head and tucking a loose strand behind her ear. "Thank you for seeing me. It won't be but a few minutes."

I blink a few times before remembering how to human. "Oh, yeah, no worries. Let's sit?"

The girl takes the chair she'd been in just a few weeks ago. Instead of kicking off her shoes and tucking her legs under her as before, she sits on the edge of the seat, her legs angled toward the door, as if she might have to take off running at a moment's notice.

"I wanted to apologize, for my behavior," she says softly, a bit tentatively.

She opens her mouth to speak again, but I hold up a hand. "Before you say anything more, I owe *you* an apology. I still think you needed the tools we worked through." I'm going to trust that I knew what I was doing before I fell into this life. "But, I also think I should've been upfront with you about the likelihood of changing someone."

Olivia shakes her head, the curtain of straight blonde hair shimmying. "I went to see Crispin and he had me build a vision board. And you know what I realized as I was doing it? That I didn't want to work there anymore."

"Oh? A vision board told you that?"

"I doubt it, but I wouldn't have left that job if you told me to do that from the start. You were right, I had to stand up for myself, even if I kept getting knocked down," she says, a smile tugging at her full lips.

"I quit. Without even a lead on another job. A few days later, I was at a coffee shop working on my portfolio, when I struck up a conversation with the girl at the table next to me. We're still working out the details, but we're going to start our own business."

"That's awesome, Olivia!"

"I'm really not going to be able to afford therapy while we get this started, but maybe you should check out what's Crispin's doing on social media," she says, standing. "There's a lot of people who need help but might not be able to afford it. You're not *just* as good as him, you're *better*." She tilts her head, her light eyes studying me. "You know, you guys oddly complement each other. Maybe you should work together on something. You don't have to do it all alone, you know."

My numb heart warmed. Sometimes we need a gentle nudge. Sometimes we need to be shoved into action.

Is that what this whole thing was?

Did Astrid's Spirits shove me through time to get to this moment, helping a young woman find her path in life, helping me find a path in life?

A partner in life.

I've had my shove.

Maybe it's time for that gentle nudge.

CHAPTER 36

I spend my third night alone in bed. I don't even bother to undress, aside from my shoes. Kick them right off and crawl between the sheets, resting my head on Craig's pillow.

His scent has faded just slightly, replaced by the peppermint of my shampoo. He still exists, right?

Did this time warp actually happen to me? Because if it didn't, and he's nothing more than a figment of my imagination…I don't think my heart could take that he's permanently gone.

That he never existed.

Just to confirm, I pull up the location app again. So much better than the stalking we did back in the nineties; driving by an ex's house, wig under a baseball cap with dark sunglasses hoping we didn't look out of place at all. Not really realizing they know our cars.

There's his dot, right over the hospital where he works.

The squeeze in my chest loosens. Not much, just enough for me to be reassured I didn't hallucinate an entire fiancé.

I open our text thread, wanting to check in on him, but my thumbs stay frozen in place, my eyes staring at the last words I texted him.

Buy more ice cream.

Which is so very me, but also heartbreaking. Because if he's doing exactly what I'm doing right now and sees that our last exchange was about my sugar addiction and not about how much he means to me…

I sit up in bed. In this whole time I've been in this timeline, I've never told him I love him.

And I *do*, right?

I always thought love was something that hit with the force of a supernova. Like sitting next to a cute boy, the first day of art class and just *knowing* we would be in love. That *I* would be in love.

Maybe love is actually something that builds slowly. Like a rising sun, it starts small, warming and illuminating. Then with each passing moment the warmth builds, *love* builds, until the light is everywhere. It fills us, chases away the fear, the loneliness.

Supernova love finishes as it starts. In a flash.

Sunrise love never fades. Even in the darkness, its warmth is still there.

My fingers move over to a social media app while my newfound epiphany rumbles around my brain.

Before I know it, I'm on Crispin's account. Olivia's suggestion echoes through my mind.

His most recent video starts playing automatically. He's seated in his office, the bookshelf behind him is both curated and casual. Books are organized by color with a half-finished Rubik's Cube sitting in front of them, as if he left it there right before the video started.

"Hi, y'all, Crispin here, with another mental health minute. Today we're going to talk about authenticity and self-acceptance," he pauses, his gray-blue eyes glancing away from the camera for the briefest moment, as if collecting his thoughts. "This is a topic very near and dear to my heart. You see, I grew up in a football family, and as the youngest of four boys, I was expected to follow the path laid out for me. The thing is, I'm incredibly uncoordinated and would have rather been in the band and only on the field at halftime.

"It was only after some really embarrassing middle school games when my parents sat me down and told me it's okay to not be good at football. Only when they gave me permission to accept myself did *I* accept myself. I was a kid, so I don't blame myself for not getting this, but what I want you to know is that acceptance begins with *you*." Crispin pats his chest, his hand lingering over his heart.

I can almost feel it, the desire to make his parents happy, to be who they want him to be. Then the relief that they'd still love him no matter what.

How different would my life be if the last conversation with my dad before I fell forward in time was him supporting me?

Even if I would've been a failure of an artist and would've likely changed my major to something else.

Would I have left brunch in an avalanche of anger? Would I have pulled into Astrid's parking lot to cool off?

Would I seek some sort of confirmation that the life I would lead was the one I wanted? If my dad had accepted the young adult sitting with him that day, would I have been as destroyed to learn Wick chased his dream without me?

Yes, but would I have been so heartbroken that I skipped thirty years of my life?

The next video in Crispin's queue starts up. This one is about setting healthy boundaries, respectfully telling people to fuck off— okay, maybe that's my interpretation—instead of letting people walk all over you.

I go back in time, watching Crispin share more advice about how to be mindful, forgive yourself and how to find peace with the choices you've made. His videos get less produced. The background changes from the curated bookshelf to beige walls. His hair gets shorter. His face softer, more youthful.

When I watch the last one, I click the link to his website and, before my brain can change its mind, I tap on the 'book appointment' button.

The next morning, I'm somewhat more rested. Instead of staring at the ceiling or Craig's empty side of the bed all night, I managed to get some sleep, albeit about as restful as a toddler on a sugar high.

I park in front of my office. Without glancing toward my building, I rush down the street. It's been a few weeks since I've been here. Since a scooter accidentally-on-purpose ended up under my back tires.

The door swings open before I even lift my hand to knock. Crispin stands there, wearing what might be the softest T-shirt ever with what might also be the softest jeans ever. How much money does this kid make?

"I come in peace," I lift my hands, showing I bear no weapons and don't plan to punch him. "I uh, I actually have an appointment?" My voice curves up at the end of the sentence in that annoying way that questions the previous night's decision. "It might not look like it's me, I booked it under—"

"Kim Gordon," he says, cutting me off. "And yes, I didn't think the real Kim Gordon was booking an appointment with me."

I blink. "Wait, are you telling me that you're a Sonic Youth fan?"

He crosses his arms, still not moving out of the doorframe to let me into his office. "Hard core."

I meet his posture. "Don't you dare tell me you discovered them on a classic rock station." The words come out low, with exactly as much menace as I intend.

Crispin scoffs. "Or what? You'll destroy my new scooter? Or my face? My mom is a fan." It's his turn to hold up a hand. "And before you hit or verbally abuse me, my mom is the coolest person I know, and this has nothing to do with age."

"Oh." Words flee from me like fish scattering in a shark's wake. "That's pretty cool. That your mom shares that with you."

He tilts his head, his gray-blue eyes narrowing. "As strange as it sounds, I think you and my mom might be friends. Anyway, why are you wasting client time?"

"I'm not wasting it, if I'm a client."

"Emily Murray is not a client. Kim Gordon has this time slot."

I drop my arms and roll my eyes. "Oh, come on. Be honest, if I had used my real name, you would've had a cop stationed outside your door."

"Probably."

"Anyway, you said it yourself, on one of your videos, that even we need someone to talk to from time to time. That there's nothing wrong with asking for help."

The little bit of his defenses that didn't melt with our bonding over a shared favorite band slides away.

"You've seen some of my videos?"

I shake my head. "Not some, all of them. And, well, I really like what you're doing. The message. Making mental health seem as normal as getting a physical."

"Because it should be."

"Yeah, it should be." A warm breeze blows through my hair, reminding me that we're still outside. "So, do you conduct all your appointments outside, or did I click the wrong button?"

Indecision flashes across his face so quickly that guilt crawls up my spine.

I'm really not a violent person. To my knowledge, I've only gotten into half a fight, and that was in middle school, and thankfully, Josie jumped in to save my butt when I was quite literally punching above my weight.

My weapon of choice is my mouth, but unfortunately, to Crispin, it's also a BMW.

"I'm sorry." The words slip from my mouth like a lover sneaking out of bed. "That wasn't me. I've just been under a lot of pressure lately."

Understatement of the century.

He steps aside, letting me into the small office.

His space is very different from mine.

Where I have a waiting area that's large enough for Mo's desk, a couple of comfy chairs and a rather monstrous size potted plant, Crispin's office is balanced between cozy and bright. The walls are painted a blue I imagine would only be found in the depths of the North Atlantic. Two chairs sit angled, facing each other without being confrontational. Thick drapes sit halfway open, looking out to a back garden.

This is definitely a place I'd feel comfortable spilling all my deep, dark secrets.

"So," Crispin says, perching against the edge of his desk. "There's probably a half dozen ethical lines and at least two legal lines we're crossing."

"Legal?"

"Your father made it very clear to me, if I come within five feet of you he'd smite me."

A smile crawls across my face, no matter how much I try to hold it back. "Did he really say smite?"

He cocks his head, his gaze studying me. "I can see where you get it. The fight in you. Standing up for yourself, the people you care about."

It's my turn to cock my head. The truth of his observation seeps into me. Aside from the fights I remember from my childhood, my mom never fought.

As a realtor, her job was all about making people happy, finding a home they'd come to at the end of a long day and instantly relax. If her clients weren't happy, they weren't buying.

So where does that leave me?

The child of a fighter and a people pleaser.

A hot damn mess.

"Well, lucky for you my bark is worse than my bite," I say, grinning just enough to bare my teeth. "Mostly. But really, I came here to apologize, and to offer a truce."

"A truce?" Crispin cocks an eyebrow.

"And maybe even talk about how we could work together."

"Work together?"

I throw up my hands. "Are you going to repeat everything I say?"

That snaps him back to reality. "Right," he holds his hand out to an empty chair. "Want to sit?"

"Like I said." I take the seat across from him. "I like how you make talking to a therapist seem so normal, and I try to take that approach with my clients, so I feel like we have a similar style in that regard." A deep breath fills my lungs. "And maybe, I'm not the best person for a teenager or twenty-something to talk to. I might be too much like their...mom."

"Let the record show *you* said it, not me," Crispin deadpans.

A laugh bubbles out of my chest. "Noted. But I want you to know while I'm far from retiring, I'd feel completely comfortable telling some of my clients that you might be the better therapist for them." I pause, picking at my cuticles. "And I'm not asking you to do the same, because—"

Crispin cuts me off. "I can think of no one else I'd rather refer clients to than you."

"Good," I smile at him. Tension melts from my body like an ice cream cone on a hot day.

"Good." He smiles back. "For what it's worth, Dr. Murray. I could've handled it all better. I'll be honest, sometimes I'm better in written form. I think it's a byproduct of my generation. We never learned how to have difficult conversations. We tend to post first and think about it after it goes viral."

"Oh, honey, leave it to my people to have all the cringey conversations." I laugh, thinking about all the over-sharing with my friends. I stand to leave, to let Crispin have a few minutes to himself before his next client.

"Did you have a favorite? Video, I mean," he asks, the haughty confidence I'd gotten used to is gone from his voice. Instead, it's tentative, like I imagine the middle school Crispin would've sounded like when he'd had that conversation with his parents about football. "Or any feedback. You know, as a peer."

I chew on the inside of my cheek for a moment. "The one on imposter syndrome. It's something that's universal, all of us feel it at some time in our lives." My hands rests on the doorknob, my heart sinking into a puddle at my feet. "What people don't realize it doesn't just infect you; it infects those who believe in you. Believe what you feel for them isn't real." I escape his office before he can see the truth etched on my face.

I might feel like everything in this strange world isn't real. That I'm not real and undeserving, but the one thing I know to be true is just how much I love Craig. Maybe it was lying there, deep in the heart of this older body I woke up inside.

Today, yesterday, tomorrow. Past, future and present. No matter which order it comes in. I love him.

And, I need him to believe that.

CHAPTER 37

"How bad does he hate me?" The words slip from my mouth like a teenager sneaking out of the house the moment Daniel opens the door.

He doesn't look surprised to see me there a full half hour before I was supposed to arrive. The plan was for me to come over at the same time Jo gets home from picking Sof up at the airport, but I need to have a conversation with Daniel alone, without my best friends hopping into fix-it mode.

I surreptitiously study Jo's husband as I follow him into the house. The last time I saw him in the flesh was our high school graduation.

Not too much has changed in thirty years. He's filled out, lean instead of lanky. His golden-brown hair is woven with gray, and his always-tanned face is still handsome with just a touch of wrinkles. Jo could have done worse.

He takes my offered wine bottle. "Actually, I think he loves you more than before."

"Sadist."

Daniel's light green eyes sparkle with humor and one side of his mouth quirks up into a wry smile. "You or him?"

I can't help but laugh. The first real laugh since I'd sent my fiancé out into the world. Since I told him that maybe we're rushing it, when in truth, nothing has ever felt more right. The laugh sounds rusty in my throat. "Fair enough."

We continue through the house and out to the back patio.

The early May evening is warm, but a cool breeze dances in the trees overhead, swaying the strings of Christmas lights strewn across the patio.

Aubrey is sprawled on one of the lounge chairs, her dark red hair spread behind her head while her gaze stays focused on her phone. "Hey, Aunt Em," she says, not even looking up.

"Hey, Aubrey, how's it going?"

She's already back into the world of her phone.

Daniel just shrugs. "You get used to it after a while. Want me to open this wine, or want a beer, something stronger?"

"Jo and Sofia will kill me if we polish off that wine without them. Maybe just a beer." Anything stronger will have me confessing the impossible.

He laughs again. "No argument there."

I study him as he goes to the outside beverage fridge and pulls out a beer for me. He looks so much like the boy Josie loved from the minute they met, but who she ultimately had to let go on high school graduation night.

Our entire freshman year of college, she vacillated between being totally despondent over letting him go and a strange sense of serenity that they would eventually find each other again.

She knew, *just knew*, they would be together.

Did Daniel know that too?

What about me?

Was there always something deep inside me that knew Craig was the one for me even before I met him?

Can our souls feel the other half out there, our paths getting closer and closer until finally we find each other?

Find each other and hold on for dear life.

Or, in my case, panic and tell him to leave.

"Can I ask you a question?" I say, taking a long pull from the beer as I settle into the comfy outside sofa.

"I figured this would be something between an interrogation and couples' therapy with just one half of the couple here," Daniel says, fiddling with the grill before turning to look at me. "Shoot."

"When did you know Jo was the one?"

He purses his lips and glances out over the pool, over the view of west Austin from my friend's gorgeous backyard. "Honestly, I think from the moment I met her, but we were kids and forever is an awfully long time when you're fourteen."

"Why didn't you say something then? Why all this time?"

He takes a long drink of his beer, his gaze on the sun sinking slowly toward the horizon. "Sometimes, the hardest thing about love is to know when to walk away and trust it'll be there when you get back. I knew, we both knew, we needed to go down our own paths before they crossed again."

"Did you ever think about not waiting?" I press, almost feeling impatient for him and her for waiting so long for happiness.

Daniel's gaze leaves mine and shoots in the direction of Aubrey.

Is he about to say something that shouldn't be said in front of minors?

"All the time, but sometimes things need to happen the way they do," he says softly.

There's something in his voice, a thread I want to pull at to see what tumbles out. From what I can tell, he never had his own children.

Is it regret for not sharing that with Josie? Or that they missed so many years together?

"How did you do it?" My voice is equally soft. "How did you know she's the one and have to wait for it?"

His gaze slides back to meet mine. "You tell me. Was it worth meeting Craig and falling in love in your late forties? Would you have rather waited to find him than never find him at all? Or, be with someone who isn't the one?"

The weight in his gaze spears my heart. There's something so unbearably raw about his stare, his words. Like a dull knife intent on skinning me alive. Not cruelly, but in a way to carve away the crust of old heartbreak.

If Craig had met me in my twenties, what would he have found?

A broken-hearted party girl with a shaved head as directionless as a deflating balloon on a windless day. He likely wouldn't have given me a second glance, or if he did, he would've been disgusted by what he found.

What about Aiden? Sure, we could have had our own children, but they wouldn't be the son he has now.

"What is this all about, Em? Really?" Daniel takes a sip of his beer. "Sure, we've lost touch those years I was…gone, but you gotta remember, I've known you for a long time. Once you set your mind to something, you don't let go. I can't imagine you're letting go, not when I've seen how hard you and Craig fell for each other."

If only I could've seen how hard we fell for each other.

Felt how hard we fell.

In some ways, I have, when I woke up all those weeks ago in a strange bedroom, in a strange life, with a man that I didn't know, yet still somehow *knew*.

Who says falling for someone has to stop? What if that's also love?

Waking up each day to fall in love all over again. To find new ways to love someone. To love how he falls asleep with his glasses askew and a laptop on his chest. To love how he sings in the shower with the confidence of someone with a much better voice. To love things about him I've not yet discovered, and not because I catapulted past them, but because no matter what timeline we're in, I'd only discover them in a moment that has yet to be written into our story.

I turn toward Daniel and scoot closer. "I'm not letting go. I'm going to hold on even tighter, so tight it might crush him, but well, he knew what he was getting himself into." I quirk one side of my mouth up into an evil smile. "Any chance you got ordained as a minister between high school and now?"

He laughs and ducks his head. "No, but thanks to the internet I can be."

Voices waft through the house behind us. I glance inside to see Josie pulling Sofia's suitcase through the living room and my other best friend laughing.

"Well, I'll leave you to catch up with the girls," he says, standing and draining the last of his beer. "Seems I need to start filling out an application or something." Daniel heads inside at the same time that Jo and Sof head outside. He pauses at his wife, his face softening as their eyes meet and something that can only be communicated between lovers passes between them.

Even in my short time with him, Craig and I have that. That silent language of glances, light touches, inside jokes.

It's just been a few days, but I miss it so much.

"Em!" Sofia shouts as soon as she steps out the back door. "I'm so going to kick your ass." Even though they are literally fighting words, they're spoken with tenderness.

Fair enough.

"Okay," I say, gripping my friend in a tight hug. "And after that I'm going to need your help."

CHAPTER 38

I t feels completely natural to sit outside with my two best friends under the canopy of stars, listening to the cicadas chide us for being up well past our bedtime.

I try not to stare at Sofia, seeing her in this new timeline for the first time. The last time I'd seen her was during summer break between our sophomore and junior years of college, before she'd transferred further away to finish her undergrad.

Weeks ago, that now feels like eons.

Then, her dark hair hung in loose waves down to the middle of her back. Now it's shorter, grazing her shoulders, still curly but the color muted with gray streaking through it.

It's not her appearance that strikes me as the starkest difference between the girl I knew and the woman sitting next to me. It's the quiet confidence, as if she'd faced the worst the world has to offer and can take on anything as mundane as Austin traffic.

"Jo, if you hadn't married Daniel, I would, just for his burgers," Sofia says, rubbing her hand against her taut belly. "I swear, I dreamt of those burgers the whole time I was in India, and felt so incredibly guilty for it every time I saw a cow."

We chuckle, as we had been for the last hour during Sofia's

catching us up on her time in a remote Indian village, serving as their doctor. Laughing at her misadventures with the animals and fear that every snake she encountered was venomous.

Josie tilts her head, studying me with her blue-green eyes. "Speaking of married…"

I cringe. We managed to make it through dinner without the topic of conversation turning toward me and my major fuck-up. "I know, I know, you can save the speech." I drain the last of my wine and refill my glass.

Somewhere around our second bottle, I'd told Sof and Jo I'm spending the night. What I didn't clue them in to was I'd planned to stay before I'd even come over. I'd thrown a few items in a bag, partly to spend time with my best friends, but mostly because I can't spend another night in that quiet home. "I've already seen the error of my ways."

"What are we going to do with you, Emily Murray?" Josie muses, staring at her nearly empty wine glass.

I lean over and refill hers, then top off Sofia's. I like this version of us. Three lifelong friends sharing wine in the quiet of a late spring evening. Josie's family sleeping inside. Sofia's easy laugh at herself. Even my own racing mind has slowed to a walk as we breeze from topic to topic, conversation meandering like a mountain road.

"Well, you're going to stand beside me as I marry the man of my dreams." I sip wine, hoping it'll steady the fear rising in me. "Assuming, he'll still have me."

"I have a feeling he will," Sofia says, her voice as soft as night. "So, what's the plan?"

"I need to show him how serious I am." The mental to-do list flashes in my mind. My wedding dress hangs in my closet, and the invitations have been addressed, but I hadn't made it to the post office.

If I'm going to do this, to pull off planning a wedding by our original date in two weeks it's going to be all hands on deck.

"Anyone want to help me plan a wedding?" I arch an eyebrow.

Jo squeals and throws her hands up in the air, lunging across the sofa to hug me.

For a second, we're back in college, friends meeting life and everything it held for us with unbridled enthusiasm.

"Yes! I knew you'd pull your head out." She grabs her glasses and her tablet from the coffee table, opening up her to-do list. "All right, you've got the dress and the venue. What's left to do?"

"Well, your dresses. The cake, we need to confirm how many people we're feeding. I should pick out Craig's wedding ring. Is it too late to get a band, or a deejay? Oh, and flowers, we'll need flowers. I wonder how much it'll be to overnight the invitations? I did send the save the date, so maybe everyone is already planning to be there…"

The world around me grows quiet. The cicadas stop buzzing. The clicking on Josie's tablet as she pecked a to-do list ceases. If we'd been listening to music, I bet even that would have scratched to a halt.

I glance between my friends.

Both are slack-jawed and staring.

"What?"

"That's…*everything*," Josie says, moving the glasses to the top of her head. "I should know, I've planned two of them."

"I've planned no wedding and even I know that's everything," Sofia chimes in.

"I've got my dress and the venue," I counter, a bit too defensively. "We told the wedding planner we'll have a full bar. And I asked Daniel to officiate this evening. So, we can knock that off the list."

"Does Craig know he's still getting married in two weeks?" Sofia asks.

"That's the top of my to-do list." I gnaw on my bottom lip. "Maybe, we should hold off on all the other items in case he doesn't want to." The wine in my stomach threatens to come back up at the thought.

"Oh, honey, you'd have to do much worse than that to push Craig away," Josie says, her voice glazed with understanding even though she directs a pointed gaze in my direction that seems to say *don't you dare even think about Wick again.*

"It's okay," I straighten, fortifying my heart with hope. "I have a plan."

Sofia smiles, both confidently and sweetly. "Of course you do. All right, Jo, this will test your organizational skills. Can we help our girl plan a wedding in two weeks?"

Josie pulls her glasses off her head and studies her tablet, the blue-white glow illuminating her face. "You have no say in our bridesmaid dresses," she points a finger in my direction. "Or, other decisions we may or may not make on your behalf."

"Did I ever?"

Sofia leans over and studies the tablet on Josie's lap. "My cousin still owns a flower shop. I can see what he can whip up, but it can't be anything exotic. Likely what he'll already have in stock."

"Do I look like a girl who wants exotic flowers?" I shrug.

That's met with a *hmm* from my friends.

"I can call in a favor with our rep at Bixby's, see if their catering department can help out with the cake," Josie says. "Hell, maybe I'll just text Jake and see what he can do."

One by one, my two best friends go down the list planning my wedding while I game plan the biggest to-do item left.

Getting the groom to say yes.

CHAPTER 39

I sink down in my seat at the flash of headlights in my rearview mirror. It's likely just another car pulling into the parking garage at Craig's hospital, but considering that I borrowed Jo's car and got here at five in the morning to get a parking spot where I could stake out his own reserved spot, I can't be too careful.

The car passes, turning a corner to climb to the next level of the garage.

As the clock inches past eight, worry settles low in my belly.

He's always at work early, catching up on his patients, prepping for rounds, reviewing charts for the patients he'd see throughout the day.

I pull up my second method of stalking, the location app, and notice that his blue dot is finally moving. Three more blocks and he'll turn into the garage.

The worry in my gut shifts to doubt.

What if he decided that he could do better than me?

That perhaps an irrational fiancée isn't good for his health. Or, spending a few nights back in his bachelor pad reminded him just how good the single life is.

His telling of the story of how we met plays in my mind. Was it relief that he saw in my face when I met him? Relief that he'd be the one to save Josie, or relief because he's *him*?

As if on cue, more headlights cut through the darkness of the garage and his SUV swings into his parking spot across from my stakeout.

A second after he parks, Craig emerges from his car, already clad in scrubs, topped with a fleece pullover. His messenger bag hangs off one shoulder with a travel coffee mug gripped in one hand, and his phone in the other.

He starts walking toward the elevator, his head bent over his phone, then he stops abruptly, head swiveling along the line of parked cars.

I sink further in the seat, hoping the headrest disguises the fact someone's sitting in the car.

I watch from the side mirror, as he starts walking back up the ramp and jabs at the elevator call button.

Seconds later, the door opens and my fiancé disappears.

A breath escapes my lungs and I sit upright. That knot of worry uncoils slightly, mostly at the sight of him. The rest of it remains wound tight, questioning if I really want to go forward with my plan.

There's a very good chance he'll tell me I was right; we *are* rushing things.

I mentally flip the bird to that knot of worry.

"You're not the boss of me," I whisper. Like it's totally normal to say that to a physical manifestation of my fear.

I wait another twenty minutes, partly to give Craig time to get to his floor, mostly to give myself the eleventy-billionth pep talk of the day.

After a quick stop by the information desk for directions, I'm on an elevator heading up to the sixth floor. The door opens and I step out, almost stepping directly into another scrub-covered chest.

"Oh, hey, Emily," the man says, stepping back. "Craig didn't say he was expecting you."

I stare up at this man, vaguely recognizing him from the foundation dinner we attended a couple of weeks ago.

Another doctor, oncology maybe? His name badge catches my eye. Alex Kilpatrick, M.D.

"Hey, Alex," I say, hoping that we're on a first name basis and I haven't called him Dr. Kilpatrick or even just Doc before today. "Oh, yeah, he's not, he, uh, forgot something and thought I'd bring it to him."

I pray to the patron saint of commitment-phobes that Craig and Alex aren't best friends and he's not aware I threw him out of the house.

Of course, this could totally work to my advantage, because aside from wandering the floor aimlessly in hopes I'd eventually run into him, I have no clue how to actually find Craig.

"By the way, you seen him around?" I add.

The man sticks his hand into the elevator to hold it open. "Yeah, we just rounded on a patient he's consulting on." He nods to my right. "He should still be down that way, you won't be able to miss him, he's the one with an entourage of residents. Oh, and guess the next time I'll see you will be at the wedding."

The elevator closes, and I loose a breath. So, seems Craig hasn't told his work colleagues that we took a break. But with a gaggle of residents? Geesh, I was hoping to be able to pull him into a quiet corner and confess my mistake.

I glance at my watch. My first client is at ten, so I have a little bit of time, but not much.

My feet carry me down the hall, toward where the other doctor had indicated. I glance at patient rooms, hoping to find an empty one I can hide in, but I stop and suck in a deep breath.

I did not come here to hide—from Craig or my mistakes.

My best friends are busting their butts to help me pull off a wedding. The least I can do is ensure there's a groom to walk down the aisle to.

I continue down the hallway, this time glancing in the rooms, not to find a place to hide, but to find Craig. Instead it's nothing but sleeping patients and busy nurses.

Picking up my pace, I speedwalk, craving his face like addict.

Quiet murmuring and the squeak of sneakers from an adjoining corridor slow my frantic pace. Out of the voices Craig's deep tone tugs at my heart, freezing my feet in place. His words wash over me, even if they're not directed at me, and instead posing questions to residents about course of treatment.

The group rounds the corner. Craig, in the lead, pulls up to a quick stop, forcing the group behind him to do the same. "Em?" Surprise lights his eyes and his mouth pulls up into a smile before it falls, as if remembering that our last words were in anger and not love.

"Hey, yeah, so I was just in the neighborhood..." I shake my head and start over. "Come here often?" My laugh is as hollow as a chocolate Easter bunny.

Craig shuffles and looks down at his feet. Someone behind him coughs, not the hacking-up-a-lung kind, more the can-this-get-any-more-awkward kind.

"Is everything okay?" he asks, his voice as soft as down feathers.

He grows watery in front of me and I shake my head again, dislodging tears.

"No, because I screwed up. I've been spending weeks asking myself if I know what love really is, and if I'm even worthy of you, of how you look at me like I'm the only girl in the world for you."

He takes a step toward me. "Because you are," he says, his face softening.

"I think I get it now, that when you love someone it's like oxygen. You may not realize it when you have it, but you definitely know when you don't." I frown. Somehow that doesn't sound quite as grand and romantic as it had in my head. "What I'm trying to say is, I think I loved you before I even knew you, which may sound impossible, but in a world full of impossible, you make me feel like anything is possible."

Even waking up thirty years in the future.

I take another step forward and drop down to one knee.

Just because I don't remember our first proposal doesn't mean I can't have this one.

"Craig Harrison, you are the man I wake up loving, go to sleep loving and everything-in-between loving." I take his hand and stare up to his hazel eyes, which are now glassy with tears. "We're not rushing things. The opposite, because I can't marry you soon enough. So much so that my best friends are currently calling in every favor to get our wedding planned in two weeks. If I go down that aisle, will you be there to catch me?"

In a quick move he pulls me up from the floor and into his arms. "I will always be there, even if I have to wait on you." His lips brush against mine, softly and tentatively at first before a week of being apart ignites something in both of us.

It's only when the whoops and cheers of residents and some nurses remind us where we are that we break away, but not before Craig whispers some very saucy promises against my lips.

"Oh," I tell him as he walks me back to the elevator. "I hope you don't mind but I commandeered one of your groomsmen to officiate the wedding."

He nods. "Daniel? Can think of no one better for the job."

The elevator dings, door swinging open to reveal a packed car.

"Hey, Em," Craig says as I step in. "How early did you get to the hospital this morning?"

"What?"

He smiles. "Your blue dot was here. I might have been keeping tabs on you."

"Stalker!" I shout through the closing door.

I carry his laugh with me for the rest of the day.

CHAPTER 40

Despite my wedding being hastily thrown together, Jo has been painstakingly planning my bachelorette party for months. Hell, it wouldn't surprise me if she's been secretly planning it for years.

"I have something I need to tell you," she said with the solemnity of someone about to deliver a terminal prognosis, a few days before the party. "There is a stripper shortage."

"All strippers?"

"Well, at least the male ones."

I bite back a laugh as I'm navigating Austin traffic to run one of the million errands. "Are they striking?"

Jo pauses, as if considering my question. "Do you think they're unionized?"

"If not, they should."

"For the healthcare."

"And the 401k." I grin.

We both break out into laughter.

At the next red light, I check my reflection in the rearview mirror, half expecting I quietly slipped back to 1996. The silly yet serious conversation with Josie feels timeless. Something we would've talked about at any point of our lives.

"But really,"I say. "Something low-key is perfect. Dinner, some drinks, a little dancing but nothing that will make our knees hurt."

That's what led me to quickly dusting powder across my face, trying to keep it from staining the silver sequined dress I'd found hiding in the back of my closet.

A low whistle from the door snags my attention.

"You look amazing," Craig says, planting a quick kiss on my neck just below my ear. "Wanna get married?"

"Sure, I'm a bit busy this weekend, but next Saturday?" I throw him a wink.

Next Saturday.

I'm freaking getting married next Saturday. Forget the fact I'd missed all of our firsts, because deep down I feel like even if I had, it would feel like the first time with every touch, kiss, embrace.

That every day with Craig will be filled with wide-eyed love.

I give him a once over. He's also going out tonight with Daniel, a few of his doctor friends and the guys he plays basketball with. Wonder if he's going to encounter a stripper shortage as well?

I chuckle.

"What's so funny?"

"Oh, just thinking about a conversation Josie and I had about stripper rights and if they should unionize for healthcare and retirement planning."

His hazel eyes are both full of humor and perhaps a little concern. "I'm so glad you two found each other. It saves Daniel and me from some awkward conversations."

I lean up, my lips nearly touching his. "I'm so lucky I found you."

Thirty minutes later, I'm in a car with Josie, Sofia and Monique, heading to our first stop of the evening, pre-dinner drinks at a speakeasy that can only be accessed through a broken bathroom stall in a gas station.

"Okay, so I know you put your foot down at wearing a bachelorette sash," Josie says, popping open a bottle of champagne chilling in the back of the car.

"Or carrying a penis-shaped magic wand," Mo chimes in.

"Where would you even find that?" Sof asks, handing me a glass of bubbly filled to the top.

"I think the term *magic wand* means it's something else," Jo snorts. "So, wherever you would buy those. That's where you find it. Anyway, we went with something classy instead."

She pulls a tiara from her bag and places it gently on my head.

"Oh, I'm a princess," I sing-song.

"You're a queen, and you deserve to be treated as one," Jo says, her blue-green eyes twinkling with tears. "I would gladly have that… *medical episode* again and again if it leads you to the love of your life."

I grip my best friend's hand in mine and squeeze, leaning across Sofia to grip Mo's as well, bringing these amazing ladies as close to me as possible. "No, you guys are the great loves of my life," I glance to Sofia, her eyes warm and watery as well. "From those who have known me the longest." A squeeze on Mo's hand, "To those who complete our circle. Without you I will never be alone."

We make it to the gas station hiding a secret speakeasy in the bathroom. A flush of a comically disgusting toilet opens the door into what is perhaps both the coolest and most pretentious bar I've ever seen.

The bartenders all have creative facial hair, the descriptions for the cocktails sound more like a mood than a drink. In what could be the strangest business decision ever, we have a time limit. We are allowed entry for exactly forty-five minutes, which suits Josie just fine, since she has our evening planned to the minute.

I take a sip of my drink, what most bars would call a Paper Airplane, this place has called Sunrise Turbulence and listen to my friends' idle chitchat.

It's soothing, really. Knowing that while my knees ache if I spend too much time in heels, and I can't read a menu in a low-lit bar anymore, there's one thing that hasn't faded with time; my friends.

Even if I woke up in this strange world to an empty bed and no knowledge of a man named Craig Harrison, I'd still feel like my life is perfect with these three women in them.

With the timeliness of a Rolex, the bartender with a villain's mustache slides over the bill and Josie announces that we're off to dinner.

Where the backroom bar was all faux pretension, the restaurant the girls take me to for dinner is all authentic charm.

We walk into the converted house and head straight back to the outdoor backyard dining area. The stone patio is rustic.

A giant Live Oak stretches overhead, its canopy covering most of the backyard. Christmas lights tightly wrapped around the branches supply most of the ambiance in this beautiful space.

"Wow," I whoosh out on a breath. "This is stunning. I don't even care if the food is good or not."

Sof laughs. "I knew you'd love it. And yes, the food here is supposed to be amazing."

We settle into our table in the middle of the patio. It's not overly crowded, only another ten tables are scattered about with mostly couples on a date.

At the back of the yard, a small stage is set up. No speaker or mic stand, but a chair with a guitar awaits whoever will provide the soundtrack for the night.

The waiter is filling our wine glasses when I feel Josie stiffen next to me.

"We can leave," she murmurs. "You say the word and we're out of here."

"What—" The rest of the question dies on my lips when I turn toward the stage.

As if feeling my gaze, Wick lifts his head up from tuning his guitar.

"Oh, hey, Em." He sets down his guitar and strides over to our table. Wick's face contorts into confusion at the tiara on my head. "Is it your birthday?"

It dawns on me then that in our short time together, he never actually asked when my birthday was. I knew his, celebrated it even with not-from-a-box birthday cake, shaped like a guitar and made with about as much art skill as I could muster, and a party with all his friends.

He'd never asked me when I was born. Like me coming into this world wasn't something worth celebrating.

I lift my left hand. "Bachelorette party."

Something passes across his eyes. Jealousy. Regret. Maybe even a bit of possession. Then his face settles back into his good-natured dude persona. "Are there going to be strippers later?" he asks.

"There's a shortage," Josie growls. I almost hear the subtext in those few words. That if he didn't back away there'd be one less musician on this planet, too.

Wick huffs out a laugh. "And here I thought when you came out to see me play…" He trails off, then shrugs. "Guess I thought maybe I could have another chance. Get it right this time."

Thirty years is a long time to wonder about what might've been. Whether it's failed dreams or a failed relationship.

If he had made it big, had been lucky enough to be one of the few who possess not just incredible talent, but incredible timing, would he have come back for me?

He never even knew my birthday.

No. He wouldn't have. I'm not a consolation prize. Not his. Not anyone's.

I stand, my napkin falling to the ground. "It's time to move on, Wick. Not just from me, but this." I wave my hand to where his guitar lies across a lonely wooden chair on a stage at the back of a restaurant's outdoor seating.

No microphone, no speaker. He's meant to be in the background. Nothing more than soft music playing on a gentle breeze.

"I won't lie," I continue. "You broke me. Not just when you left, but even while we were still together. I molded myself to fit into your life. I was young, and didn't know any better, but I do now. Love isn't about fitting yourself into someone else's box, it's about being with someone whose love helps you grow." I smile to soften the bite in my voice. "As much as it hurt me, I wouldn't be where I am today if you hadn't let me go." I glance down at Monique.

Her knowing nod tells me she realizes I mean this much more literally than figuratively.

"Good luck, Wick," I say, taking my seat with my best friends. "Both with your set tonight and everything after."

He flashes a tight smile and, with a quick nod, heads back to the stage where he plays a muted set, mostly unnamed tunes to accompany a perfect evening dining under the Texas stars.

Never once through the dinner does my gaze wander to the stage, or does my mind think about what could've been if he'd just picked me.

Because really, my destiny shouldn't be up to him. I know that now, and just wish I could have told my twenty-year-old self that instead of feeling brokenhearted I should've felt grateful.

After dinner and dessert, I lean back in my chair, swirling the last of the wine in my glass. At some point in the evening Wick packed up, the stage now empty, aside from that single wooden chair.

I never saw him leave, never felt a disturbance in the universe.

"What's next?" I ask.

Mo leans on her forearms, drumming her perfect red nails on the table. "Something I think will be right up your alley," she says, mischief gleaming in her eyes. "Nineties night at a club on Sixth Street."

"Are we going to party like it's 1999?" I ask, suddenly uncaring if my knees are going to ache into next week.

"Hell yeah."

That's exactly what we do. With these three amazing women at my side, we sing and dance and dance and sing until we are sweaty and my tiara is as gone as our voices.

It doesn't matter that I lost thirty years of my life, because everything I've found since I woke up is exactly where I want to be.

CHAPTER 41

"I don't understand why we have to have a rehearsal dinner when we're not having a rehearsal," I whine with the fervor of a teenager, which isn't that hard since I'm pretty much one.

Mentally that is, despite spending two months living an adult life.

Craig shrugs as he switches the toothbrush to the other side of his mouth.

I can almost read the relief in his eyes that he can't answer me.

Josie was insistent we have one, even if the instructions for tomorrow is as simple as *don't trip while walking down the aisle, breathe and repeat after Daniel until I say, 'I do.'*

Easy peasy.

Which is why complicating things by bringing our families and wedding parties together for what Jo swears will be a casual, fun evening makes getting a root canal without Novocaine sound more pleasurable.

Craig spits and wipes his mouth. "Twenty-four hours from now, we'll be married, and then two days after that, we'll be on a plane heading to the other side of the world."

I huff out a laugh. "You make it sound like we're running away."

"We are." He presses a minty-fresh kiss on my lips. "Just keep your eye on the prize."

"Which is being married, or on the other side of the world?" I glance to my suitcase, yearning to be filled with tropical clothes for a two-week trip to the Maldives. So far, all that's in it is four large bottles of SPF 100 sunscreen.

"Yes," he deadpans. "It's just dinner, with all the people who love us most. How bad can that be?"

I grunt. "Spoken like a man who's never been in the same room with my parents. Together."

Jo called in a favor with my dad, who'd reserved a private dining room at the country club. The very club where, thirty years earlier, my father had chastised me for not being serious about my future.

This feels like a bad metaphor.

Or at least a bad omen.

I note the differences in the drive up to the club. The trees are more towering; azalea bushes line the driveway where the last time I was here, it was tired rose bushes.

The porte-cochère is new. Thirty years ago the poor valet guys had to stand out in the sun or rain waiting on Austin's elite. Now, they can do it under a protected pitched roof. With fans even. Maybe they unionized, like the strippers.

Josie wanted us to arrive after everyone else, but I'd put my foot down. Under no circumstances were my parents to be left alone together. They needed to be under adult—well, almost adult—supervision.

My best friend is arranging name cards around the tables when we walk in.

I watch her for a minute, dropping placards down, then backing up as if to imagine the people sitting there, only to pick them up and shuffle them, like a dealer trying to dole out a winning hand for a change.

The room itself is more a wine vault than a dining room. Instead of walls, the room is lined with glass-encased shelves of wine bottles, all lit with a soft yellow glow. Because free booze is still a novelty, I give one of the handles a gentle tug, only to find the wine to be safely locked away.

"I can't decide if it's safer to put all the kids together at one table or to spread them out with their parents," Josie says, tapping the edge of one place card against her bottom lip. "It would probably keep the adults on good behavior if their children are watching."

"Does that include my parents?"

"Yep, sorry babe, it's your wedding so you have to sit with your parents. But don't worry, your dad sprung for a full bar with all premium liquors. We should be all set."

Since we're having a small wedding, the rehearsal dinner is even smaller. Just a few tables fill the private dining room. Seated with Craig and me, is Mom, Geoff, Dad and Monique. Josie, Daniel, Aubrey and Ben are seated with Craig's ex, Diane, her wife Veronica and Aiden. The next table is Sofia with a few of Craig's doctor friends.

Jo shoves a glass of champagne in my hand. "My job is to never let your hand or your glass be empty. Trust me, it'll make the evening tolerable." She pulls the glass back out of my hand. "Oh, but you can't drink too much of it. You don't want to be all puffy and hungover tomorrow." She hums. "Maybe my job is to alternate you between water and booze."

She finishes the placement of the name cards just as the first guests arrive.

Sofia comes in on the arm of a handsome man with rich ebony skin. His face is so familiar, yet...not.

"Em, it's so good seeing you," he says, wrapping me in a hug. "Crazy to think what a small world it is. Of all the women Craig could fall in love with, it's one I went to high school with."

It hits me then. High school.

This guy who now stands nearly as tall as Craig was once a short, nerdy teen.

"Holy crap, Matthew Fraser!" I squeak, going in for another hug. "You got hot. And tall." I snap my mouth shut, in case I actually see Matthew regularly. "Sorry, Jo's mission tonight is to get me drunk. And we all know what an overachiever she is."

He laughs and squeezes my shoulders. "It's all good. It's been ages since I saw you. You stayed hot…and short." Matthew adds with a wink before following Sofia to the bar.

Daniel arrives next, with Aubrey and Ben in tow.

Aubrey beelines to the bar, glancing over her shoulder as she smiles brightly at the young bartender. If anyone here can talk her way into underage drinking my money's on my best friend's oldest kid.

I recognize Craig's ex the minute she walks in. Not because I've seen pictures of her or met her, obviously, but because she's the other half of Aiden's genes. Her blue eyes are absolutely stunning. Where my own eyes are more glacial blue, hers are the warm depths of the ocean. Set against the silver of her bob and perfectly smooth skin, Diane is gorgeous.

"Hey, guys, thank you so much for inviting us," Diane says, warmly hugging Craig as he plants a kiss to her cheek. She turns her attention to me and pulls me in for a tight hug. "Thank you for loving him," she whispers in my ear.

Her wife, Vanessa, introduces herself, saving me the embarrassment of wondering if we know each other.

Aiden steps up next, but his head is down on his phone.

"Hey, sup," he says. "Deleted any apps and think they fell on the counter lately?"

A perfect retort perched on my tongue is interrupted by redheaded tornado plucking my champagne glass from my hands.

"Cover me," Aubrey says, taking a swig. She goes in for a second drink, but freezes when her gaze lands on Aiden.

A heartbeat passes where the two teenagers simply stare at each other. If this were a movie, there'd be dramatic music, intense close-ups, cheeks reddening.

Since this isn't a movie and instead, my non-rehearsal rehearsal dinner, Aubrey breaks the spell and downs the rest of my champagne. She stifles a small burp, hands my empty glass back and is off.

Aiden's gaze follows where Josie's spawn goes as she works her way to Sofia.

"Need I remind you that her stepfather has some sort of super-secret government job," I say to the breathless boy. "And while I might not be able to work my phone, I can easily hide a body."

He pulls his gaze from Aubrey. "Does my dad know you're a pyscho?" Aiden says on a laugh.

"You're right, I should worry about you, not her." I flash an evil grin. "But seriously, Aiden, I think she has a boyfriend. Or, did. Proceed with caution."

Before he could retort shuffling at the doorway catches my attention.

Because the Spirits like to stir shit up, they decided that my parents should arrive at the same time.

"Please, after you," Dad says, gesturing for my mom and Geoff to enter ahead of him.

"Well, this might be the only time you ever put me first," Mom snipes. "Geoff, post something on the Face Place."

The older gentleman next to her clears his throat and attempts to stand as tall as his hunched back allows. "I believe they call it Face-book, my dear."

"Really, Abigail," my father says. The tightening of his jaw is visible from across the room.

I jump in to intervene. "Hi, welcome, let me show you guys to your corners."

"Don't give me that, Paul," Mom says. "You never put us, Emily, first, so don't make a show of it this weekend."

"Mom," I bark the word, hoping it'll snap her out of whatever mood she's in.

"I couldn't give you the lifestyle you wanted *and* be there at your beck and call," Dad says.

"Dad."

"So, you choose neither?"

I push between them. This is the argument they have every time they're together, rehashing what broke them up.

Looks like thirty years did nothing to change that.

"Okay, so the divorce was settled a long time ago and I think the statute of limitations for this argument is officially over. Craig and I can go to the courthouse tomorrow instead of a wedding if this is how you're going to behave."

Josie comes up behind me. "No, you can't," she stage whispers.

"Hi, Paul, Abigail, let me get you to your seats and we'll get dinner started."

The appetizer and salad courses pass with no drama. Mom and Geoff are regaling Craig with their latest travels.

I listen closely, waiting to hear my mother struggle for a word, or call someone by the wrong name, but she's clear and crisp as a stout martini.

Dad and Monique have their heads together, discussing a court case he's preparing for.

I glance around the room. Unsurprising, Aubrey must've upended her mother's handiwork and put her chair next to Aiden. While Craig's son is chatting animatedly, my goddaughter plays it cool.

Jo was right. Everyone here loves us, wants us to be happy. Everyone here knows me, at least some version of me, and put together in this room they make me feel whole.

As if the Emily Murray sitting here, the eve of her wedding, is a college student, a daughter, a friend, colleague, future family, and lover.

"So, we need to talk about the ceremony," Dad says, pulling me back into the room.

"What's there to talk about? Daniel's got it."

My father shakes his head. "No, I mean the procession. What time do you want me to meet you at your dressing room?"

"Meet me for what?"

"To walk you down the aisle, of course," my dad says, his gaze on the filet he's sawing away at.

I look at Craig, my mouth dropping open. It's not that I'm skirting tradition, but my father giving me away never crossed my mind.

My mother scoffs. "If there's anyone who should give her away it's me."

"I'm not a piece of property," I say, just short of a snap. I can't help it.

"Well, I certainly paid enough for your school to own more than a few houses," Dad snorts.

"Because that's the only way you acknowledged your daughter."

Mom leans across Craig and points her steak knife in my father's direction.

My fiancé scoots back from the table ever so slightly.

"That's the only thing you wanted from me." He points his knife back at her and I scoot back as well. "Even tonight. Would I be invited if you didn't need my membership?"

"Is that what you think?" My voice drips with disdain. "That all I want from you is your money? No, that's not it at all, but you never took the time to ask *me*. All those times I came to spend the weekend with you, and you were never there, or if you were, it was to see you at breakfast and again at dinner." I push up from the table. "I am not yours to give away," I tell my father before turning my gaze to my mother. "And not yours either, because you're not without fault. But it doesn't mean I love you guys any less. That's what love is, forgiving your parents for their imperfections, because deep down, I know you were doing the best you could. So no, I'm not being *'given away'* tomorrow." I wipe at the hot tears running down my face. "Instead, I'm walking toward someone who will be there, no matter what." I throw down my napkin and jog out of the silent dining room, ignoring my parents calling my name.

CHAPTER 42

I'm starting to seriously rethink a lot of my decisions the morning of my wedding. Not that I'm actually doing it, not that I'm marrying a man who feels less like a stranger and more like a piece of me. My heart.

No, I'm starting to seriously rethink the decision to have an outdoor sunset wedding in May on the exact day that Mother Nature cranks up the thermostat on the Texas Hill Country.

Josie and Sofia are running the last few wedding errands, so it's just Monique and me in the car heading to the wedding venue. Something tells me she leapt at the assignment.

"Are you okay with this?" Her voice is soft, like what she'd use with her son. "I mean, in some ways, this is an arranged marriage to an older man, just one arranged by you, to someone who really isn't that much older than you." Mo lets out a low whistle. "Damn, Doc, how does your mind not explode every day you get out of bed?"

"Who says it doesn't?" Truthfully, every day is becoming less jarring. Sure, I think there will always be moments when I feel like I've missed out on so much life, but I also know that every moment, like this one with Mo and every moment I'll have today, as I marry a man

I've seemed to wait my whole life for, are incredibly precious, whether I have a thirty-year gap or not.

"And I know it may seem like an arranged marriage, but I think past-me made a pretty good decision when she snagged this fish from the sea." The city turns to countryside outside my window. "Where do you think she is? The older me? Do you think she woke up on my old apartment's bathroom floor thinking she's living some stress dream? Freaking out that she can't wake up and get back to Craig?"

My chest squeezes. A version of me could be back in my past desperately missing the man I'm—we're—about to marry.

I let loose a long breath and sink deeper into the passenger seat, my stomach folding in on itself.

"Is that second thoughts?" Mo says, worry pinches her face.

"No, just trying to keep who I am straight in my head."

The wedding venue is a beehive of activity. Staff is busy putting white folding chairs on the limestone patio. A florist is weaving what looks like wildflowers into an arch, the exact place where Craig and I will promise to love and honor each other for the rest of our days in just a few hours.

A sea of blooming lavender waves in the wind beyond the patio, the sound like a thousand tiny hands applauding for me making it to this day.

I was never one of those teenagers who dreamt of her wedding. Even when I thought Wick and I would get married, I always imagined it would just happen, maybe a super casual affair, me barefoot in a short white dress, him in an ill-fitting second-hand suit, Josie and Sofia beside me and just a few close friends.

Standing here watching it all come together, it hits me. *This* is my dream wedding. To my dream man.

Mo's phone dings and she glances down at it. "All right, let's get you inside. Craig is en route and he can't see you yet. It's bad luck."

"Too late, I saw him over breakfast."

"Doesn't count. The clock only starts when you're at the wedding venue."

"According to who?" Not that I'm looking for reasons for bad luck. I just want to have all my facts. "Is there some secret society judging whether or not we make it based on how well we follow these outdated traditions?"

She tsks. "Twenty-year-old you is insufferable." Mo reaches for my wedding dress garment bag draped over an arm. "You're going to wrinkle it." Her face is bright, eyes glistening, betraying her chastising words.

I let her take the bag. "You've been hanging out with my dad too much."

We make our way into the bridal suite. It's every bit of a place for girlfriends to spend an afternoon sipping champagne and gossiping while one of those lucky ladies is doted on. White and plush and frilly. Both cozy with thick, upholstered sofas and armchairs, but also light and airy with plantation-shuttered windows letting light stream in. To complete the fantasy of the perfect day, a bottle of bubbly sits in a bucket of ice.

"Tell Craig we're getting married in here," I say on a sigh.

Mo hangs up my dress and the door pops back open, Josie, Sofia and Aubrey burst in on a wind of excitement.

"It's your wedding day!" Jo throws her hands up and high knees herself over to hug me. "Oh my gosh, I'm so excited for you." She pulls back, her eyes shiny with tears. "Shit, I've already cried twice, and I thought I'd gotten it out of my system. Don't worry, I'll dehydrate myself, so I won't embarrass you."

"Or you'll pass out and fart in front of everyone," Aubrey says, her fingers flying across her phone.

Jo sighs. "It's moments like these when I think I came home with the wrong kid."

Oh, she absolutely came home with the right kid, and I love that child more and more every day. I really hope I had some small part in influencing this sass.

With champagne bubbling in our glasses, including a small pour for the small pint, we all wrap up in soft robes and bare feet, and wait while the makeup artist and hairstylist takes turns with each of us. After all of the ladies are beautified, not that it took much work, it's my turn in the chair.

"What do you think about an updo, but we'll pull out some face-framing strands?" The stylist asks, playing with my hair like it's clay to be molded. "This will hold through the wedding and reception, especially outside. Plus, those earrings." She adds, nodding to the diamond and sapphire earrings Craig bought me for a wedding gift nestled in their jewelry box.

At my nod, she goes to work, and when she's done, the makeup artist takes over, murmuring how well-preserved I am, and she must get the name of "my guy." Once the hair and makeup is done, Jo helps me into the dress.

It's still perfect. The corseted bodice holding my pounding heart in place, like, well, like armor.

Astrid's words from all those weeks ago play in my mind like naughty children.

I see you standing there, wrapped in armor.

Was that what she saw? My wedding dress?

I turn and gasp at my reflection. Eight weeks ago, this reflection startled me. Like looking at a funhouse mirror version of myself. Someone I knew, but who also felt completely foreign.

Or like that time in high school when I'd borrowed one of my mom's suits. It was too big, and not just the cut of it, but the aura of it. Like I had yet to become the person who could wear it.

Waking up to the older version of me was just like that. This version of myself is much bigger than who I was when I was in college, but I've grown into it.

Into her.

"Oh, no, it's happening again." Jo fans her eyes. "I can't ruin my makeup before we even step out of the room."

Sof steps up. "Aubrey brought extra makeup in case we need to do touch-ups."

Jo laughs through her tears. "Okay, *that's* the child I brought home." She sniffles and fans her eyes again. "I owe you an apology," she adds, her expression sobering.

I shake my head. "What? I don't—"

"All these years, I thought you were still hung up on Wick and thought you were afraid to open yourself to love." Jo squeezes my fingers. "What I didn't understand is that you were brave enough to wait for the one. Anyone can settle, only those courageous enough to know that their soulmate is out there will wait for him."

I pull Jo into a tight hug, but really, I'm hugging myself. The me who gave me, us, the gift of not settling into a bad relationship, or even just an okay relationship, but who knew that someone better was out there.

A knock on the bridal suite door interrupts the moment.

Aubrey pulls it open and I hear her speak to whoever is on the other side.

"Yeah, we're all ready. Mom's already cried three times. I know she has at least one more in her and then you're going to have to pay up."

"What?" Josie says on a breath. "Are they betting on how many times I'll cry?"

Daniel pops his head around the partially open door. The light flooding his eyes when he sees his wife is hard to miss.

I remember seeing a version of that in high school, just a few years ago to me, and my heart turns to goo, seeing that three decades of time only made that love grow.

"Em, you look beautiful. Craig won't be able to breathe when he sees you," Daniel says. "Speaking of, it's time. Ready to marry the love of your life?"

I'm ready.

Ready for forever to begin.

CHAPTER 43

The breath I'd been holding as we gather up our bouquets, and Jo makes sure for the fiftieth time she has Craig's wedding band, threatens to erupt from my lungs in a plume of smoke. Seconds earlier, I'd been ready to run into Craig's arms and skip all the vows we'd written to just get to the part where I say 'I do' and kiss him silly.

Now, something feels off.

Missing.

"Daniel?" I call, while he's shutting the door. "Can you ask my dad to come in here?"

"Everything okay?" His brows knit a worry sweater.

"It will be. Tell Craig I just need my dad and I'll be right out."

As if understanding the conversation I'm about to have, Josie clears her throat. "All right, ladies, let's go ahead and get lined up."

A moment after the girls leave with Daniel, the door opens again and this time the slightly stooped form of my father fills the doorway.

"You asked for me?" he says by way of greeting. His voice is tentative, almost afraid. A far cry from the man who commands courtrooms, who dines with judges and travels with senators.

Then again, being told off by his daughter in front of family and friends will do that to a person.

Dad pauses and his gasp echoes in the now quiet room. "My little girl," he says, more to himself than me. He shakes his head and closes the door behind him. "I used to tell everyone I can recall every closing argument I've ever given. It was mostly true, but only because no one ever challenged me on it," he says, coming to stand just feet away from me. "But what I can absolutely remember like it was yesterday, is holding you for the first time." My dad laughs. "I told the nurse I was having a heart attack. Your mom thought I was flirting with her, but you know what the nurse told me? 'Dad, that's love, and fear, and hope.' And she was right."

A sob I didn't know was building in my chest gurgles out of me. I fan my face, not wanting to be a mess when I finally come out of this room.

"I didn't know how to father you from afar, and that's my failure, not yours," he continues, lowering himself into the closest chair.

It was then I really noticed how much he's aged.

"My first way to parent you was by providing, so I bought you everything you could need. Want. And then you were in college, and I thought this is where I could make a difference. Guide you." My father mindlessly rubs one of his knees. "I could help you be successful; not make the same mistakes I made."

His blue eyes, the same he passed down to me, lift to mine and my blood freezes in my veins.

"I over-rotated. I went from being the providing parent to the domineering guardian and it was awful. For you, for me." Dad takes a deep breath. "I still remember that terrible brunch, when you walked out and I didn't see or hear from you for three years. Thankfully, your mom still had a shred of kindness toward me in her heart, and she at least told me you were still alive. Albeit without that gorgeous head of hair.

"I screwed up, and I thank whichever deity was kind enough to let me back in your life. I understand, Emily, why you don't want me part of your wedding—"

"But I do," I finally find my voice and cut him off. "I want you to be. To walk with me down that aisle. But, you're not giving me away—"

"Because you're not mine to give away," he finishes for me with a wry smile. "Also, Emily, why would I want to give you away, when all I've ever wanted to do my entire life is keep you close to me?"

The levee of my emotions snaps in half and I fling myself into my dad's arms, catching him off guard.

Good thing he's sitting or we both would've ended up on the floor.

At first, his arms hang limply by his side. Then slowly, tentatively like coaxing a scared puppy out of its hiding place, his arms wrap around my shoulders.

Have I ever hugged my dad?

I'm sure we did at some point, maybe when I was little. Sitting there felt equal parts natural and novel. A bit of déjà vu.

Like I *should* have a memory of hugging my father, except for the fact I have no actual memory of hugging my father.

"I must've been an infuriating child to parent," I murmur into his shoulder.

He laughs, the sound rumbling through me. "Actually, the opposite. You were far too well-adjusted for the drama your mom and I put you through. I realize now it was your defense mechanism. That as the child of parents too wrapped up in their own careers you became your own parent."

I pull out of the embrace and stare at him. I didn't need to be an actual therapist to know that's exactly what happened.

"My therapist told me that," he adds, as an answer to the question on my face.

"You go to therapy?"

My father nods. "I started when you changed majors. I won't lie, I went in there with the intention of proving it was bonk. Now, I can't imagine what I would be like without it." He stands, pulling me up him. "I'm so incredibly proud of you, Emily. Even when you were standing up to me, I was proud of you for standing your ground. Now, let's get you married." Dad adds, tucking my arm in his.

The shift in the air is palpable when we emerge from the bridal suite. A string quartet plays outside, the gentle notes from their music drifting among the guests and floating out over the fields of lavender. The sinking sun casts the field and patio in a warm orange glow.

My gaze catches Josie's and she rushes over to me.

"Good?" Her blue-green eyes scour my face.

"Great," I say on a breath and my best friend visibly relaxes.

"Good," she says again. And then a little louder. "Let's get this party started."

On cue, the quartet moved from a classical tune to a peppier one, more modern, so modern that it's one I've heard a few times but couldn't name it or who sings it.

"What's this?" I laugh.

"You put me in charge, so I decided you and Craig don't need no stuffy Wedding March. This is a damn party, so we're going to treat it like one."

My mouth drops and I wipe away an errant tear. *This* is also love. Friends who take charge to make me laugh, to make this moment in my life absolutely unforgettable. Even if Josie doesn't know I'm missing half my life, she's committed to making every moment special. For me.

Jo takes her spot at the end of the line of bridesmaids, with Aubrey setting the tone sashaying and skipping down the aisle, swinging her auburn waves. Even from my tucked-away vantage point, it's not hard to see stoic Aiden go slack-jawed at the dancing redhead.

What are the chances that my goddaughter and stepson end up together?

Monique follows, whipping the crowd into a frenzy with her shaking hips and whoops of excitement.

Sofia follows, throwing a Latin flare into her moves as she sashays down the aisle.

Before Jo heads out the door she turns and our gazes meet again. She crushes into me, engulfing me in a fierce hug. "Love is about leaping and trusting that it will be there to catch you," she whispers into my hair. "Jump, Em. And I'll always catch you. We all will."

Then, my best friend takes off for her turn down the aisle, pulling out some of our favorites from our youth; a little Running Man, some Roger Rabbit, and just to make sure my future husband has tears of laughter running down his face, she Cabbage Patches into her place as Maid of Honor.

"Not to disappoint you, dear, but I have no dance moves prepared," my dad deadpans, although there is just a lilt of humor to his voice.

"Neither do I. Shall we wing it?" I step into the doorway and the music shifts, just a bit louder; the beat a bit faster, to signify that the bride is about to come down the aisle.

Away from the air conditioning of the inside, the heat of the setting sun blasts into me.

Craig wipes his eyes and straightens when his gaze falls on me; his smile widens when he sees my dad standing beside me.

We step onto the carpet leading me to my future, and I can't stop the joy flooding my entire being. Before we step further toward my fiancé, Dad twirls me and I thrust my bouquet into the air, my smile so wide my face hurts.

My gaze is stuck on Craig's, and buzzing fills the air. There must be a whole colony of bees taking advantage of the blooming lavender.

With each step toward my almost-husband, my vision narrows. This man who I've come to love in just a few weeks but really, deep down, I feel like I've loved him most of my life.

This man who laughs at my corny jokes, who remains unfazed when I act more like a natural disaster than a human being. This man who I shoved away but was there to hold me when I reached for him.

Every moment of my life led me to now.

To him.

It doesn't matter one bit that I missed thirty years of it.

He's worth it.

We're worth it.

Dad twirls me again and heat rushes over me.

Why did we think it was a good idea to get married outside at sunset in May in Texas?

The buzzing gets louder, overtaking the strings. Are we under attack?

I let my eyes dart from Craig long enough to check if our guests are ducking or covering their heads, but no.

They're all smiling and laughing, basking in the joy of two people celebrating their love.

I fan myself. A sign that could mean I find my fiancée hot, which I do, but in reality is meant to cool me. Am I going to have sweaty pits in my wedding photos?

Dad twirls me once more, and the world goes sideways as he pulls me close to peck a kiss on my cheek. "I love you, my baby girl. It's time for you to go to the other man who loves you."

He takes our joined hands and holds them out to Craig, encouraging me to step forward.

I let go of my dad and reach for Craig's outstretched hand.

The buzzing grows louder.

Sweat trickles down my back and my stomach backflips.

Did I eat today?

Probably not, but those few sips of champagne shouldn't have made me this loopy, right?

I feel the buzzing at my feet, an electrical pulse that zips up my body. My smile slips, just slightly, like a figure skater hitting a slick spot, but enough that Craig's brow knits in confusion.

Oh no.

No, no, no. This can't be…

I'm being pulled apart. Atom by atom, cell by cell.

Breath by breath.

I need to touch him.

Craig will tether me to now, but just as our fingers nearly touch, I slip further.

"I love you." I force the words out before the darkness steals him.

Steals *me*.

CHAPTER 44

"Em! Oh my God. Emily, wake up, please." Josie's worried voice is engulfed in sobs.

I jolt awake and sit upright, chilled from lying nearly naked on the bathroom floor. Nothing but shaved hair surrounds me. My best friend kneels next to me; panic splashed across her face.

My hand lifts, as if still reaching for Craig, but…

"Where is he?" I glance around my tiny, old bathroom. So stark compared to the one I'd become accustomed to over the last couple of months.

This one dingy, small, musty as if it's never been cleaned. Which, it probably never has been.

I glance at my hands. The engagement ring that once weighed so much is gone from my left hand. My right palm burns from an angry red streak bisecting it.

"He's gone." My words are flat, defeated.

Jo gathers me in her arms. "I know, sweetie. I heard the message on the answering machine. He's an ass, and if I ever see him again, I will absolutely murder him."

The best friend holding me isn't the one who hugged me just

minutes ago before dancing herself down the aisle for my wedding. It's the one who cleaned shards of glass out of my hand thirty years ago.

The man I'm crying for isn't the loser ex-boyfriend.

It's a man Josie's never met. Not yet.

A man I can't even begin to explain.

"I've got to find him," I say, jumping up and nearly knocking Josie on her butt.

"Em, wait, you…um, you missed some spots."

I glance into the mirror and jump. Not at the haphazardly shaved head, but at the face I'd forgotten. It's the same as the one I'd gotten used to seeing, but closer to youthful fullness, the little lines I'd shrugged off nowhere to be found, and, from what's left of my hair, it's still a rich brunette.

"Let me…help you," Jo's voice breaks.

I nod, recalling her retelling of this story. How she found me on the floor. How I'd missed some spots, and she cried alongside me as she finished shaving my head.

Josie switches the razor on, and buzzing fills my ears. The same buzzing as the bees in the lavender fields around our wedding venue.

Maybe this is a dream.

It was hot. I hadn't eaten and had too much champagne. Dad twirling me down the aisle got me dizzy. Did I breathe any on my way to Craig?

As the final few strands of my hair fall around me, understanding settles in low and deep in my stomach.

This is real.

As much as *that* was real.

Jo turns off the razor and chucks it into the trashcan.

A sob bellows from my mouth and I kneel to the floor.

My best friend follows me down, once again putting her arms around me, holding me close. Holding me together.

"I need to find him," I say again. She has no clue who I'm talking about. She won't for many more years.

"Are you sure it's a good idea?" Jo asks.

I don't answer her.

"Do you want me to go with you?" she adds.

I shake my head.

"You're not…you're not going to hurt yourself, are you?" Her voice breaks like shattering glass.

"I won't, I promise. It's just…something I have to do."

Someone I have to see.

I have no clue what time it is. How long I've been lying on the bathroom floor. From the light streaming into my bedroom window, it's still daylight.

I pull on cut-off denim shorts and a sweatshirt, not even bothering to dig out a bra from the piles of clothes around the room. Before heading out of my room, I grab a baseball cap. Geesh, this is going to be awful as it grows out.

Seeing Scarlett waiting for me nearly launched another wave of tears. Despite having a car that knew its way to my office and could park itself, I missed my Jeep something fierce.

It's so stark seeing the other cars on the road. No longer sleek, futuristic.

Austin traffic still sucks, even late on a Sunday afternoon.

I whip into the parking lot just as a now-familiar figure closes the front door behind her.

Astrid looks up as I hop out of my Jeep, not even bothering to turn it off.

"Send me back," I shout.

The woman stares at me, taking a step back before the shock erases from her face, likely one of her Spirits whispering some bullshit at her.

"You."

"Yeah, me."

She glances over her shoulder, the scowl on her face deepening.

"You really should've given me a heads up," she snaps at her Spirits. "Come."

I follow her inside the shop that feels so much fresher, newer than it did the last time I saw it.

"Want to tell me about it?" Astrid doesn't go to the room at the end of the hall, instead she falls into the armchair that's several shades brighter than it was thirty years from now.

"I guess your prediction came true. I did go on a long journey.

Thirty-years-into-the-future long." I cross my arms. "And, just as I was about to marry the most amazing man in the universe I pass out and wake back up here."

Her craggy face furrows, deepening the lines. "The Spirits say that sounds about right. You'd surrendered. That's what brought you back."

"I didn't surrender. I wasn't giving up on anything."

"You misunderstand, that's not giving up. You learned to love, to let others love you. To let them be human, make mistakes. To ask forgiveness. To forgive." She opens both hands, her lined palms facing upward.

"Well, that's bullshit." My eyes burn with fresh tears. "Astrid, you have to send me back." I glance around the shop, hoping somewhere the Spirits are huddled nearby. "Please, I know I was petulant and temperamental and all that, but Craig is probably freaking out. I need to get back. I *want* to get back."

The woman shakes her head and sorrowful eyes meet mine. "It doesn't work like that. I can't."

I drop my arms and stiffen my spine, then stiffen my resolve. "Okay, fine. Fine. I'll just do this the old-fashioned way. I'll go to him now."

My mind takes off in a sprint, whirling through the information I know about Craig, hoping to snag on where he was in August 1996. Was he still in college, or was he already in med school?

He took a gap year to backpack across Europe, but was that before college or after.

"You can't," Astrid's quiet voice cut across the noise in my brain.

"Of course I can," I counter. "I mean, it might not be as easy as it will be in a few years, but I can do this." My feet start pacing the length of the shop, dragging my torso along. "I'll just run into him, and of course I won't tell him that we're destined to get married or something, but it makes sense. Why waste so much of our lives not being together?"

"You. Can't," the psychic says again, louder, firmer. "It would put too much out of balance in the world. If you find each other now, it won't be the love you have if you wait. You're a different person. He's a different person. You're not ready for each other."

I stop dead in my place.

My *heart* stops dead in its place.

It's only been a couple of hours, but I feel the time stretching between us like a piece of gum. How much longer until the bond between us breaks?

"But…"

The woman sighs and pushes herself to standing. "Who wouldn't exist if you and your man got together now? Your kids? His kids?"

Aiden.

He's a haughty, judgmental little shit, but he's also Craig's son. Maybe even will become someone special to my future goddaughter.

"What do I do?" I whisper.

"You live your life. You become the person he falls in love with. And you trust in the Universe that when the time is right, you will find him."

I'm surprised Scarlett is still there waiting on me, considering I left her running while I was in Astrid's shop.

The drive home is much slower. The breakup with Wick feels so insignificant compared to the loss of Craig. Of the future that was within my reach. Silent tears fall down my face, clouding the twilight road ahead of me.

I don't know every twist and turn that got me to Craig. Just the big decisions, but even then, we met when Josie had a medical emergency.

What if on this new road I'm on now, she doesn't? Not that I'd ever wish any sort of illness on my best friend, but if Josie doesn't end up in the hospital, how else would I meet him?

Or, what if he makes a different decision? What if he and his ex-wife stay together? What if he doesn't move to Austin? Or, he does and Jo ends up in his hospital, but when we meet there's nothing there.

It's dark when I get back to our apartment. The lights are on and I know that Jo will stay up however long it takes to make sure I'm okay.

I turn off Scarlett and watch the rising moon.

There's no guarantee Craig and I will find our way back to each other. There's also no guarantee the world will keep turning after today.

However, there's hope. Hope will motivate me to get out of bed tomorrow. To go down to the registrar's office and change my major again.

For the final time.

Hope will drive me, as I spend late nights studying to be a therapist. As I work my ass off to build a practice of helping people.

Hope will protect my heart, save it for the man I pray will still be there, will still want me, when the time is right.

Even in this moment when I feel like I have nothing, I do have hope.

I'm going to hold on to it like my life depends on it.

CHAPTER 45
TWENTY-EIGHT(ISH) YEARS LATER...

My ringing cell phone buzzes in my desk, the sound filling the awkward silence of my new client, who sits as closed up as a cold clam.

It stops. Seconds later, starts again. Only to stop once more, before a series of single sharp vibrations reverberate off my desk.

Client forgotten, my mind goes immediately to Josie. Her voicemail about finding out her son of a bitch almost-ex-husband was making a play for full custody shattered my heart, but with back-to-back clients, I've barely had time to pee, much less check to see how she's doing or find out if she needs help hiding the body.

The ringing starts up again.

Maybe she's in the midst of dragging his body to her car. Surely this client can understand a little accomplice to murder among friends.

"Do you mind—"

"Do you need to get that?"

I'm not sure who was more relieved, my client or me.

"I'll just be a second, and I promise you, this is not normal," I say, launching myself toward my desk.

The name on my missed calls is not the one I expected.

Peter Gardner.

I don't listen to the voicemails right away. Instead, I thumb open my text messages.

PETER GARDNER

> Something happened to Josie.

> She's in an ambulance on the way to the hospital.

> She won't wake up. I don't know what's happening.

> Can you meet me there?

> I'm still her emergency contact.

> What am I going to tell the kids?

I can feel his panic through his written words. As much as I was looking forward to hiding his body, Peter's not a bad guy. He just wasn't *the* guy for Josie. Also, I can't hate the man who gave me my godchildren.

My heart speeds up.

Not just because of concern for my best friend.

But…for what else this could mean.

"I'm so sorry, there's been an emergency," I pull my bag out of my desk and shove my laptop inside. "I have to go, but I'll tell Monique there's no charge for today and to book you for another appointment, also at no charge."

I know there will soon be a new therapist moving in down the street, and while I plan to welcome him with open arms and a fruit basket, I figure it wouldn't hurt to go ahead and up my client service.

It takes everything in my power to not run every red light and break every speed limit on my way to the hospital.

Peter's in the waiting room of the Emergency Department. He's pacing, running his hands through his salt and pepper hair. Kirsten, his new girlfriend, sits quietly to the side, gnawing on her thumbnail.

How awkward is this for her?

To see her boyfriend panicking over a medical emergency of his ex-wife?

I'll have to pull that out of her later, help her process her feelings.

"Em." Peter rushes over to me, his voice thick, and pulls me into a hug. "They don't know what happened. She was in her office and then they found her passed out on the floor. She's breathing. They're checking her heart, but she hasn't woken up yet."

"She'll be okay," I say, hugging Peter back. My words are more than vacant assurances. Unless the Universe is sticking a middle finger at me, I *know* Josie will be fine.

"I'm still her emergency contact," Peter repeats what he texted me.

I've seen this before with divorcing couples. The time it takes to unwind someone from another's life can be unending. It's not as simple as flipping a switch.

I have a client who found out her ex-husband still had her as his beneficiary of his 401k when he died suddenly, more than a decade after their divorce. It took us several appointments to work through the guilt of the financial and emotional windfall.

"It takes time to update things."

"She's still mine," Peter says, his voice low and guilty. "Emergency contact that is."

I nod, understanding what this really means. "What can I do? Do you need me to get the kids?"

"Not yet, not until we know more. Can you just…sit with me? Us?"

I take deep fortifying breaths. Over the past few years, it was all I could do to avoid online stalking, but one lonely night, when I accidentally had a bottle of wine all to myself, I did indulge in a quick search to reassure myself he really was a neurologist here in Austin. At this very hospital.

He may not be working today. He may be about to take his son off on a spring break camping trip. Or he's tending to another patient and one of his colleagues is evaluating Josie.

Or…A thought that makes my stomach curl in on itself.

Maybe this is far more serious, and instead of a neurologist, an emergency room doctor is trying to keep my best friend's heart beating.

The automatic doors open, and a tall figure in blue scrubs strides through.

My breath catches. It's been twenty-eight years since his hazel eyes met mine. Since his full lips brushed mine. Since I rested my head on his chest and felt his strong heartbeat under my ear.

"Mr. Gardner?" He extends a hand to Peter. "Dr. Harrison, the neurologist attending to your wife."

Peter blanches but doesn't correct Craig.

I'm drawn forward, like a magnet, and my movement catches Craig's attention.

"Hi," he says; his voice softens at the loss of doctoral authority. His focus is fully on me, a feeling like coming home.

The coldness of worry for my best friend, for nearly three decades of missing this man, fades away under his warm hazel eyes.

Josie is going to be okay.

I am going to be okay.

"Hi," I breathe, fighting back tears. "Finally…I found you."

EPILOGUE

TWO YEARS LATER...

It's only natural to forget things in thirty years. To forget the silly inside jokes between my best friends, as we got dressed for my wedding.

How my dress, still bought at the very last minute, was made for me. How love shone in my dad's eyes when I ask him to walk me down the aisle.

The day feels like a dream I've had, maybe part anxiety dream, also part anticipation. A moment I've waited my whole life for.

To marry someone I've waited my whole life for.

We line up just out of view of my husband-to-be and all of our friends and family. It's like I dreamed.

Remembered?

Or did I imagine it?

The string quartet switches from the song I'd half-heartedly chosen to walk down the aisle to. Half-hearted because I *knew* they'd end up playing something else.

My goddaughter dances her way down the aisle.

I peek around the corner just enough to see a cartoon heart pop out of Aiden's chest. Yeah, that kid's got it bad.

My other bridesmaids dance down the aisle. Every one of our guests are now up on their feet, dancing with them.

When it's Josie's turn, her words to me are like a long-forgotten memory.

A flash of fear spears my heart. What if? What if I hear the buzzing again? What if this is just one big cycle I'm doomed to repeat?

A little voice whispers in my head, in my heart. *Vulnerability is surrender. You can't love, and be loved, if you don't surrender your heart to another. Your future is waiting. All you have to do is reach for it.*

I look at the second to last row, at the back of a head with its long white hair plaited in a French braid. Astrid is the only person who knows everything.

While the Spirits were done with me after my trip back to 1996, I continued to visit the psychic. In the beginning, to pester her to tell me where to find Craig so I could hurry *forever* along, then because she gave really good advice, no psychic ability needed.

I like to think I learned as much about being a therapist from her as I did from any of my professors and mentors.

I glance to the back of the head of the person seated next to her. Crispin's mullet curls around the collar of his navy jacket. Too bad he still chose that haircut, but when he showed up at my practice to introduce himself, I might've welcomed him a little too warmly with a tight hug.

The music changes again, a signal that it's my turn.

"Not to disappoint you," Dad says, words that feel vaguely familiar. "I have no dance moves prepared."

"Me either, but I think we can wing it."

My dad twirls me down the aisle, not like I'm his middle-aged daughter finally getting married, but like I'm four years old again and he's finally allowing himself to be a father.

I let the glacier between us melt not long after I'd made it back to 1996. My father was never my enemy. He was just a man trying to parent a child from a distance.

When I'd explained I was changing my major for the final time, and the good I'd hoped to do with it, Dad was wholeheartedly on board with it.

I won't say we've had it easy, but we tried and, I imagine in this timeline, I've had many more happy memories with my father.

That's the thing about life; we only have these moments to grab on to, to make them mean something. Like clouds passing overhead, there will be another, and it might be similar, but it won't be exactly the same.

That's okay, because life is a mosaic of belonging and loneliness, joy and sorrow. However, life is mostly an accumulation of love. Not just for the man I'm mere feet, minutes, away from marrying, but everyone who fills my life and my heart and my soul.

My father gives me one final twirl and murmurs in my ear. "I'm so proud of you, and I love you, my baby girl. Now, let's get you married to the other man who loves you."

I look at my fiancé, almost afraid he'll be swallowed by the Universe. That the Spirits were only distracted for the last thirty years but decided to wake up today and whisk him away to another time.

Craig holds out his hand, and I tentatively put mine in his. I feel no zap of electricity, well, nothing more than the usual rush I feel every time we touch. The ground beneath my feet as solid as every step before it.

"Hi," he says, a bit breathless, as if he forgot to breathe as I made my way toward him.

"Hi," I say, also a bit breathless, because I also forgot to breathe. "In case I haven't said it lately, I love you."

I had said it lately. That morning over breakfast. Last night, as I was falling asleep. Yesterday afternoon for no reason other than I just wanted to taste the sweetest words that I can give him.

Every time I say it, it feels like the first time.

The End

A NOTE TO MY READERS

Wow! Here we are. Lucky number seven.

It feels appropriate to have Emily's book as my seventh, because in some ways luck is a driving force into getting us exactly where we need to be.

For example, I was lucky to have wonderful parents who encouraged my love of reading and writing. I was lucky to find an incredible community of writing friends — strike that, writing *best* friends. Because I can't imagine my life without them.

And, lucky to have readers like you who spend your hard earned money and harder earned time reading my stories.

If you enjoyed *Feels Like the First Time*, please tell a friend. Heck, tell an enemy. I'm not choosy. I'd also be forever grateful if you share a review on Goodreads, BookBub or wherever you bought this book.

What's next? Well, my romance friends continue to rub off on me (not like that!) so my next book is a fun rom-com involving the Greek Fates. Sign up for my newsletter or follow me on Instagram to learn more.

xoxo,
Kim

BOOK CLUB DISCUSSION

If you're reading *Feels Like the First Time* for your book club, feel free to use this as a discussion guide.

1. *Feels Like the First Time* looks at how much we change, or not change, from when we're on the cusp of adulthood to midlife. How have you changed? Are you where you thought you'd be?

2. Emily goes from the mid-90s to modern times and had to quickly learn how to navigate the 21st century. What would be your biggest challenge if you woke up thirty years in the future? How do you think you'd learn the new technologies?

3. One of the challenges Emily faces is a younger therapist who thinks he can do a better job. Emily is initially defensive but eventually realizes that they can work together. Is this something you can relate to? Do you think that's due to her immaturity, or is that a common reaction?

4. Emily is heartbroken and at a low point in her young life when she gets a glimpse of her future self, which leads her

down a path of helping others. Is there a time in your life when flashing forward would have been helpful to you?

5. *Feels Like the First Time* is a sequel to *This Time Around*, in which Emily's best friend Josie goes back thirty years. If you have time travel ability, would you rather go back in time or forward?

ACKNOWLEDGMENTS

This book is only here because my amazing friend and editor, C.A. Szarek, casually said to me when sending edits for *This Time Around*, "I think you have a sequel." Since she planted the seed, it only grew from there. Thank you for that nudge for Emily's story. And, I hope you're still not mad about that series of 6 a.m. texts when the story hit me. (Sorry, not sorry)

Thank you to my parents, for not just supporting me now, but all the way back to when I was just a little kid with her nose in a book and a penchant for telling stories. To my sister, Angie, and brother-in-law Mike, thank you for being so awesome and giving me the coolest niece and nephew on the planet.

To Colby, thank you for letting me lock myself away to spend time with my imaginary friends, even on vacation.

Thank you to my wonderful mother-in-law, Claudette, for your support and long talks about the books we love. I got lucky when I found Colby, and even luckier you came with him.

And, thank you, dear reader. I wouldn't be here without you, and for that, I am forever grateful.

ABOUT THE AUTHOR

Kimberly Packard is an award-winning author of women's fiction and romance.

When she isn't writing, she can be found planning her next trip, asking her dog what's in his mouth or curled up with a book. She resides in Texas with her husband Colby, a clever cat named Oliver and a precocious black lab named Tully.

Her debut novel, *Phoenix*, was awarded as Best General Fiction of 2013 by the Texas Association of Authors. She is also the author of a Christmas novella, *The Crazy Yates*, and the sequels to *Phoenix*, *Pardon Falls* and *Prospera Pass*, her stand-alone titles *Vortex* and *Dire's Club* and her duology *This Time Around* and *Feels Like the First Time*.

She was honored as one of the Top 10 Haute Young Authors by Southern Methodist University in 2019. *Vortex* was the 2019 winner of the Pencraft award in Women's Fiction, and *Dire's Club*, was awarded the 2021 General Fiction of the Year by the North Texas Book Festival. Her most recent novel, *This Time Around*, was an America Book Fest finalist in romance and winner of a 2025 Stiletto award from the Contemporary Romance Writers.

ALSO BY KIMBERLY PACKARD

The Phoenix Series

Phoenix

Pardon Falls (Phoenix Book 2)

Prospera Pass (Phoenix Book 3)

Standalone Titles

Vortex

The Crazy Yates

Dire's Club

This Time Around